THE GREEK LIFE

If this were New York I'd be totally fine with hopping on the train and checking out some museums or walking in Central Park or window-shopping. But in Athens? I don't know if I'd make it two blocks. Not that people aren't nice, but I can't understand them, even when they speak English; if they talk to me in Greek it's like listening to Elvish or something. The words slide through my head before I can grab on to anything. My made-up sign language is improving, though, so I guess that's something.

Maybe I'll become a street mime. Though probably that's more of a Paris thing.

This Just In: Teen Unable To Function Without Certain Necessities

A care package was dispatched to Athens earlier this week in response to the desperate pleas of a recent and now frantic 15-year-old transplant. Upon her arrival, she discovered that drugstores there (which are all disguised as churches, with big green light-up crosses instead of signs) do not stock normal tampons. If you can't read Greek letters, there's no way to tell the difference between dish soap and shampoo, since all the bottles look the same. Not a mistake you want to make.

Plus, grocery stores were found to carry weird scratchy toilet paper, and paper towels are impossible to find at all. Forget about ranch dressing or Corn Pops cereal. And instead of pudding cups, Greeks eat something called "spoon sweet," which is kind of a cross between candied fruit and marmalade. (It's not bad on yogurt, actually. But it's still not pudding.)

Filed, 12:34 p.m., Athens.

Other Books You May Enjoy

Anna and the French Kiss	Stephanie Perkins
Cindy Ella	Robin Palmer
Freshman Year & Other Unnatural Disasters	Meredith Zeitlin
Goddess Boot Camp	Tera Lynn Childs
Just Listen	Sarah Dessen
Oh. My. Gods.	Tera Lynn Childs
Prom	Laurie Halse Anderson
S.A.S.S.: When Irish Guys Are Smiling	Suzanne Supplee
Sleeping Freshmen Never Lie	David Lubar
Sophomores and Other Oxymorons	David Lubar
The Truth About Forever	Sarah Dessen

SOPHOMORE YEAR IS GREEK TO ME

meredith zeitlin

speak

SPEAK
An imprint of Penguin Random House LLC
375 Hudson Street
New York, New York 10014

First published in the United States of America by G. P. Putnam's Sons,
an imprint of Penguin Group (USA) LLC, 2015
Published by Speak, an imprint of Penguin Random House LLC, 2016

THE LIBRARY OF CONGRESS HAS CATALOGED THE G. P. PUTNAM'S SONS EDITION AS FOLLOWS:
Zeitlin, Meredith.
Sophomore year is Greek to me/ Meredith Zeitlin.
pages cm
Summary: "Fifteen-year-old Zona Lowell is finally comfortable in high school when her
father tells her that they're moving to Greece for the second half of her sophomore year,
and she will be forced to meet her mother's large extended family there against her will"
—Provided by publisher.
ISBN 978-0-399-16746-1 (hc)
[1. Moving, Houshold—Fiction. 2. Family life—Greece—Fiction.
3. High schools—Fiction. 4. Schools—Fiction. 5. Single-parent families—Fiction.
6. Journalism—Fiction. 7. Greece—Fiction.] I. Title.
PZ7.Z395Sop 2015
[Fic]—dc23
2014015974

Speak ISBN 978-0-14-751793-7

Printed in the United States of America

1 3 5 7 9 10 8 6 4 2

This book is dedicated with love to every person who
read the first one and asked me to write another.

And to the YA blogging community: you guys rule.

1

Just before the clock ticks over into a brand-new year, one that is going to be completely different from any I've experienced before, my dad and I get on a plane—my first overseas flight—heading to Greece. I look out the window, take a deep breath . . . and then we soar off into the sky.

Fourteen-Hour Trip Not Nearly As Awesome As Anticipated

During the course of the seemingly endless journey from New York to Athens today, Zona Lowell, 15, realized she was on the verge of jumping out the plane window.

"It was two different flights and both were delayed, my little TV was broken for one of them, and reading made me feel like I was going to throw up. The food was horrible, and my dad was snoring practically the entire time. Based on my TV commercial–focused research, I thought travel abroad would be fancy and exciting. As usual, field reporting reveals that real life is not as glamorous as anticipated."

Zona's father, well-known international journalist David Lowell, had this to say: "I love my daughter, but she seems to have trouble distinguishing between actual problems and slight inconveniences. Hopefully seeing a bit of the world

By the time we land in Athens, I'm so keyed up and restless from endless cups of coffee and sitting in a deceptively uncomfortable chair for so many hours that I want to lie down in a nice soft bed and run laps around the airport at the same time.

My dad, on the other hand, is just plain cranky. He hates long flights, which makes his choice of career kind of ironic.

Well, he'll get no sympathy from me—this was his idea, after all. I wanted to stay in New York where I belong.

We collect Tony, our exceptionally grumpy Scottish terrier, stumble through customs, get our passports stamped (my first stamp!), and retrieve our luggage. Frankly, I didn't think it would all make it, but I suppose miracles happen every day.

Dad is riffling through a sheaf of papers, looking for the one that will tell us how to get to our sublet. It's in a neighborhood called Kallithea that is supposedly not hard to get to, but suddenly I'm not even sure I can make it to a bench before collapsing. Does jet lag set in immediately?

As we head out of the airport arrivals area, the first thing I notice is the signs: they're in English and Greek, those strange curly letters that look like hieroglyphics to me. I thumbed through an English-to-Greek dictionary back in New York, but I couldn't make heads or tails of it, so seeing the English signs is a huge relief. Maybe I won't be hopelessly lost after all . . . or at the very least, I can just hang out in the airport if I get desperate.

There's a big glassed-in smoking area in the middle of the airport, which is weird to see—in New York City, smoking is banned everywhere. My dad, who smoked like a chimney before I was born (and sometimes has been known to sneak a cigarette when he thinks I'm not looking), gazes at it longingly. "Dad!" I scold him. "This is no time to revert to atrocious habits. Pull it together."

We changed a bunch of money at JFK before we took off, so we plunk down eight euros apiece for train tickets. Eight euros is roughly eleven dollars, I believe, which I find to be completely insane: that much money for a subway ride? According to the not-very-friendly woman at the ticket window, a regular ride (not from the airport) is only €1.20, but still. I sort of thought things would be dirt cheap in Greece, what with the economic difficulties. Apparently not.

We roll our suitcases (and poor, miserable Tony) down a long tunnel until we get to the platform. The subway is really simple here, unlike the rat's nest of colors and numbers I'm used to at home. In Athens there are three lines: blue, red, and green. It would be incredibly straightforward if not for the fact that I can't pronounce—and therefore remember—any of the names of the stations. But it's only my first hour here, so I'll try to give myself a break.

We sit down to wait for the train, which arrives at the airport every half hour according to the electronic sign. I reach into Tony's carrier to pet him; he's still groggy and looks even grouchier than usual. Poor guy. At least in Greece pets don't have to be quarantined after entering the country—then we might not have been able to bring him at all.

The train platform's waiting area is bright white and has plants all around. With the sun shining in from overhead, it actually looks like an atrium in here, minus the birds. Definitely not like any subway platform I've ever waited on, that's for sure. Maybe I'm hallucinating?

The train finally arrives. We lug our stuff through the doors, and right on cue, Tony starts howling. A nice lady offers me her seat so I can put him down, which is a surprise. My sleep-deprived brain wonders when more traditional passengers will put in an appearance, like the NYC subway staples "lady eating sunflower seeds and spitting the shells on the ground" or "guy with no pants screaming about the apocalypse." Shockingly, their Greek counterparts don't appear; only tidy, quiet passengers fill the train. The seats are covered with fabric and totally spotless, and there isn't a single piece of litter on the floor. Even the poles look especially shiny. But, like I said, it's possible I'm just delirious from exhaustion.

After twenty minutes or so, we switch trains at a stop called Monastiraki (once again, I'm relieved to see the station names spelled out in English letters) for the green line. Four more stops and we've reached our final destination. We walk out onto a sun-dappled platform filled with potted trees and drag our belongings up the escalator and out of the station.

So this is it: my first official view of Athens, and my new home.

If you want to know the truth . . . it kind of looks like Brooklyn.

There's a cobbled platform with steps (and a ramp, thank the lord) leading from the station down to the sidewalk, and straight ahead is a store that looks like a typical deli. Past that and on the other side of the street are more shops and a restaurant, and what I'm guessing is a church, because it has a big lit-up green cross on a sign. It's a neighborhood. Just like my neighborhood in New York, really.

I guess I was expecting some massive ruins or something. Or for everything to be white from a fine layer of ancient dust. People feeding one another grapes. Something more, well, *Greek*.

To our left is a ramp leading to a highway overpass. The cars look different—boxier—and they have strange-looking license plates. And everywhere I look, people are walking, riding scooters, talking, or picking up newspapers. Not a single person appears to be wearing a toga. If it weren't for the fact that everyone's speaking a language I don't understand, we could be pretty much anywhere.

So far.

My dad has his stack of papers out again, and Tony is barking his head off at two dogs who are hanging out by the door to the station. They have collars and tags, but no leashes or obvious owners. Tony is losing his mind, scrabbling against the sides of his carrier.

"Anthony Oliver Lowell!" I reprimand him. He knows better than that.

He looks chastened and switches from barking to a low growl. I'm tempted to let him out of his carrier to stretch his legs—I'm sure he's been miserable cooped up for almost an entire day—but the other dogs make me nervous. Instead I apologize to him profusely.

"Can we get a cab? Do we even know where we're *going*?" I whine. This has been fun and all, but I think I'm ready to wrap it up. Dad is sitting on top of his big suitcase, looking like he's about to fall over. One of the strange dogs comes over and sniffs his leg.

"Dad? Dad!"

He starts, snorts, and looks back at the papers. He is holding them upside down. I sense I'm going to have to take charge.

I snap a piece of paper out of his hand and look it over. "Okay, Dad, this isn't far at all." I look up from the directions and point. "That way, I think. Let's roll."

I'm looking for street signs, which, after getting to the verge of bursting into exhausted tears, I eventually realize are cleverly hidden by being attached to (and camouflaged by) the buildings. No steel rods helpfully sticking out of the sidewalk here. We turn down the wrong street, which has almost the exact same name as the *right* street, and after correcting our mistake finally get to a building that looks like, well, a building. Where are the columns? Where are the decorative urns? Where are the goats?!

Wait—you know what? Hang on. It occurs to me that I may need to back up. After all, a good reporter should start a story at the beginning so that her readers have all the facts.

Let me try this again:

My name is Zona Lowell. I'm fifteen, from New York City, and a month ago my father decided to turn my entire world upside down in one fell swoop.

I've been kind of freaking out about it.

2

Dad Blindsides Innocent Daughter At Breakfast Table

In an unprecedented display of cruelty and sneakiness, internationally renowned newspaper journalist David Lowell announced today over a bowl of Frosted Mini-Wheats that he would be completely ruining his daughter's entire life by forcing her to go live in Greece for six months, effective January 1. The aforementioned daughter, Zona, 15, could not believe it when her father (known for being somewhat eccentric but marginally cool nonetheless) told her she was being uprooted from her life and forced to live halfway across the world where she didn't know a soul except for Lowell himself (a man to whom she would never be speaking again, thank you very much).

Zona's plans to emancipate herself were thwarted by the realization that she had recently spent all her hard-earned baby-sitting/birthday money on an iPad mini and wouldn't be able to pay rent or buy food. Her insistence on moving in with her best friend Hilary's family was scoffed at by Evil Dictator Lowell.

Lowell's paltry excuses that this story "could be his legacy" and that "any normal teenager would jump at the chance for such an exciting adventure" fell on deaf ears.

Filed, 10:37 a.m., Lower East Side, NYC.

"You're kidding," Hilary said, looking at me in disbelief over the round, sticky table in the Starbucks on 26th and Sixth. The Bauers live on the Upper West Side, which is kind of a pain to get to from my neighborhood (the Lower East Side), so in these kinds of dire circumstances—when a phone call will simply *not* suffice—a convenient meeting place is essential.

Anyway, I'd just told Hilary the horrible, unbelievable, unavoidable news. We were supposed to be making winter break plans, but instead were talking about my impending and total disappearance. Hil shifted in her seat. "Zo, you can't *move*. It's the middle of the school year. And, I mean, what about—"

"What about the fact that I'm going to be stuck for half a year—at *least*, by the way, he said 'at least'—in a country where I have no friends, don't like any of the food, and can't even read the street signs? What about *that*? Has the man even considered the ramifications of his unilateral decision? This is an affront to—"

"Okay, Captain Vocab. Calm down," Hilary chided sweetly. I tend to go into what she lovingly calls my SAT Prep Mode when I get upset; I just can't help it. I've been reading the Sunday *Times* out loud with my dad (aka the enemy) since I was five. Everything distressing is better expressed in multisyllabic words, or at least my brain thinks so.

But I digress.

I took a hearty swig of my peppermint mocha latte and got whipped cream up my nose. *Perfect,* I thought as I attempted to regain my composure. "They probably don't even have Starbucks there." I was about to burst into tears . . . over *Starbucks. In* a Starbucks. How tragicomic was this going to get?

"Well, everywhere has Starbucks," Hilary said helpfully. She looked down at her hot cider like, if she focused on it hard enough, she wouldn't cry, either. Great. Hilary's the more sensitive of the two of us (I try to be objective at all times, like a good journalist), so if she broke, I would, too. And I wasn't even leaving for three more weeks.

"I just don't understand why he's doing this," I fumed, trying to get away from sad and back to furious. "I mean, I get it: Greece, economy, political upheaval, crisis, whatever, huge story . . . but why do *I* have to go? Doesn't he realize I have stuff to do? Like, doesn't he get that being the only sophomore ever chosen to be features editor is kind of a *huge deal*? I'm trying to carry on the Lowell legacy, and this is his response? I've only gotten to work on two issues! And maybe, I dunno, I'll actually manage to have some kind of social life this year."

"Hey! No offense to me, I'm sure," Hilary interjected.

"Come on, you know what I mean." I poked her arm apologetically. She gave me a wry smile in return.

"Yeah, yeah, of course I know what you mean: guys." She sighed. "Me too."

"I have *plans*, Hil, is the point," I continued. "Intentions. A life. A small life, but a life all the same. Doesn't that count for anything?" I dropped my face into my hands in despair.

Okay . . . so maybe I should make something clear before I go on: I'm not actually this horrible. I mean, I knew that my dad writing his new magazine piece—which he thought could be the basis for an entire book—was a much bigger deal than my working on the school newspaper (and maybe, as a bonus, finally figuring out a way to make gorgeous editor-in-chief Ben Walker realize I was alive). But one measly hour after finding out I had to pick up and leave everything that mattered to me behind didn't seem like the time to act like a mature adult.

Usually I *do* act like a mature adult, though. Some people would probably say I've never really acted any other way, even when I was a little kid. I guess it's because of my dad and how it's always been just the two of us. For one thing, Dad is old—not, like, Methuselah old, but he's older than most of my friends' dads by a lot. Before I was born, he was a freelance journalist and traveled all over the world for stories, including during the Vietnam War. He's won two Pulitzer Prizes—one's hanging in the bathroom of our apartment. The other Pulitzer was *supposedly* lost in a poker game with a famous dictator, but I think it was just lost, period. My dad's a bit on the disorganized side, except when it comes to his writing. Then the mess is referred to as "organized chaos." Our whole apartment is basically stacks of papers and discs and flash drives and other objects that are *not* to be touched by anyone except the person who put them there (and occasionally Tony, who doesn't care much about personal space).

It's precarious, but it's home.

Anyway, Dad was forty-six when I was born—which was after he met my mom, obviously—and he agreed to stay put in NYC for a while. I personally don't think he ever really intended to stay, and probably he wouldn't have . . . if my mom hadn't died right after giving birth to me.

So it's been just me and my dad for the last fifteen years. And for the most part it's been pretty cool, actually. Growing up with a dad who writes for newspapers and magazines is great. He'd take me on all kinds of trips when I was a baby and use my extreme cuteness to disarm tricky sources and interview subjects. I used to hang out at his office and play on the old typewriters. And of course I had a million crazy "aunts" and "uncles" all over the city—local informer types and other writer friends of my dad's.

Oh, and his nickname for me is Ace—as in "ace reporter." Sensing a theme yet?

World Totally Unsurprised To Learn Of Girl's Predisposition To Writing, Journalism

In a truly unshocking turn of events, Zona Lowell, daughter of acclaimed writer David Lowell, wishes to pursue a career in journalism like her dad.

"You know that saying, 'Like father, like daughter'? Turns out it's a real thing," said the owner of the deli near the Lowells' apartment.

As the masses recover from this extraordinary revelation, we will continue our exclusive coverage of how the sky is blue and gravity is real.

Filed, 4:13 p.m., NYC.

Now that I'm older, we're more like roommates in some ways than father and daughter: we take turns doing the grocery shopping and staking out a machine at the Laundromat down the street, share cooking and cleaning responsibilities, and fight over what makes it onto the DVR. We maintain our piles of important personal property with only a once-in-a-while argument over who stole whose copy of *Newsweek*. We treat each other like equals, really. My friends are totally jealous of me for having a dad who gets so involved with a project that he doesn't mind if I do whatever I feel like doing as long as I check in. (Not that I'm running around town doing anything particularly nefarious, but still.) He trusts me. And I *used* to trust him.

But now?

Forget it.

13

Because I knew that this wasn't just about researching his work. He could stash me somewhere for six months instead of interrupting my sophomore year of high school. I was supposed to be gathering up grades for AP classes and preparing for the SATs. How was I supposed to do that in Greece?!

No, this was a straight-up trick. Because I knew who else was in Greece: my mother's family, whom I'd never met and, to be honest, never wanted to meet.

3

I never knew my mom, obviously. She lived her whole life in Crete (which, according to various accredited sources, is the largest and most populous island in Greece. Also, Zeus was born in a cave there. So, my mom . . . and also Zeus) until the day she ran off with my dad. She died just twenty hours after I was born, and I just don't feel any connection to her. I mean, I love her, in that sort of vague way you'd love anyone who was related to you and gave you half your DNA. But that's kind of it.

Don't go thinking this is all sad or anything like that. It isn't. You can't miss what you've never had, and in my family there's a dad and a daughter and a dog.

And I like it that way.

Here's the thing, though: in the last couple of years, my dad had started tossing around random comments involving me meeting this slew of relatives. I would just laugh and change the subject, saying I was sure they're fine people, but I didn't *know* them. I have nothing in common with them. I don't speak Greek. I pointed out that they've never come over to meet us, or even sent a card. I was fine with things the way they were.

And honestly, I was.

There's another part to this story, as I guess there usually is when it comes to family stuff . . . but I don't like to think about it. Not if I don't have to.

Anyway, I put my journalism skills to good use and came up with a theory about why Dad had been pushing the Greece angle: he's afraid of something happening to him and me being left alone.

I know, super morbid—but I'm not an idiot. I mean, why else would he be doing this? And of course I've thought about the possibility of him . . . dying. I can't even imagine life without my dad, much less being an *orphan*. It's just . . . too much. And maybe that's an immature attitude, too, but I'm only fifteen, for God's sake. This is the time to *have* an immature attitude, isn't it? And besides, I don't think fear of something that hasn't happened is a reason to just pick up and move to another freaking country to hang out with people I happen to be related to.

So when he said we were moving to Greece—*moving!* Not even just taking a vacation!—I saw through the whole scheme right away.

Hilary knew all this stuff, of course. (Well, almost all of it—the part I don't like to think about is the only secret I've ever kept from her. More on that later.) But I just knew that, somehow, I'd think of a way out of this mess. And then it'd all just . . . go away. And I wouldn't have to talk about it at all. Right? Don't things sometimes happen that way?

So. Back to Starbucks and me not taking the news very well at all.

"Maybe he's just testing your level of loyalty to the *Reflector.* See how hard you'll fight to stay here, you know? Like, a co-journalistic ethics and devotion test or something . . . ?" Hil trailed off. I raised my eyebrows skeptically, and she wrinkled her nose. "Yeah, I guess that sounded better in my head. Ugh, this is so unfair! What am I going to do without you?!"

Hilary Bauer and I started hanging out at the beginning of fourth grade, when we got partnered up for a book report project involving hand puppets. (Seriously, where do teachers come up with this stuff?) Hil was new in school, and we bonded immediately over her notebook, which had pictures from the *Narnia* movie on it. Before we met I'd been really shy and mostly kept to myself; I was used to things being quiet at home, with just one parent and no siblings. Plus, I go to a pretty swanky private school with mostly well-off Manhattan- and Brooklynites. My dad and I are considered . . . eccentric, to put it nicely. Poor, to put it bluntly. The parents of my kindergarten classmates weren't rushing to set me up with playdates once they found out we lived in a less-than-pristine two-bedroom rental apartment in a (gasp!) non-elevator building—at least, not until they figured out my dad is *that* David Lowell, the one who wrote the famous piece on 9/11. And by then I'd kind of learned to do my own thing, anyway. I never minded sitting by myself with a book, but meeting Hilary was just . . . serendipity.

(In case you're wondering how I could afford to go to a Manhattan private school, the answer is: after my mom died from blood toxemia, the hospital settled out of court with my dad. He was pretty messed up, obviously, and didn't want to touch the money. He had a lawyer put it in a trust for my schooling, and that's the only thing it's ever been used for. Again, pretty morbid . . . but like I said, it's the only life I've ever known. No pity parties, please, okay?)

Anyway, my friendship with Hilary has not only been awesome and silly and *necessary,* but it survived the middle-school-to-high-school transition, mutual crushes on at least four guys, her parents almost getting divorced last year, a terrible text message misunderstanding in eighth grade involving one of the above-mentioned mutual crushes (too long and boring to explain), and one of us growing boobs and the other not (I'm the "not," unfortunately). And now we're going to be parted by a giant body of water?!

Hilary was drawing a sad face on the table with Splenda. "And what about Matty?" she continued. "He needs you as much as I do!"

Matt Klausner is the third member of our trio, who

joined the ranks in seventh grade during a mind-blowingly boring school dance. He's super smart, gay, spectacularly irritable about almost everything, and I love him to pieces. What would I do in Greece without him to make me laugh when I got sad about not having kissed anyone since someone's visiting camp friend shoved his tongue down my throat at a party last spring? Who would let me copy their chemistry homework?!

My latte was gone and I felt worse than ever. Hilary blew away her Splenda portrait. She looked as glum as I felt.

"I don't know, Hil. I mean, at least you guys will still have each other. What will I do without *you*?"

"Maybe your dad will change his mind and decide to write about something else," she suggested quietly.

I didn't bother replying. We both knew that'd never happen. When David Lowell decided to write something, he wrote it.

4

When I got home, Dad was in his study working with the door closed—probably looking up ways to further sabotage my high school career/life. I headed to my room and found a Post-it note stuck to my computer monitor. It said: *Ornery Daughter Comes to Senses, Celebrates Impending Adventure.*

Interesting.

This is a thing my dad and I have done since I could write: leaving headlines around the apartment instead of regular notes. Usually I think it's pretty clever, but not this time.

I got out my own pad of paper and scribbled down: *Despondent Daughter Ignores Father's Annoying Note; Father Withers Away Unvisited in Bargain-Basement Nursing Home.* Not the world's most concise headline, but it'd do. I dashed down the hall and stuck it on the door to his study.

The next morning, there was a new Post-it plastered to my forehead when I woke up. It said: *Come on, Ace. Look on the bright side. For me? . . . For you?*

I crumpled it up, tossed it in the trash, and headed to school.

"You guys. Guess what?" Matty said, sliding in next to me at the lunch table later that day.

I eyed him warily. Despite the fact that I'd spent an hour on the phone with him the night before lamenting the unwelcome turn of events at Chez Lowell, he seemed to think that other topics were up for discussion. And when Matt Klausner leads with an open-ended question, you never know what path you might be lured down.

"If this has anything to do with that piercing place in the Village, the answer is still no," Hilary said.

Matt grinned. "My cousin Paulette got her tongue pierced there, and when my uncle saw it, he helpfully removed it *for* her . . . with pliers. Then she watched the hole close in the mirror. She said it took two hours."

"This is what you wanted to tell us?" Hilary asked, horrified.

"No, it is *not,* so if you'd just—"

I glanced up from my grilled cheese, which I'd been bitterly picking at instead of eating. "Your cousin stared at her tongue in the mirror for two hours? What's wrong with her?"

"Well, she's not that interesting." Matt shrugged, stealing some tater tots from my plate. When I scowled at him, he opened his mouth to reveal the disgusting mess inside.

"You're seriously the worst," Hil said.

"Oh, I'm *so* sorry. Were you two sitting here moaning about the fact that Zona gets to leave this cesspool and live in one of the most gorgeous places on the planet? Are we having a cry-athon in the caf?"

"Hey!" I snapped. "If you want to switch itineraries with me, feel free to—"

"Because if you're done with sad-sack time, I have something of *great import* to share with you. But maybe . . . maybe you don't even *care*." Matt glared at us, folding his hands on the tabletop.

"Sorry, sorry," Hilary said. "What's up?"

"Well, now I'm not sure you deserve to know . . ." He sniffed petulantly.

I knew when a battle had been lost. "Pleaaaaaase, Matty, most handsome of men. Please, *pretty* please, tell us the exciting news. It's all we want in the world." Hilary and I batted our eyelashes at him dramatically.

We're dorks, but it's so *fun*.

"Okay, you've forced it out of me!" Matt exclaimed at last. "The news is: I. Like. Someone."

Silence.

"Hello? Anyone? This is a landmark event. I'd *like* a reaction." Matt folded his arms across his chest. I looked at Hilary. She looked at me.

"Is this a joke?" Hil finally said.

"How dare you! I've never been so insulted in my—"

"It's just that . . . you *never* like anyone. Ever," I pointed out quickly. "I mean, is it someone at this school? The

22

school filled with 'horrible, hideous, juvenile, totally unin-spired guys you could never in a million years imagine touching with a ten-foot pole'? Because I definitely remem-ber that speech."

"Ugh, of course it isn't someone from this freak show. It's"—Matt leaned in conspiratorially—"the counter guy at the Starbucks on 12th Street. I'm in love, I'm in lust, I don't know what to *do* with myself!" He flung his arms in the air triumphantly.

Today's Special Interest Story: Deluded Teen Professes Love For 30-Year-Old (Minimum) Barista

Matthew Klausner, a Man-hattan resident, revealed today that he thinks he has a snowball's chance in hell of go-ing on a date of any kind with the much older and most likely not looking to be put in prison Scott NoIdeaLastName.

Klausner's friends tried to say encouraging things after the young man's revelation, including, "Well, it's great that you figured out your type!" and "Have you completely lost your mind?!" but the subject of their best intentions remained un-moved.

For more information, please see "Mary-Kay Letour-neau" and "Truly Terrible Ideas."

Filed, 12:18 p.m., Manhattan.

"Should I say 'Is this a joke' again?" Hilary asked. "Because I totally will."

"Scoff all you want, but we have a connection. He gave me a free package of those chocolate-covered graham crackers today," Matt said smugly.

"Wow. Did he hand them to you through the window of his white van before asking you to climb in?" I said. Hilary laughed. Matt did not look amused. "Matty, come on. You can't be serious. This guy is like . . . *old*. Too old."

"Love knows no age restrictions. Weren't your parents, like, twenty years apart or something?"

Twenty-five years, actually. *So* not the point.

"Besides," Matty went on, "he's not old, he's *mature*. And I'm sixteen, not nine. He can get me into clubs. And maybe you guys, too, if you're good."

"Gee," I said with wide eyes, "I can't think of anything I'd enjoy more than hanging out with you and your new faux-boyfriend in a—"

"What do you call a cougar if he's a guy?" Hilary interjected thoughtfully. "A lion?"

"—club, but I have to move to another continent instead. Thanks for the invite, though."

"Oh, here we go. Back to Sadsville." Matt slumped in his chair. "Can't you take a minute to be encouraging? Should I ask him out or what?"

"*NO!*" Hilary and I said together.

Hil flung her sandwich crust at him. "Definitely *not*," she added.

"You two just want everyone to be as miserable as you are." Matt narrowed his eyes and flung the bread back.

"Matty, that's not fair. Of course we want you to meet someone. Just not someone who is elderly and works at

Starbucks," I said, trying to be diplomatic. I knew Matt got bummed out because there were basically no other gay guys in our school—well, not many who'd admit it, anyway—and he wanted to hook up and have crushes like everybody else.

"He's not *elderly*! He's probably, like . . . twenty-four!"

Hilary and I gave him the exact same look. He scowled at us again. Then the bell rang and we all heaved a collective sigh. "Well, this was fun," Matt said morosely. Then he brightened. "I've got a free period . . . Anyone want to go get coffee?"

"Seriously, though, you guys, what's a male cougar?" Hilary asked again. "A tiger?"

"I have no idea, Hil. I'm gay, not an expert on gay terminology. Zona, why don't you do a little undercover journalism and find out for us? I'll ask Scott where you should look for leads."

"I have History," I said firmly, scooping up my tray and ignoring Matt's suggestion. "Also, you've had enough coffee for today, sir. Hilary, I'm leaving you in charge."

"Gee, thanks." Hilary rolled her eyes resignedly and looked pointedly at Matt. "No coffee for you." He sniffed haughtily and started doing something on his phone—probably tweeting about how no one understood him. I winked at Hil and headed to class.

5

Young Journalist Daydreams Through Entire Meeting

Instead of paying attention during what would likely be one of the last opportunities to contribute in her official capacity as features editor, Zona Lowell spent the entire weekly *Reflector* meeting wondering if she could somehow make her dad change his evil, stubborn mind. She also gave some thought to what the paper's editor-in-chief, handsome senior Benjamin Walker, would look like with his shirt off.

When called on for her thoughts, Zona managed to say, "Oh, yeah—totally agree," which made absolutely no sense, since the question was "What are you thinking for the features theme next month?"

Filed, 2:24 p.m., Manhattan.

It was hard to believe I was sitting in our usual Friday meeting like I hadn't had my world upended a few days earlier. And yet, here I was, same as always.

". . . and that pretty much covers it, I think," Ben said. I was too busy focusing on how his deep, chocolaty-brown eyes crinkled at the corners when he smiled to hear his full speech. (I'd been obsessed with him since last year.) Unfortunately, he A) had a girlfriend and B) didn't care about me even before he had a girlfriend.

This reality was one I had to live with daily as I plodded through the sad desert that was my romantic life. The only bright spot to my Greece trip, really, was that maybe there'd be some cute guys there. Guys who liked reading biographies, and utilized correct punctuation, and didn't have to *try* to be cool. Basically, exact replicas of Ben, only Greek. And single. And not oblivious to my love.

But I wasn't putting money on it.

Hilary was on the other side of the room chatting about a new article with über-gorgeous staff writer Lexi Bradley (also a sophomore, but looks like she's about twenty-five), and I was just about to go over and join them when I felt a tap on my shoulder.

"Hey, Zona—can I talk to you for a sec?" It was Ben. Touching me. On my actual body. My heart stopped beating for a second, but I made a quick recovery; I knew this wasn't going to be a "Let me reveal my love for you" speech. It was going to be a "What the hell? I chose you to be features editor over all those juniors and seniors and now you're leaving the country?!" speech. I'd sensed this was coming, but I'd kind of hoped it would be a few more days before I had to talk to him about it. Of course, news travels fast in high school.

I trudged behind him to the big desk where he did all the layouts. Why did he have to be EIC? I'd much rather disappoint last year's chief, back when Ben was just a snarky junior with a camera wandering around school. For one thing, it was way easier to pretend he had a secret crush on me in those days, because you could never be sure who he was taking pictures of. But then again, that's exactly how he ended up with his girlfriend, Kelsey, so . . . Ugh—why was I thinking about this? I had more important things to focus on, like—

"Zona? You in there?" he asked. Oh, *terrific*. He was doing the crinkly-eyed smile thing.

"Yeah, sorry, just spacing," I said.

"Seems to be your thing today," Ben replied.

I blushed furiously. "Yeah, sorry about that—I guess I've been a bit distracted." *By your chiseled good looks. Run away with me?* "So, um," I continued, "I guess you heard through the grapevine about my dad's new story—"

"Don't you mean the *olive* vine?"

Ben grinned and looked at me expectantly, but I was blank. Finally, after an endless moment, I got it. "Oh," I mumbled, "is that a Greece joke?"

"Not a very good one," he conceded, shrugging. He looked down at the desk and moved a few index cards around. *Great. Now he hates me*, I thought. *Why didn't I just laugh hysterically?* He looked back up. "Anyway, it sounds amazing. I'd kill to be there with your dad while he's researching—I mean, talk about the opportunity of a lifetime, right? You must be pretty psyched."

"Yeah, I guess . . . but I'd honestly rather stay here."

He looked genuinely shocked. "Seriously? Why?"

"Well, I have responsibilities, um, to the paper, and—"

"Oh, yeah—our beloved *Reflector*. Nice that you're worried about her, but I promise we'll soldier on while you're living it up in freaking *Greece*. And working on actual news that isn't about someone running a bra up the flagpole. Again." Ben held up his iPad, which had a photo-editing program open with a picture of a bright blue bra flapping in the wind.

I laughed, but didn't feel very funny. I started fiddling with the zipper on my Brooklyn Industries hoodie. Maybe I *should've* been more psyched . . . but all the kids who were excited on my behalf didn't actually know the whole story.

Maybe Ben would offer to go with me. He could help carry my suitcase. Dad would probably be completely on board with that plan.

"Anyway, I guess you know we're gonna have to replace you as features editor. It's too bad—your work on the last two issues has been awesome. I was really excited about having you on my team this year."

He was?! How excited, exactly?

"I kind of don't have a precedent to follow for this sort of thing," he continued. "If you want to recommend somebody . . . Or I could just go through the other applications from the end of last year and see if anyone is still interested in the job . . ." He trailed off, his attention suddenly distracted by his phone. Probably a romantic text from Kelsey. He cracked a smile and started typing a reply.

I was ready to get the hell out of there and go write some subpar, heartbroken poetry on the wall of the girls' room.

"Yeah, so," I began, scrambling for something to say before dashing away, "I'm honestly devastated about leaving you in the lurch like this, especially because I was elated about getting the position . . ."

He glanced up at me. (I continued fidgeting like a six-year-old.) "Sorry, Zona, that was totally rude. Um, yeah . . ." His eyes flicked back to his phone. "But don't feel bad. You'll be back next year! Have an amazing time in Greece—seriously, I would love to be in your shoes."

And . . . he was back to texting. 'Kay. Bye.

I slunk out of the room, waving to Hilary and Lexi on my way. Hil followed close behind me.

"Did he already know?" she asked.

"Yeah. He's going to replace me. I mean, I knew he would. It's just all happening in five seconds, you know? I don't leave for another two-ish weeks!" I thought about the absurdly expensive spiral notebook with the hard metallic cover that I'd bought at Kate's Paperie when I found out I'd been chosen for the job. I'd already filled up half its silver-lined pages with my ideas for features articles, interesting layouts, surveys, interviews . . .

"I'm sorry, Zo. This totally sucks." Hilary scuffed the ugly linoleum tiles with her studded Converse high-top sneaker. "Want to come over later? My mom's on call and my dad will be at some meeting, I think. We can order in Thai and hang out on the terrace and they won't bother us."

I love going to Hilary's. She lives in a gorgeous penthouse with massive floor-to-ceiling windows, a view for days, and every gadget in the world. They have a fridge that's about the size of my bedroom, and it's always chockfull of fancy cheese and desserts that her parents never eat because they're always at work or charity events. Oh, and did I mention the enclosed, heated terrace that's bigger than my entire apartment? Don't get me wrong—the Lower East Side is more my style, and I honestly wouldn't trade . . . but the Bauers' is a *very* nice place to visit.

I smiled. "Thanks, but I have to go home and try to convince my dad to reconsider. Again. And that could take all night . . ." I trailed off, feeling depressed.

She squeezed me in a quick hug. "If you change your mind, just text me. 'Kay?"

I couldn't believe I'd have to be without my incredible best friend for six months. I was never going to make it.

6

I poked my head around the door of Dad's office, my backpack still slung over my shoulder. He was at his desk, sticking tiny Post-its to things. His computer was on and there were at least fifteen tabs open on the screen—working on a new outline, probably. But I had to risk interrupting for the sake of familial peace and general group sanity. "Can we talk?"

He looked up and slid his reading glasses onto his head. "Well, that depends. Did you replenish the pudding cup supply? Don't think I didn't notice the sudden total depletion of said cups in the last couple days." He stuck a Post-it to the edge of his desk. It read: *Man Bereft of Post-Breakfast Dessert Option!* "Not cool, Zona," he continued.

I knew he was trying to be silly to break the tension, but I was determined to have a serious talk with him. "I'll get more tomorrow after school, I promise."

"Well, all right. Lucky for you I have dinner plans tonight." He looked down, found another Post-it, and stuck it next to the first one. It said: *Overworked Journalist Dines with Editor in Attempt to Secure Halfway Decent Advance; Will Daughter Manage to Feed Self? Story at 11.*

I had to laugh. "Dad, really? How far in advance are you writing these things?"

"I gotta write what's foremost in my thoughts at the moment it comes to me," he said. "Can't fight the muse."

"Right, okay." I cleared my throat.

Dad clasped his hands on top of his papers and smiled, sort of lopsided. It's my favorite Dad smile, and my heart hurt thinking about having an argument with him, but there was nothing else to do. "So, what's shakin', kid?" he asked.

I stood just inside the door frame and took a deep breath. "I've done a lot of thinking, and I want you to know I understand you have to go to Greece for the new project, and I support your work, and you, and it's not my intention to be a jerk about it."

This was rewarded by a big Dad smile, with both sides of his mouth engaged. "Well, Ace, I'm thrilled to hear it. I know we'll both—"

"But," I said, keeping my voice steady, "I'm not going. I don't want to leave school, and my friends, and the paper. I don't want to meet Mom's family. I'm not going, and I won't change my mind."

Dad's smile deflated, as I knew it would.

"Zona. Come sit, okay?" He put his thumb and finger

against the bridge of his nose and pressed, as if he had a headache. "I don't blame you for not wanting to go. I know this wasn't your plan for the year. And I try—I've always tried—to treat you like your own person and not tell you what to do . . . but you don't get a choice. We're going. *You're* going. It doesn't matter if you want to or not—"

"How can you do this to me?" I burst out. I'd promised myself that I wouldn't get upset, but this was just so *unfair.* When he'd ambushed me with the news at the breakfast table, I'd been too shocked to do much more than simply refuse to go.

I knew I needed to make a calm, clear, and concise argument now if I had any hope of making him understand. But I couldn't put the words together. I felt myself filling up with dread and the knowledge that nothing I said would make a difference—this thing I couldn't bear was going to happen whether I liked it or not. And that thing wasn't losing my position at the paper, or being away from Hil and Matt. And the worst part was, Dad knew exactly why I didn't want to go, and he was making me do it anyway.

I ran out of the room and flung my bag on the floor of the living room, startling Tony, who went lurching under the couch. I could hear Dad pushing his chair back, but I knew it would take him a few minutes to extricate himself from the piles of books and papers around his desk.

I managed to drag Tony from underneath the couch with little to no snuffly growling and snapped his leash into

34

place. I carried him down the stairs at a run and stepped into the bitter chill of the late December afternoon. I shook with relief.

I knew Dad wouldn't follow me. But I also knew I'd have to talk to him again, if not that night, then soon.

I took Tony the long way, by the water. It was still light-ish out, and I knew a walk would give me a chance to clear my head. Besides, we both needed the exercise.

By the time we got home, Tony was beat, we were both starving, Dad was gone—presumably to dinner with his editor—and I'd made a decision. It was time to face this Greece thing head-on.

All of it.

I fed Tony, grabbed peanut butter and a box of crackers, and went back into my dad's office. It's not off-limits, but I didn't usually go in there when he wasn't home unless I needed to grab a book or something. On the bottom shelf closest to his desk (the whole room is basically floor-to-ceiling bookshelves) was a light-blue wooden box that used to hold my mother's jewelry and keepsakes. Now it was filled with those things, plus letters and pictures.

I sat down on the floor with the box. Inside was a whole stack of envelopes, covered with my mother's familiar spiky handwriting. Of course, I couldn't make heads or tails of the Greek addresses. I *could* read the faded stamp on each one, however, since that was in both languages: **RETURN TO SENDER.**

The letters were all unopened, except for the bottom one in the pile, which was in my dad's writing. It was addressed to my grandmother and similarly stamped. My dad had written the letter to tell my mother's family what had happened—that their daughter was dead but they had a healthy granddaughter.

And they'd sent it back. The only person who read it was me, years later.

After that, there were no more letters.

My dad showed me the blue box when I was seven or eight and had started asking questions about my mom. It wasn't easy to do a second-grade family-tree project with only one branch and a single leaf. (Well, two if you count Tony, and my teacher didn't.)

By then he'd already told me how they met and fell in love. It's actually one of those stories you might hear and think, *Come on. That doesn't happen in real life.* But in this case, it did. My dad had been working in Turkey and a friend of his, another journalist, insisted he come to Crete to blow off steam before heading back to the States. They went exploring, my dad saw my mom, Hélenè, walking down the street with some girlfriends, and BOOM.

Love at first sight.

Well, at *his* first sight, anyway. My dad had been immediately smitten (shocking everyone, as he was a forty-five-year-old self-proclaimed bachelor) and followed my mother into a café. He sat down with her and her friends and refused to leave until she agreed to go to dinner with him. Luckily for him, she spoke a little English and one of his journalist friends spoke a little Greek.

After that . . . they really did fall in love.

She agreed to go back to New York with him two weeks later, even though he never thought he'd get married, she'd never been to America, and her English wasn't very good. Even though he was much older and her family was furious about the whole thing.

Dad told me my mother hadn't been surprised when the letters came back. She said it was typical Greek behavior, that they were old-fashioned and stubborn. They were trying to make a point, to show her they were still in charge of her life. She was confident they'd come around once I was born. She would laugh about it, he said, and tell him to enjoy the peace and quiet before the apartment filled up with noisy Greeks demanding to hold/feed/raise the baby.

But they never got the chance to find out if she was right.

After Dad got his letter back unopened, he never wrote again. He was barely holding it together between losing my mom and having to take care of a newborn, and the years just went by. I was never even sure they knew I existed, but I was happy to write them off. If they didn't want me, or my family, why would I want them?

So that was my big secret. The part none of my friends knew, and the reason I couldn't find any way to be excited about going to Greece, despite the opportunities for adventure that everyone so eagerly pointed out. That's why this trip was the worst idea on the planet, and why I'd do anything not to go. Because what kind of people refused to open letters from their own daughter?

Or worse . . . never followed up when the letters stopped coming?

7

When I heard the key in the door, I looked up at the office clock—it wasn't even seven P.M., way too early for Dad to be back from dinner. I scrambled to get up, the letters spilling over my lap.

"Zona?" Dad called. Our apartment isn't that big, and the office is on the way to the kitchen. He stopped in the doorway when he saw me. He had a plastic bag from the deli; I could tell it was full of packages of pudding cups. He set it down on the floor. "Zo, what are you doing in here?"

"Nothing," I said, pointedly shoving the blue box back on the shelf in the wrong place. A huge, dusty thesaurus fell over. I ignored it. "I thought you had a dinner."

"I canceled it," he said quietly, sitting down next to me on the floor. "We need to talk about this, Ace."

I dragged the heel of my hand across my eyes when I felt angry tears spring to the surface. Dad handed me the cloth handkerchief from his pocket. I took it, but didn't use it, clenching it between my fists instead.

"Look, I know you don't want to meet them, kid. I don't blame you. But they're part of who you are. They're part of who your mother was—"

"They rejected and abandoned her!" I shouted, practically ripping the cloth square in half. "Seriously, *screw* them—they *aren't* a part of me. I don't want them in my life!"

Why couldn't he understand?

Dad's voice was quiet. "I'm pretty pissed at them, too, Ace. You know that. Things might have been very different if they'd reacted another way to your mom's marrying me. Who knows what might've happened if she were still here—maybe her parents would've come around like she said, and then you would've grown up with a whole other kind of family. I don't want to deprive you of that chance."

"Well, she's not here and things aren't different. And I like our family the way it is."

"So do I." Dad reached over and took the crumpled handkerchief back, then attempted to wipe my cheek with it. I pulled away. He sighed and shoved it back in his pocket. "Look, Zona. I'm not gonna be around forever, and they're your only living relatives. You may need these people someday."

"Is this your way of telling me you're sick or something?" I felt my throat starting to constrict. I reminded myself to breathe and not panic. "Because you have to—"

"No, no, no—stop. I'm not sick. I'm *fine*. I swear."

My dad's never lied to me, ever . . . but I had to be double sure. "Swear on the Gray Lady and her legacy?" I managed to squeak.

"Yes. Times ten." He smiled wanly. *Now* this *is our family*, I thought. Bad newspaper jokes and all. And that's all I wanted.

Dad went on. "But I also can't see the future. There's cancer in our family, and heart disease, diabetes . . . I'm just trying to look out for you."

"Do they even know I exist? What are we going to do, show up and yell sur—"

Dad's cell phone buzzed angrily in his jacket pocket, long and loud; since I was here with him, I knew it was probably his editor. If he ignored it, the house phone would start to ring.

"Just answer it," I said. "I want to be by myself for a while, okay? I need to think."

Dad nodded solemnly as he stood up. I could hear him answering the call in the kitchen. I retrieved the blue box from the shelf, straightened the cover, and put it carefully back in its correct place.

I didn't know what to do next. But it was clear that my plans to dissuade Dad had failed—and I suppose, deep down, I knew they would.

Maybe it was time to try something else.

8

Best Friend Discovers She Doesn't Know Everything After All

Hilary Bauer, 15, learned tonight that her best friend Zona had been keeping a pretty major secret from her, which is kind of unbelievable considering they know everything about each other. Plus, Hilary taught Zona how to do the monkey bars and use tampons.

"Seriously, I couldn't believe it!" Ms. Bauer told our inside source. "You think you know someone and then . . . well. I guess it's her business, but I'd be lying if I said my feelings weren't a little hurt. I mean, how could she not trust me with something this big?!"

Ms. Lowell declined to comment, preferring instead to suck down five pudding cups in a very impressive display of gluttony.

Filed, 4:12 p.m., Manhattan.

I never told Hilary about the blue box, even though I tell her everything, because I didn't know how to explain it. I didn't want her to feel sorry for me. It's one thing to whine about missing school or having to leave New York. It's another to tell your best friend that an entire group of people rejected you before you were even born and now you're going to show up on their doorstep.

I guess I could've told her, or Matt, sometime, even shown them the letters . . . but there was never really a good moment to. Why make everyone pity you for no reason? And now it felt like it was too late, like I should've told them before and I was going to look like a freak.

But at least I'd be a freak whose best friends understood her. Which seemed like it might be what I really needed right now—because being depressed and angry with my own personal "Greece Is Awesome!" cheerleading squad wasn't working out so well.

Hilary came over the next day after school. Matty had taken up residence at his favorite Starbucks, and I figured it would be easier to do this one person at a time, anyway. We grabbed snacks and went up to my room, where I'd left the blue box on my bed.

I didn't explain, just handed it to her. I knew she'd understand when she saw the sealed letters and the one my dad wrote.

"So . . . does this mean these people don't even know you *exist*?" Hilary gaped at me after she'd finished reading my dad's heartbreaking letter. Her mouth was actually hanging open like a fish.

"Well. I guess they do now," I mumbled around a mouthful of pudding. "I mean, right? I don't actually know."

Hilary plucked out a picture of my mom and dad in

Greece. My mom was super tan, with long, wavy dark hair and wearing a blue bikini. My dad was wearing board shorts that looked absolutely ridiculous and holding a bottle of beer. They were both laughing.

"Wow, awesome picture," Hilary said. "Your dad looks so young!"

"I know. And look at his long hair! I don't know *what* they were thinking back then, seriously."

Hilary rolled onto her stomach and fished another photo out of the box. A picture of my mother, hiding her face behind a big hat on the beach. My dad took it the first week they met.

"How come you never showed me this stuff before? I mean, obviously you can do whatever you want. Family stuff is, you know, it's private, I get that. It's just, you talk about your mom like it's no big deal, so I never guessed . . . I just didn't, I dunno. I'm rambling. Sorry."

"No, it's okay." I slipped the old picture of my parents back in the box and took out an even older one of my mom posing with a bunch of people—her brothers and their wives, probably. My dad wasn't sure who they all were, and the label on the back was in Greek, of course. "Honestly? I guess when I learned about the letters I was upset, but you and I didn't know each other yet, and then later . . . there was just never a time to mention it, I guess, without it seeming overdramatic or whatever. I mean, I didn't think about it much—why would I? It never occurred to me I'd ever have to meet these people."

"Have you looked them up online yet? I bet you have cousins. What about getting someone to translate the stuff on these pictures? It might give you a better idea of what you're up against, you know?"

"Who do you know who speaks Greek?"

"Zo, seriously? You live in New York City, for crying out loud. We'll find someone. Now let's look online." She grabbed my laptop. "What's their last name?"

"Marousopoulou," I said slowly. It was the first time I'd ever said it out loud, actually, and I had no idea if I was pronouncing it correctly. Hilary looked at me, her fingers suspended over the keys.

"I'll type it," I said with a laugh, and carefully punched it in.

Hilary and I stared at the seemingly endless list of entries on the screen—page after page on Google, and half of them in Greek. "Maybe 'Marousopoulou' is like 'Smith' in Greece?" she finally suggested.

"No clue." I sighed. "Maybe I'll just ask my dad. I mean, he must have some kind of plan to contact them, right? If he hasn't already?"

"*You* didn't find out all the facts? Shame on you, and on your dad for letting you get away with it!" Hilary chided, smiling.

"Yeah, yeah, okay." I rolled my eyes. "Anyway, no need for us to stalk random people like this."

"What else is there to do?" Hil asked, flopping back onto my bed. She had a point.

She took out her cell phone and scrolled through while I picked a playlist for us to listen to. Suddenly, I heard her gasp behind me.

"You okay? What's wrong?"

She was staring at her phone like she'd seen a ghost.

"I, um . . . I just got an e-mail." she said slowly.

"Okay . . . Hil, what's going on?" I asked. "Is everything . . . Hil, talk to me. You're scaring me!"

She looked up and swallowed. I braced myself for the news that something terrible had happened.

"It's from Ben. Ben Walker. He . . . he asked me to be features editor. For when you leave, I mean," she said, her words tumbling over one another. "But, you know, I didn't . . . I mean, he had to choose someone, and he says all the upperclassmen who applied are doing other things by now, so . . . But of course if you . . . I mean . . . Um. Zona? Are you . . . are you okay?"

I sat down heavily in my desk chair.

"Yeah, I'm okay," I managed. I was trying very hard to remain calm and rational, like a good newspaperwoman should. (And which lately, it seemed, I was less and less good at doing.) After all, this wasn't a betrayal. I was leaving. They couldn't hang up the features editor position like a retired football number. Though the fact that Ben chose another sophomore to replace me made me far less special . . . But like she said, my previous, older competitors were committed to other extracurriculars now. It made sense.

And Hil is very organized, and she's a pretty good writer.

And she's my best friend.

And yet.

"This is totally unfair of me, and I'm not mad at you, but I . . . I just need a second. I'll be right back. Okay? I just—I gotta go."

I dashed across the hall into the bathroom, turning the sink on full blast. I sat down on the toilet lid and started taking deep breaths.

I knew I was being unreasonable. It's not like there was some nefarious plot to take my job. (A job I worked very, very hard to get, as you may recall. A job that was a jumping-off point, part of a trajectory, and the most important thing I'd ever achieved in my young life, just to review.) Hilary obviously felt terrible about being asked to take over. This wasn't personal.

Although, an evil little voice inside my head said, *she could say* no. *She could tell them she refused and that they should let me do the job from Greece. Why didn't she suggest that right away? Maybe she wanted the job all along!*

A sensible voice chimed in. *Hilary doesn't even* like *writing!* it said. *She's only working on the* Reflector *because her parents made her. You know that.*

The sensible voice had a point. Hilary is an incredible artist. She can draw and paint and make jewelry and create mixed-media pieces—you name it, she's amazing at it. But her parents think art is "nice, but not an appropriate choice for a serious future." They want her to be a lawyer

47

or a doctor, like they are. So instead of working on the arts magazine or taking photography lessons or designing her own fashion line as an independent study, Hilary works on the *Reflector*—because the Bauers think it'll look like a "more serious endeavor" (they're *obsessed* with serious endeavors) on her college applications.

Of course it wasn't her fault—but then, whose was it? Ben Walker's? My dad's? Mine?

I felt like a bad friend, and a bad person. All I wanted was to have things be the way they were a couple of weeks ago, when my entire world was two best friends, my dad, writing, and living in New York City. When my biggest problem was Ben Walker not being in love with me. When things were essentially perfect.

I turned off the water and went back to my room. Hilary was still sitting on my bed, looking lost.

"Any more pudding cups in here?" I said, coming inside. I sat down next to her on the bed.

"I think you ate them all," she said hesitantly. "Listen, Zo—"

"If there's no pudding, then we're out of distractions. So let's plan your reign as features editor," I interrupted. I reached over to my desk and snatched up my precious silver notebook. "I'm going to give you this." As I handed it over I wondered if I was insulting her—if she'd assume I didn't think she could handle the job on her own. "If you want it, I mean," I added quickly.

"Oh my God, yes *please*," Hilary exclaimed, clasping it tightly to her chest. "I know these ideas are your babies, but I have no idea what I'm doing. Or what *to* do. I haven't written back to Ben yet. Should I say yes? If you don't want me to, I won't." She looked at me, and I could see in her eyes that she was totally panicking.

"Of *course* you should. I'm sorry about how I reacted; I just . . ."

"I know," Hilary said. "You don't have to explain. Ugh, why is everything so *complicated* lately? Your dad is kind of ruining our lives."

"Tell me about it!" I laughed and pulled Hil into a bear hug. She hugged back, hard, and I knew in that moment, despite everything, that it would all be okay. Because we had each other.

"Honestly, Zona," she said, "if I do this, I'm gonna need your help. This feels like a disaster waiting to happen. I can barely put an article together without you, much less a whole section, and editing other people's stuff—"

"It won't be a disaster, I promise," I said, giving her my most reassuring smile. "You're going to be brilliant. We can Skype every day and work on it together, okay? I'm going to be your right-hand man. Woman. Person? Right-hand person."

Hilary smiled tentatively. "I would love it if you'd be my right-hand person. This just isn't what I'm good at, Zo. I don't know what Ben was thinking." She stopped smiling and looked down at the notebook in her lap. "This is supposed to be *your* job, not mine."

"Well, it's your job now," I said. "You're going to do a *phenomenal* job, Hil, even without my help. But if you want it, I'm all yours."

And I really meant it.

9

I crashed backward into the door of the girls' room at school on Monday morning, gasping with laughter, Matt hot on my trail.

"Matty! You can't follow me in here, you idiot! This is a safe zone!"

He hooted dramatically and turned on his heel. "You can't hide forever, woman! I will have my revenge!"

I escaped into the safety of the bathroom, wiping away tears of laughter.

Teen Attempts To Wash Boots In Sink, Fails To Consider How Disgusting School Bathrooms Actually Are

It was an odd scene today in the first-floor girls' room at the end of second lunch. Kelsey Finkelstein, 15, was discovered standing barefoot and pantsless with a turquoise sweater wrapped around her waist. She was observed angrily scrubbing leather ankle boots, socks, and dark-wash jeans in the sink; all items were covered in what appeared to be cement.

The water was running in one of the sinks. I figured someone who cared nothing about the future of our planet left it on, so I went around the tiled corner to shut it off . . . and there she was, standing at the sink with intrepid reporter Lexi Bradley. My rival for Ben's affections: Kelsey Finkelstein.

"Uh . . . what are you guys doing?" I asked.

Kelsey heaved an enormous sigh, shaking her head, and Lexi giggled. "Oh, Kels just thought it would be a good idea to stomp through a newly poured sidewalk during a free period. NBD."

"I didn't *know*. There was no *sign*. How many times do I have to tell you this?" Kelsey muttered bitterly. Lexi rolled her eyes at me, and I tried not to laugh.

"Do you . . . do you mean the sidewalk across the street? They've been doing construction there for—"

"Apparently the guy who was supposed to be putting the new cones down ran to get a snack at the exact time Kelsey decided to go to Barnes and Noble. By the time I got there to help her, he was back. And yelling a lot," Lexi explained.

"He yanked me out. *And* he was *very* rude. I should totally sue," Kelsey grumbled.

"He lifted you out because when you tried to *step* out you lost your boots and ended up making it even worse!" Lexi insisted. "What was he supposed to do, leave you there til the cement hardened?"

Trying not to laugh wasn't going well at all. You know, maybe she's earned Ben Walker—I've never heard of someone with worse luck than Kelsey Finkelstein.

"Do you need . . . shoes? I might have—" I offered.

"I've got sneakers and some gym pants in my locker," Kelsey cut in. "But thanks, Zona, that's really nice. Unlike *some* people, who just think this is hilarious," she continued, glaring at Lexi.

"Well. It is *kind* of hilarious," I agreed tentatively. I didn't really hang out with Kelsey, and I didn't want her to think I was making fun of her. "You want me to write an article about it? 'Student Cruelly Accosted by Quick-dry Cement'?"

Kelsey smiled wryly as she stepped into her half-wet pants. "Thanks, but no thanks. My tenure at the *Reflector* is over, thank God. Good headline, though," she added, wringing her socks out.

"You okay?" Lexi asked me while handing Kelsey a bunch of paper towels to dry her feet with. "Did you . . . come in here to pee, or . . . ?"

"Oh! No, no. Just hiding from Matty. Matt Klausner," I clarified. "We were . . . never mind. Had to be there." I felt awkward now, standing by the door watching Ben's girlfriend wriggle into wet socks.

"Oh my God, this is . . . disgusting," Kelsey exclaimed. "I'm just not going to wear socks." She stripped them off and shoved her bare feet into the wet leather boots. "I'll probably get some kind of rash and have to have my feet amputated. Why do I even leave the house?" Lexi helped her up and handed her the turquoise sweater.

"'Kay, well, see you later. Hey, you doing anything cool for New Year's Eve?" Lexi asked on the way out the door.

"Oh, I'll be . . . I'll be in Greece. Well, in a plane on the way to Greece, actually. I'm moving there. For the rest of the year," I added hurriedly. Saying it like that sounded so final.

"Really? That's amazing! I think Ben mentioned that, actually," Kelsey said. "Have an awesome time."

"You gonna do a foreign correspondent column for the *Reflector*?" Lexi asked, pausing with her hand on the door.

"I . . . Actually, that's a great thought," I said slowly. "I don't know what I'm going to do. Hilary's taking over for me as features editor, so . . . I may help her, or—"

"Just thinking out loud." Lexi shrugged. "Anyway, see you later!"

There was still a little time before the bell, and it was nice to be alone for a minute. I took a look at myself in the mirror of the now quiet bathroom. The bathroom I share with my dad at home is pretty small and has terrible lighting, so I didn't usually spend a whole lot of time in there taking stock.

I thought about the pictures of my mom in the blue box. I know I look like her, but I usually don't mull it over much. I wondered what the rest of her family looked like, and how it would feel to be in a room with a bunch of people who all look . . . related.

I didn't think I was going to like it. Just thinking about it made me feel pressured and claustrophobic. Saying "I'm moving to Greece" just then, like it was the truth (even if I still didn't want to accept it), and having it feel not so scary was one thing. But the other part, the family part . . . I didn't think I could do it. I didn't think I should *have* to do it.

But with every passing day, it was becoming more and more clear that I really *didn't* have a choice.

Hilary was right: I *should* have all the information. Knowledge is power, after all.

10

"Okay," I said, flopping into a chair at the kitchen table. "I want to know."

Dad looked up from the sad-looking Hot Pocket he was trying to eat without burning his tongue. It was Tuesday afternoon, just six short days before we were leaving for Greece, and also Christmas Eve. Why school made us come in for a single day I will never understand. Probably spite. Anyway, since we don't celebrate Christmas (Dad was raised Jewish, and I was raised nothing), he had pointedly left a hideous suitcase in my room with a Post-it attached that read: *Daughter Packs.* I was pretty sure the suitcase had been made from a tapestry in 1937 and may at one time have had a family of anthropomorphic voles living in it. I shoved it under my bed and hoped it wasn't haunted.

"You want to know what?" he asked, his mouth full. "I'm going to need a bit more to go on, Ace."

We hadn't talked about Greece—other than logistics—since the night I cried in his office. I knew he was giving me space to sort out my feelings and waiting til I brought it up again. I also knew the clock was ticking and the situation wasn't going to change. So now I was ready.

"I want to know what the plan is. With the Marousopoulous. Are we just going to ring the bell at Mom's old house and be, like, 'Hi, we're your long-lost relatives!' or something? Do they even speak English? I mean, do you know anything *about* these people, other than that they are awful and mean?"

Dad started twirling a fork over his fingers; it's a nervous habit of his, which he usually does with a pen. "They speak English," he said, more to the wall than to me.

His tone made me immediately suspicious.

"Okay . . . and how do you know that?" He didn't respond, but switched the dancing fork to his other hand. I reached over and plucked it away. "Dad. What are you not telling me?"

He looked up. "Well, I know your cousins speak English, at least. And no, we're not just going to show up randomly. They know we're coming and they know all about you."

Father Continues To Drop Bombshells, Scar Only Child

During a conversation that was already pretty high-stakes as far as she was concerned, local resident Zona Lowell was floored when her father revealed a piece of information he'd been keeping secret for two entire years.

"TWO YEARS? ARE YOU FREAKING SERIOUS?!" Ms. Lowell was reported to have screeched in horror.

David Lowell, known best lately for his capacity to shock and dismay, explained thusly: "You have a cousin named Yiota . . . I think I'm saying that right. Anyway, she's in college, and she was taking a course, you know, in genealogy or something, and she was asking her mother, Angela—your mother's brother's wife—about the family . . . and then she wanted to look up Hélenè, because no one ever talks about her, and her mom didn't think that was a good idea, but she told Yiota my name and she looked online and found me. And then she found you."

Ms. Lowell did not have a comment when this article went to press, as she was too busy sitting with her mouth hanging open in disbelief.

Filed, 5:14 p.m., Manhattan.

"How could you keep this from me for two whole years, Dad?!" I finally said.

"I tried to bring it up several times and you refused to talk about it! And then you were starting high school and I didn't want to . . . Look, Ace, this isn't easy for me, either, okay? In fact, it pretty much sucks. But maybe it doesn't have to. And this isn't only about you, as hard as that may be for your teenage brain to accept."

"Hey!"

"This trip isn't only about the Marousopoulous. I really want to write this story. Greece has had a massive impact on my life, too, you know? And right now it's enmeshed in a multilayered, fascinating, financially dire situation. I want to tell *Greece's* story. Greeks are different, and they care about different things. I want to be the one to really uncover what's going on, if I can." He folded his hands on the desk, breathed deeply, and looked me in the eye. "This is very important to me. But so is your getting to know your mom's family. And it's happening. Period."

I slumped a bit, defeated but not so angry anymore. What's important to my dad is important to me, too—we're a team, after all.

"Can I at least get my bearings before I have to meet the entire family? I hear you, okay, and I know we're going and I'm . . . not *cool* with it, but resigned, anyway. But this is a *lot* all at once."

"That's not unreasonable," Dad said. "They've had time to adjust to this on their end. Yiota talked to the family. Your grandfather died years ago, but your grandmother wants to meet you very badly. You're family, and Greeks love family. It's literally the most important thing to them: not money or jobs . . . family is *it*."

"Could have fooled me," I muttered under my breath. Dad ignored me.

"We'll be in Athens—where your school is—for the bulk of the winter, and most of the relatives live on Crete. You can meet them on your spring break. But you have to reserve judgment and see who these people actually are, all right? No reporting without a verifiable source?" He was looking at me almost pleadingly.

"Yes, I know." I paused. "But that goes for you, too, right?"

"Well," he said, retrieving his fork and flipping it around again. "Actually, they don't want to meet *me*. I'm still the enemy."

I jumped out of my chair again. "Then forget it! We're a package deal—"

"Zo, I'll be working anyway. Look, I know you're pissed. But I also know how important these people were to your mom, and she would want you to meet them. She loved them, and they loved her."

"Wow. Cheap shot, Dad."

"I know. I'm sorry. But my only other go-to is 'I'm the father and I said so,' and that one hasn't worked since you were nine."

I smiled before I could stop myself. Dad visibly relaxed.

"So can you just cooperate?" he said. "Maybe it'll be fun. Maybe you'll learn something. I mean, this is a pretty cool opportunity. I bet every kid in your class is jealous as hell."

"I guess." I picked at a loose thread on my sweater. "I told Hilary about the letters."

"Okay."

"I don't know why I never told her before. I just . . . I thought she'd feel sorry for me. And that would really suck, you know? Because I don't feel sorry for me. It just makes me really mad. At them, I mean."

"I know. And you can tell them that. But at least be willing to hear what they have to say."

"I'm gonna go . . . pack." I heaved a dramatic sigh and got up to leave the kitchen.

"Hey, Ace?"

I turned back.

"We're in this together, okay? You and me, just like always. I swear on the Gray Lady and her legacy."

"Thanks, Dad," I said. I knew he meant it, so I'd try to mean it, too. *Try* being the operative word, of course.

11

When I got to my room, I found a catalog for a school called GIS, Greek International School, on my desk. Ugh.

Leafing through, I thought it looked pretty standard, as private schools go. Smiling kids (artfully arranged to show off versatility of race, age, and size) "hanging out" in classrooms, on benches, and at sporting events. There was a mission statement explaining the importance of bringing American school systems to Greece. It said that everyone who attends GIS must speak fluent English. That was a relief, at least.

Starting high school the year before, dealing with new people and buildings and teachers . . . that was hard enough, but I had Hilary and Matty with me. In Greece I'd be completely alone. And as for writing, who knew what opportunities I'd have there?

I flopped onto the rug next to my bed and peeked underneath. Yup—the suitcase was still there. I dragged it out and stared into its dusty interior.

I picked up the copy of *Let's Go to Greece!* Dad had given

me during his initial breakfast announcement, and which I had subsequently also shoved under my bed. It didn't say anywhere in there if they had Duane Reade drugstores in Athens or Crete or anywhere. *They must have something similar, though, right?* I thought.

But what if the bad economy shut down all the stores and there's nothing left? Should I pack six months' worth of SPF 15 facial moisturizer? What about ketchup? Did they eat ketchup there? Should I bring some? What if all they had was olives? I would slowly starve to death. Should I bring a few hundred Nutri-Grain bars with me?

I imagined what my mysterious relatives would think if I showed up with a suitcase filled solely with breakfast bars and face lotion. They'd probably tie me up in the back-yard and let the goats eat me. If they had goats. Maybe the goats and Tony would develop a beautiful symbiotic relationship heretofore unseen in the wild, and I'd make a YouTube video that would go viral and I'd have to come home to make appearances on the late-night talk show circuit.

Now I was going to be seriously disappointed if there were no goats in Greece.

Well-Meaning Bffs Attempt To Help In Relocation Disaster

Hilary Bauer and Matthew Klausner, friends of soon-to-be-displaced high school sophomore Zona Lowell, tried valiantly to help their pal prepare for her trip abroad—with mixed results.

"This is our last real time

together before she leaves, and she isn't even being fun. And I am not discussing that heinous suitcase. Or helping to pack it," Mr. Klausner commented disdainfully.

It seemed that the Greece-oriented agenda planned by Ms. Lowell's friends also went underappreciated. "But I hate musicals! Why are you doing this to me?" Zona scowled ungratefully when presented with a DVD of *Mamma Mia!* Despite admiring the admittedly gorgeous scenery, Lowell refused to budge on her opinion that the film was "beyond lame and embarrassing to all parties involved."

A follow-up viewing of *My Big Fat Greek Wedding* was better received, mostly because there was limited singing and lots of John Corbett. However, Bauer and Klausner are now seriously reconsidering the plan to take Ms. Lowell to a local Greek restaurant to try some traditional fare, as Ms. Lowell is indeed being a "total downer who isn't even trying to see the bright side, especially since [Ms. Bauer and Mr. Klausner] are the ones being abandoned for half a year!"

Ms. Lowell refused to comment further, but was observed collapsing in a heap on Ms. Bauer's family room floor in despair. Luckily, the room has very fancy, thick carpeting, so no injuries were sustained.

Filed, 12:43 a.m., Lower East Side, NYC.

And then, before I could fully process it, there was no more time left. Holiday gifts were exchanged, Matt and Hil left for winter break trips with their families, and my bag was actually packed (and not just with ketchup and goat treats).

New Year's Eve arrived, freezing cold and daunting. This was it. Everything was about to change, for better or worse. And I was still afraid that *worse* was the direction we were heading in.

I e-mailed my cousin Yiota right before we left for the

airport. I felt like I should, now that I knew about her role in this whole reunion. I wrote three versions of the e-mail, each time thinking I should sound less (or more) enthusiastic or tell her less (or more) about myself . . . or not write at all.

Ultimately I went for a middle ground, just a friendly-ish introduction. Short and sweet. I shut down my computer for the last time on American soil and added the laptop to my carry-on. Then I said good-bye to my room, and our apartment, and my life as I'd known it for the last fifteen years. We doped up Tony, loaded our luggage into the trunk of a cab, and . . . we were off to the airport. Just like that.

12

And now here we are. In Athens, on a little cobbled street in Kallithea. We buzz the fourth-floor apartment, load everything into an elevator that looks suspiciously unstable, and head up to what will be our home for the next six months. The woman we're subletting from opens the door and ushers us inside, cooing over Tony and rushing around, bringing a platter of olives and grapes and cheese to the table in the living room.

She seems really nice, but I am suddenly rendered speechless by the proximity of both food (*not* the olives—gross) and a bed to collapse onto. After some small talk, a quick tour of the place, a lesson on how to turn the hot water on with a red switch, and a short speech about what is definitely the most confusing washing machine I have ever seen, she gives us keys, wishes us the best, and leaves.

So. Now it's real.

. . .

Time Difference And Father Both Impossible To Deal With, Study Shows

New research indicates that jet lag is a real and incredibly debilitating condition, according to sources from the Lowell Institute of Discomfort. Lead scientist Zona Lowell, 15, explained that "jet lag sounds like this ridiculous concept—I mean, just sleep at a different time and get over it, right?—but it's actually a crushing, unforgiving reality that ruins lives and, possibly, father-daughter relationships."

Her research partner in this venture, David Lowell, proved to be even more susceptible to the misery of not being able to sleep (a problem not helped by the fact that mattresses in Greece are only three inches thick and not squashy at all). Coffee consumption was noted as having increased, as did irritated comments about "teenage girls who need to get out from underfoot when people are trying to do serious work."

As the study is only a few days old, it is presumed that circumstances will improve based on further data collection, including but not limited to: figuring out what anything at the supermarket actually is, which euro coins are which in under five minutes, and how cell phones work in this country.

Adjunct consultant Matthew Klausner of New York City commented, "This whole thing sounds like a hot mess. How hard is it to figure out Google Voice, seriously?" This opinion was not well-received by either member of the research team.

Filed, 6:39 p.m., Athens (11:39 a.m., NYC).

It turns out that in Greece, students have their final exams *after* winter break instead of before, which sucks for them (can you imagine having to study for tests during vacation?) but is pretty great for me. I don't have to actually go to school—meet anyone, sit alone like a total outcast, etc.—til late January.

On the other hand, I don't exactly have anything to do. If this were New York I'd be totally fine with hopping on the train and checking out some museums or walking in Central Park or window-shopping. But in Athens? I don't know if I'd make it two blocks. Not that people aren't nice, but I can't understand them, even when they speak English; if they talk to me in Greek it's like listening to Elvish or something. The words slide through my head before I can grab on to anything. My made-up sign language is improving, though, so I guess that's something.

Maybe I'll become a street mime. Though probably that's more of a Paris thing.

This Just In: Teen Unable To Function Without Certain Necessities

A care package was dispatched to Athens earlier this week in response to the desperate pleas of a recent and now frantic 15-year-old transplant. Upon her arrival, she discovered that drugstores there (which are all disguised as churches, with big green light-up crosses instead of signs) do not stock normal tampons. If you can't read Greek letters, there's no way to tell the difference between dish soap and shampoo, since all the bottles look the same. Not a mistake you want to make.

Plus, grocery stores were found to carry weird scratchy toilet paper, and paper towels are impossible to find at all. Forget about ranch dressing or Corn Pops cereal. And instead of pudding cups, Greeks eat something called "spoon sweet," which is kind of a cross between candied fruit and marmalade. (It's not bad on yogurt, actually. But it's still not pudding.)

Filed, 12:34 p.m., Athens.

• • •

"So, what actually happened to the Greek economy, any-way?" I ask Dad over lunch about a week after we arrived. While I'm glad my internal clock has finally adjusted to the time difference, I'm sick of reading. I'm also sick of the three TV channels they have here, and of exploring the five-block radius around our apartment. (I'm too chicken to go any farther by myself, and Dad's too busy to join me.) So I guess if I'm going to be here, I might as well participate in Dad's project. Maybe I can be his secretary. That'll at least give me something to *do*.

"Well, it's complicated—"

"I should hope so, if you're gonna get a whole book out of it," I tease him. I toss Tony a piece of chicken from my sandwich.

"Har har. I don't know what it's gonna be yet. Quit with the pressure, kid!"

"Sorry," I say. "Anyway, go on."

"Well, to put it in very simple terms, before Greece joined the European Union and started using the euro, they had their own money system, using drachmas. They didn't have property taxes, and they didn't have to claim everything they owned, either. So if someone owned six acres of olive trees and made oil from them, they might tell the government they owned one acre. Or half an acre. And that was what they paid taxes on."

"How could they do that? Who paid for roads and schools and . . . stuff?"

"Well, exactly. The government paid for it, borrowing, building up debt. It's a different culture here, more . . . relaxed. I'm not saying they don't care, but that stuff isn't a priority. Living is. Again, this is all very broad. But basically, once they were in the EU, they suddenly had to pay property taxes. People had owned land for years and never anticipated having to pay another dime—so they didn't have the money. Plus all the prices had to be jacked up to match other countries on the same system, so things suddenly cost three or four times what they had, but the amount people were earning stayed the same. Businesses closed, people lost jobs . . . Suddenly there's this massive unemployment problem, homelessness . . . and no one knows what to do."

"I guess they can't just go back to the old system, huh?"

"Well, that's what some of the riots were about, but no, they can't. Because the world knows about the debt now. It's too late. On top of all those things, there are claims of massive political corruption. There are a lot of facets to the problem. And it's a pity. Greece was—is, as you'll see, if you ever leave our street—a beautiful place, with so much culture and so much *love* of that culture . . . and now many people just think of it as a place where everyone screwed up."

"That should be the name of your book."

"Very helpful, Ace. Thanks. Now get out so I can do some work, willya?"

My father wants me to call my cousin Yiota—aka the one who started this mess—and ask her to take me on a tour of the city. I'm tempted, since I'm bored and maybe a *tiny* bit interested in my new surroundings, as a good journalist always should be.

The longer I sit in the apartment reading my friends' status updates, realizing that Skyping with them all day and pretending to still be home is practically impossible with the seven-hour time difference, the more my resolve to avoid the Marousopoulous weakens.

I guess it can't hurt to ask her how to use the subway. Or say a few key words in Greek, such as "Sorry, I don't speak Greek" or "Do you speak English?" or "How do I get to New York from here?"

On the eighth day, I cave. I reopen Yiota's exuberant response to my e-mail and look at her long, strange phone number. She seems pretty cool in the e-mail, and very excited about meeting me. How bad could it be, really? It's just for an afternoon . . .

13

I'm standing nervously by the steps at the Monastiraki train station a couple days later, wondering if I've made a huge mistake. I scan the faces of people milling around, trying to see if one of them maybe looks a little like me. Then, just as I'm considering ducking back onto a train to go home, I feel a tap on my shoulder.

Yiota is tall and broad-shouldered, with perfectly clear olive skin, black eyes, and thick black hair that flows down to her waist. She looks kind of like Princess Jasmine from *Aladdin*, actually.

"I knew it was you right away, Zona!" she says breathlessly, pulling me to her and kissing me on both cheeks. Her voice is deeper than I expected, and she speaks English in a way that is both melodic and clipped, drawing her vowels out and cutting her consonants short. And once she starts talking . . . she doesn't stop. Not even for breath, it seems.

"It was so long before your father wrote back to me, and then so long again before he said you would be coming here to Greece, and I didn't know if I would get to meet you any time!" she gushes, linking her arm through mine and steering me down a cobbled side street.

Monastiraki turns out to be more than just a major train station. It's a huge area with a giant flea market full of tourists. Yiota points out everything as we pass by: tables topped with rows of Doc Martens and studded boots with six-inch platform heels, all kinds of clothes and pictures and creepy toys and leather jackets. There's one store selling nothing but dream catchers and crystals.

"Don't go to there for that stuff, Zona," she instructs, interrupting her own story about first contacting my dad. "They raise the prices too much, trust me. Come on, come on, *eksadélfi*—we're almost there now!"

Her energy is contagious; I scurry after her, trying to take in my surroundings at the same time.

Many of the walls outlining the maze of alleys and side streets are covered with colorful murals or just random pictures, and some merchants incorporate them into their shops.

"This one I like very much—is artistic, yes?" Yiota comments as we zip by. It's a graffitied wall with different light fixtures hanging all over it. I can't tell if the fixtures themselves are for sale or not—we're moving too quickly for me to ask—but it looks awesome.

One of the coolest things about walking around Athens is how there are modern buildings interspersed with these incredibly old—and in some places totally falling down—buildings. Like, on one corner there's an office building with a view of the Parthenon right behind it. On another there's an apartment house standing next to a thousand-year-old column that looks like it's about to fall over. An ancient wall might have a painting of anime-style women on it. The contrast is unlike anything I've ever seen; sure, New York has some old buildings, but nothing like these. I start snapping away with my phone at everything; I know Hil will love these pictures.

Finally, when I'm certain I'll never find my way back to the train station again, Yiota stops in front of a crumbly-walled building with two iron tables and a bunch of scattered chairs out front. "Ah, finally we are here!" she exclaims, tossing her purse onto one of the chairs and herself into another. "Sit, Zona, sit. This one, it is my favorite place in this neighborhood. No one knows about it—is a secret place, yes?"

I sit down, looking at the dusty ground and bunches of vines (grapes?) clinging to the wall, trying to figure out what could possibly make this café so special. But I can feel my mouth twisting into a big grin; honestly, it wouldn't matter if our final destination had been a big pile of garbage. Yiota's so excited that I can't help having fun, too. And she's still talking, talking, her voice rich and joyous, telling me how she can't wait to show me *everything* in Athens.

If this is what having a cousin is like, I think, *maybe this Greece thing won't be so bad.*

Maybe.

By the time we've had two cups of coffee and a delicious honey and nut pastry called baklava, I feel like I've known Yiota forever. I'm comfortable enough to tell her I was surprised by her super sunny attitude—I guess I thought people in Athens would be kind of miserable, since there are so many problems.

"I don't want to make light of our situation in Greece," she explains. "It *is* serious, and it *is* scary. So many people lost their jobs, or will lose their jobs . . . politicians are stealing and no one can do anything, the debt, homeless people . . . But this is the thing of Greek people: we try to be optimistic. We can't let the bad luck stop us from living. You know what I mean?"

I'm not really sure if I do, but I'm definitely interested in her perspective, and I know Dad will be, too. I wonder if everyone in Athens shares it.

As we walked through the flea market on the way to the café, I saw some people sitting on the sidewalk holding signs (presumably asking for money or food) and empty stores with broken windows. It's weird—maybe if I were from a small town, those things would be shocking. But being from New York, it just doesn't seem that extreme. Honestly, if I didn't know anything was going on with the economy, I might not have guessed it.

I can't decide if that's good or bad. Maybe it's neither. Or both.

Yiota goes on, telling me that the stray dogs we see everywhere were abandoned by their owners, which is why most of them have collars and tags. This news makes me want to cry. How can people just leave their dogs on the streets?!

"Before the Olympics in 2004 there were people sent to round them up and fix them, you know, like"—she makes a gesture like scissors cutting, and I laugh—"then they put them back to the streets. They all get fed and are happy, so don't feel too bad, okay?" Yiota says when she sees how upset I'm getting. I don't know if I really believe her, though it is kind of cute to see dogs looking both ways and crossing the streets together in the middle of a bustling city. But still, it hurts my heart to think about so many pets who've lost their families, and I want to believe the owners had no other choice.

To distract me from the plight of Greece's pet population, Yiota insists on teaching me some Greek words. The sounds are so different from English, and I need her to write them out phonetically (in Greek-lish, as she calls it) before I can say them correctly.

"I'll start with the basic things that you need to know most, okay? So: *kalimera* is 'good morning.' *Kalispera* is 'good evening.' *Kalinikta* is 'good night.' *Kalo mesimeri* is 'Good afternoon.' Now you say it back," she instructs.

"Why isn't 'good afternoon' *kali-something* like the other ones?"

Yiota looks stumped. "Because . . . it just isn't!" she finally says, laughing. "Now repeat them back, Zona!"

Once I've got those straight (the trick is to remember *M*

76

for "*mera*/morning" and *N* for "*nikta*/night"), Yiota moves on. "*Efcharisto* is 'thank you,'" she says. "Now you can say that when you order a coffee next time, yes?"

I repeat the word back to her a couple times—the *ch* is tricky to get right; it's pronounced sort of like a *K*, but with more phlegm. Like the *ch* in *challah*.

"Very good!" Yiota crows excitedly. "Next is *nay*, which means 'yes,' and *ochi*, which means 'no.' *Ochi* has the same sound like *efcharisto*. Get it?"

"*Nay* means 'yes'? That's totally confusing!" I exclaim. And here I'd been feeling so good about my progress.

Yiota laughs again. "Remember, Zona, Greek existed long before English. So maybe it is English that is more confusing?"

Well. I suppose she has a point there.

Luckily the next word she teaches me is *signomi*, which means 'sorry.' I have a feeling I'll be using that one more than any other.

I'm excited to finally be able to speak a little Greek instead of just looking like a dumb American who can't be bothered to learn the language.

After we pay the bill, Yiota leads me back through the market and we come out at a side street buzzing with cars. Since I've basically perfected the art of jaywalking over the last decade, I don't hesitate to step right into the street instead of waiting for the light. After all, there's no way anything could be a bigger pedestrian threat than NYC cab drivers and tourists on rental bikes.

Turns out NYC has *nothing* on Athens. Yiota yanks me back by my coat just before six different cars almost flatten me simultaneously.

"*Never* assume that a car will stop to let you cross the street! They don't stop, cars here, sometimes not even for lights!" she gasps. "We are crazy drivers," she adds with pride when we've both gotten our breath back.

She's not kidding. Greek drivers seem to be on their own race courses. It's like the main goal is not to get where they're going, but to find someone to curse at or run over on the way. I'm glad I'll be taking the train and not attempting to drive or ride alongside these maniacs.

Transit System Completely Nuts, Operates On "Honor System"

Intrepid world traveler and hard-boiled reporter Zona Lowell was stunned today when she discovered the total inadequacy of the ticketing system for the Athens subway.

"Wait a second," Lowell was heard remarking to her cousin Yiota Marousopoulou, who has gone along with this charade for years. "You're telling me you're supposed to buy a ticket and scan it through those machines *[here Lowell indicated the three parking meter–shaped machines in the middle of the station]* and then . . . that's it? Seriously?

There's no barrier? Nothing to stop you from just walking through without scanning anything at all? Why would anyone ever buy a ticket?"

"Well, when you scan your ticket it's stamped with a time, and then you can use it for ninety minutes," Marousopoulou explained, unfazed. "Because . . . well, you have to scan it. Sometimes there's a man who asks—"

"'Sometimes there's a man'? Couldn't you just say you were American and didn't know? This is the silliest system I have ever heard of, honestly," Lowell scoffed.

By the time Yiota heads home to do some schoolwork, I adore her completely. I can't believe I was afraid to meet her—it feels incredible to be related to someone so pretty, so cool, so generous of spirit. It makes me wonder if everyone in our family is just like her, or if that's too much to hope for.

After our first meeting, Yiota and I spend the whole next week exploring Athens. The first few days she takes me to see all the obvious places that *Let's Go to Greece!* told me to check out, both of us pretending to be tourists just for the fun of it. We trek up to the famous Acropolis, which is actually the name of the site where the Parthenon is— *acropolis* means "highest city." The Parthenon is the monument everyone recognizes from postcards: an enormous white marble temple with massive columns that was built to honor the goddess Athena, for whom the city is named. (Full disclosure: I never even *thought* of that, despite having done an entire unit on Greek mythology in sixth grade. Fail.)

We tour the Old Palace in Syntagma Square, which is the biggest building I've ever seen and houses the current parliament. Past Museum Mile we check out Ermou Street, where all the fancy shops are. Every woman we see is dressed to the nines, and I feel very shabby in my UGGs and gray puffy jacket. We walk through Omonoia, the center of Athens, and visit the National Library and the college square on Panepistimiou Street. Students and teachers are picketing (separately) outside one of the buildings, and nearby there's a whole slew of policemen with very intense-looking rifles. I get pretty freaked out at first, but Yiota just laughs and tells me demonstrations are just what Greek people *do*.

"Look over there, at these police right here," she whispers in my ear. Lo and behold, the cops are all on their phones, texting. Interesting.

"What do the signs say?" I ask her, pointing to the protesters.

"Ah, well—the teachers, they want more money, of course. And the students don't want to have to pay for the books. They used to be free, you know." She sighs, sounding frustrated. "My college was closed for two weeks during exams last year," she continues. "It happens like this every year, mostly. This is one big change with the economic problems, having to pay for school supplies."

Apparently *before*, the country paid for everything— college and books and housing . . . I couldn't believe it. Imagine college being free!

"But here is what, Zona," Yiota adds. "There are always, historically, demonstrations in Greece. Now we are on the world stage, people are paying more attention, it seems like a new thing. But really it isn't."

I make a mental note to tell my dad all of this for his research, then snap a picture of one of the cops texting. Unfortunately, he spots me and yells something in Greek that sounds angry, so we quickly move on.

The second half of the week, we explore places that aren't on the tourist maps, like coffee shops down tiny alleys where Yiota and her friends hang out for hours even though they only buy one cup of coffee apiece. I explain that in New York the manager would kick them out after an hour if they weren't buying anything else, but they just crack up laughing and tell me that isn't the way Greeks do things.

We get gelato (like ice cream, but somehow *more* ice creamy) and gyros, which are meat sandwiches on pita bread with a yogurt sauce called tzatziki. Of course, we have those in New York, too, but Yiota is quick to point out that *real* gyros have french fries on top, which I admit I've never seen before. Yiota gives up on making me try olives and makes spanakopita (amazing flaky pastry pie filled with spinach and feta cheese) in a funny little oven that sits on top of the counter in her tiny, light-filled apartment. It's absolutely delicious.

We spend one night walking around by a gorgeous marina in an area called Floisvos, where everyone in the city seems to be hanging out, even at midnight—kids my age, college students like my cousin, old people, mothers with tiny babies asleep in their carriages . . . and everyone just commingles. It's so odd to see, somehow, and yet it just *works*. No one is cooler than anyone else or doesn't belong.

The water at the marina is lit from below with blue lights, and there are giant black fish swimming around that follow us as we walk past. We sit at the edge of the water drinking coffee, looking at the massive ships docked at the harbor, and talking—about beaches we can get to by ferry when it gets warm out, and about school, of course. I tell her how nervous I am. She tells me about the guy she's sort of dating, and her college classes, and her friends, and how she isn't sure what she wants to do after she graduates.

"Does the economic crisis make you more worried about what comes next? It must, right?"

She pauses to think a moment, looking out over the beautiful dark water.

"You ask about this a lot, Zona," she says, sounding a bit sad. "The answer is that I truly try not to think about it too much. Greeks want to work to live, not live to work. We aren't letting this 'crisis'—what you call it—get to us or change our lives or stop us. We can't move ahead this way, you understand? So we just don't think about it. Well, not more than we have to."

I can't decide if this is an incredibly silly and uninformed way to go through life or a refreshingly positive one.

Good thing my dad is the one writing the story about this, I think. Yiota puts her arm around my shoulders and squeezes, so I know she isn't upset. We sit together like that for a while, each of us quiet with our own thoughts. And then, of course, Yiota bursts forth with another dozen ideas of things to see, to taste, to explore. And we're off again.

And throughout our week together—our fun, informative, exciting week—she keeps trying to tell me about the family in Crete. But I keep changing the subject. I can't explain it; even discovering how fantastic she is, and how nice and easy to talk to, it's still too scary to think about this big looming *family* out there waiting to pounce on me.

I'm just not ready to talk about them. Yet.

14

I've been trying to describe the marina at Floisvos to Dad, but as usual when he's working on a new project, he's only half listening. Not because he doesn't care, but because he gets so focused on his work that it's all he can think about. He's been wearing the same sweatpants and T-shirt for three days, sitting at what used to be the living room table but is now officially his work space. He's acquired a scratchy-looking beard and is starting to smell a bit . . . well, ripe.

"You drag me all the way to Greece to get in touch with my roots and now you don't even want to hear about it? What kind of father are you?" I ask, pretending to be stern.

Dad sighs and surveys his makeshift desk covered with papers and strips of what look like pieces of film. "The kind who has to sift through a thousand miles of microfiche looking for buried treasure. The kind who may never get up from this chair again. The kind whose wonderful daughter should be understanding and maybe also make him a sandwich?"

I give him my best furious glare, but he's already focused

on his papers again. "*Exceptionally* Understanding Daughter Stores Latest Moment of Injustice Away for Future Use," I grumble as I head toward the kitchen.

I'm bursting to tell Dad about Yiota and how great she is, not to mention all the places I've been exploring. Of course, I realize the Acropolis has been around for a while and he's seen it before. But still, now that we're in Athens and I'm actually having fun, I want to *share* it. Especially since this little respite from reality will be over in a few days and I'll be at my new school, trying to find my way.

But I also know that when Dad's finished, all his effort will be worth it. And I'll be part of it, which is exciting.

I bring Dad a hastily made sandwich and a big bunch of grapes (I still haven't been able to find Hot Pockets at the grocery store) and put it on the edge of his "desk."

"Ah!" Dad looks up at me and takes a horribly chewed-up pen out of his mouth. "Darling Daughter Serves Adoring *Pater* in Time of Need, Will Someday Be Handsomely Rewarded!" he headlines.

"I accept cash, you know," I offer, perching on the arm of his chair.

"Nice try." He grins, sticking the pen back in his mouth and making a quick correction on the keyboard. He looks up again, leaning his head against my arm affectionately. "I'm sorry I've been so busy, Ace. I just have to get the pre-liminary stuff in shape before I start interviewing . . . but I do want to hear more about Yiota and what you've been up to. Are you feeling totally neglected? Tony is."

I look over at Tony, who couldn't look more disinterested in the two of us, much less neglected. "I'm okay. I just . . ." I consider mentioning my nerves about school, or telling him how Yiota keeps trying to talk about the relatives on Crete . . . but he's obviously on a roll with his work. "I just have to run," I finish. "I'm going to finally Skype with Hil and Matty."

"The Dynamic Duo, eh?" Dad says.

"God, you're old," I say, narrowly ducking a flying, saliva-coated pen on my way out the door. I holler *"Kalispera!"* and dash into my room. On the far side of the room is a wall that is not actually a wall at all. It's sort of a really big, heavy-duty wooden blind—or maybe more like a pegboard?—that goes up and down with a pulley. It leads out onto a terrace. (Definitely the most amazing thing about this apartment. I mean, private outdoor space? In my neighborhood in NYC, you get a fire escape and consider yourself lucky.) I haul the wooden panel all the way up so I can take in the view of the sky, bright blue and cloudless as usual. I like to do that even when it's kind of chilly; I just put on a scarf and big sweatshirt and pretend it's not cold, because I'm in Greece and it's supposed to be warm here, dammit. In the morning the light streams in through the little holes and wakes me up—so much nicer than an alarm clock.

I flop onto my bed and open my laptop. It's about eleven A.M. in NYC. We haven't been able to coordinate a group session since the first week I got here because of the time difference (seven hours earlier in NYC) and their having tons of schoolwork and commitments while I've been gallivanting around Athens with Yiota. E-mail is simply not the same. Thank God Hilary found out about a phone app that lets you send international texts for free, or I would most likely die. When my dad found out how much data plans cost in Greece I thought *he* was going to die, and if I couldn't text Hil all day as usual, the results would be catastrophic.

Actually, my swanky new Greek cell phone is probably cheaper than my American one—the plans are prepaid, so you can't go over. The plan itself is called Whatsup, which I think is hilarious.

Op Ed: Life Before Skype— Was It Worth Living?

For today's media-savvy teens, a world in which it took weeks, hours, or mere minutes to communicate seems impossible. The idea of sending a letter overseas and having to wait for one in return instills a look of horror on the average e-mailer, who is used to immediacy being a key factor in correspondence.

"If I have to wait three minutes for someone to text me back, I pretty much lose my mind," said Matthew Klausner, 16. "The thought of not having e-mail and Skype is . . . traumatizing. I can't even contemplate it."

Mr. Klausner and his peers aren't the only ones affected, of course. Older people who grew up with landlines and long-distance pen pals have quickly gotten used to being in touch 24/7, and most of them wouldn't go back.

"Of course, I loved getting

letters when I was young. And the anticipation of waiting for an exciting phone call can't be matched with a text," said David Lowell, 62. "But do you have any idea how much easier it is to do research online instead of relying on library resources alone?"

Check out the next installment in our technology series: "Walking, or Segways for Everyone?"

Filed, 11:54 p.m., Athens.

I see Hilary's screen name pop up in a window. One click and there's her familiar face, with Matt's right next to it. Tears prick up behind my eyes; even though I've only been gone a couple weeks, and I haven't exactly been miserable, I miss them so much it's physically painful. Also physically painful is the high-pitched screech they emit simultaneously when my picture pops up on their screen.

"Ohmygod, you will not believe what has been going on here," Hilary starts, with Matty overlapping her.

"Scott and I have been hanging out—not at Starbucks, mind you. He is just . . . he's *dreamy,* Zona, and I don't use that word lightly. You wouldn't even—"

"Ben has been really cool and he *loved* the ideas I pitched for the new issue. I mean, most of them were yours, so *of course* he did, but I suggested covering the new exhibit at the MoMA and he—"

"—haven't kissed or anything, but I almost don't care. It just feels so good to have a crush on someone who might *actually* like me back, you know? I'm just so sick of—"

"—finally talk about art, and he said I could possibly illustrate the article—"

"—going to the gym more? What if he invites me to Fire Island?"

Hil turns to Matt. "If you bring up Fire Island one more time . . ."

"Developing a six-pack takes time, you know. It's already mid-January! I—"

"He is not taking a high school kid to Fire Island!"

"Zona's younger than I am and she's been hanging out with her cousin, and she's twenty! Zo, tell Hilary how—"

I can barely understand what they're saying, but I'm bursting with happiness to hear their voices and see that nothing has really changed. And to see that they genuinely miss me. I'd be lying if I didn't admit that a teensy slice of my brain was terrified that I'd leave and they wouldn't even be sad.

"You guys, hang on!" I cut in, laughing. "I can't respond to six things at once! Hil, that is fantastic—I knew he'd love the art angle, and it's so you. Matt, what do you mean you're 'hanging out' with Scott? Like, in his apartment? I don't know how I feel about that. Do your parents—"

"My parents?! Woman, give me a break. As long as I occasionally show up for dinner and don't wear makeup and a dress to the table, those two don't even remember I live at home. They have my brothers to mold, which is fine by me. And yeah, he lives in Hell's Kitchen, which is basically the new—"

"Zo, you would not believe how hard English Lit is already. Sinett gave us a ten-page—"

"Are you seriously talking about homework right now?!" Matt says. "Zona, tell us more about Yiota. Am I saying that right, like Yoda from Star Wars? Oh, and give us a Skype tour of your apartment! Can you see the Acropolis from your terrace?"

It's almost like they're in the room with me: Matty would be sprawled out on the floor playing with one of the 3-D brainteaser puzzles he can solve in five seconds, Hilary maybe sitting at my desk sketching the Athenian skyline on a little notepad, all while talking nonstop.

But they're a million miles away.

The reality sinks back in that I won't see them for at least *five more months.* In just a few days I'm not going to be palling around with cool cousin Yiota, either. I'm going to be at a school with strangers, who are probably all as cliquey and drama-obsessed as the kids at my old school. And I'll have to navigate it all by myself.

I swallow the lump that has formed in my throat and pick the computer up. I give them a 360-degree tour of the room, then go out to the terrace to show them the gorgeous sky.

"Just like New York, right, guys?" I quip.

"We hate you," Hilary grumbles. "It's been sleeting for two days and it's freezing and gross. I'm seriously wearing about six sweaters right now. We were going to go check out this stand-up thing at Sweet later, but Matt doesn't want to ruin his hair by going outside."

"Yeah, *I'm* the one who doesn't want to ruin my hair," he says, rolling his eyes at me. (Hilary is obsessed with maintaining her curly, untamable hair.) "Listen, Zo, you okay? You seem a bit . . . subdued."

"I'm . . ." What do I say? Telling them I'm scared for school won't change anything—they can't magically be here to save me from being alone. "I'm fine."

Hil and Matt look at each other, then back at me. "You know you're going to be fine, right?" Matt says. "You're awesome, and smart, and fantastic, and—since you've let fabulous *us*"—he pokes Hilary in the arm, and she smacks his finger away—"rub off on you, you're way less shy than middle-school Zona. So don't freak out."

"Just be your amazing self, Zo. Do your thing like always," Hilary adds.

I sigh. I can't fool them, obviously. I feel the lump in my throat getting bigger as I fight back tears. I'm so lucky to have two friends as supportive and wonderful as my besties are . . . I don't care if I ever meet another person for the rest of my life, honestly. Except that I have to, and I have to hope that at least one of them likes me—or at least wants to sit next to me at the lunch table.

"I just feel so discombobulated, you guys."

Hilary smiles, not-so-subtly mouthing *SAT Prep Mode* to Matt. I pretend I don't see her and continue.

"Sure, maybe my cousin turned out to be cool, but what if she's just an exception? Maybe the rest of the family is divisive and hateful! What if my school's full of snobs who don't like strangers, or everyone there is obsessed with, like, Greek goth metal—"

"Is that an actual thing?" Matty interrupts.

"—or something and I don't fit in and have to sit alone?"

"Zona," Hilary says, "no entire school is any *one* thing, and you know it. And even if they are, I have no doubt you can research the hell out of Greek goth metal and talk about it all day long. So stop panicking. You will make a friend. Maybe even two!"

"They won't be as awesomesauce as *we* are, of course," Matty chimes in. "But they'll be okay for a few months. Now, tell us more about Athens! I thought it was going to be a ghost town, but it sounds pretty rad."

I settle onto a lawn chair on the terrace with the computer in my lap. Tony pads out and flops down next to me with a large wheeze of contentment. I pat his head affectionately, and he starts chewing on the leg of my jeans.

"Yeah," I say to my friends, who are so far away, yet still so close to me. "It really isn't what I thought it'd be like at all."

15

Suddenly there's no more time left to run around Athens playing visitor—or new resident, anyway. It's my first official day at the Greek International School.

According to my handy brochure, it's K–12, state of the art, has students from all over the world (including Greek kids who want a better education than the public schools offer), everyone is required to speak fluent English . . . and I don't want to go.

Please let me find one person to hang out with, I think as I sit on the train clutching my backpack against my knees. *Just one.* I feel strongly that the universe should grant my request, especially since I didn't also wish for there to be a super cute guy who will immediately fall in love with me. That has to count for something, right?

I get off at my stop, check the map on my phone for the eighteenth time, and start walking through a small plaza. I can feel my heart racing and I try to tell myself to calm down: *It's just school, it's just what you've been doing for pretty much your whole life, only in a different place. Talking to people is not hard, and you will be fine. Pretend it's all research for a story.*

My internal pep talk isn't helping. My mouth is dry and my palms are wet. I try to imagine Hilary and Matty walking beside me. Trying to calm my nerves, I think of the most complicated vocabulary words I can: *Abnegate. Rapacious. Extrapolate. Persiflage.* I turn down a little path and come to a massive gate; it reminds me of prisons I've seen in movies.

This doesn't look very promising at all.

I walk past a security guard booth and into a big courtyard with a lawn surrounded by a bunch of buildings. Little kids with giant backpacks are being herded by teachers, older kids are in clusters comparing homework and laughing. It looks . . . well, it looks a lot like my school in Manhattan, actually. I relax a bit.

I have only a vague idea of where I'm going as I try to find the administrative office to get my schedule and check in as a new student. I get sucked in to the sea of students who, as I look more closely, all appear to be dressed like the kids back home. Another notch of tension dissipates—at least I won't be the weird new kid dressed totally wrong.

For the first time since I got to Athens, everyone around me is actually speaking English. It's crazy how that sounds strange all of a sudden, being able to understand people's conversations and not just letting the sounds drift over me.

When I get to the third floor, I ask a tall girl where to find the admin office, and it turns out I'm actually in the wrong building. I feel like an idiot, but she tells me her name is Maria and offers to walk me over to the right place, which is really sweet. I feel less awkward having someone to walk with.

"You just moved here?" she asks in totally unaccented English.

"For the rest of the year, yes. I mean, not permanently," I stumble.

"Oh, interesting. Parent's job or something?"

"My dad's, yeah. He's a—" Before I can explain, Maria's cell rings in her bag.

"Sorry—forgot to turn it to vibrate. Hang on." She fiddles with her phone for a second, and by the time she looks up at me again, we're outside.

As we head into the correct building, an older woman points at her wrist as if to say *Don't you miscreants know you're late for class?* but Maria just smiles and we turn down a corridor. The walls are covered with pictures painted by little kids.

"They moved the admin offices to the Lower School last year—it's confusing," Maria explains when she sees me looking. "Anyway, here you are. Good luck—I'm sure I'll see you around. I gotta run to class." And with another big smile, she's gone.

Well, at least she was nice. And I'm not lost. So far, so good.

This Just In: School Is Pretty Much School, Meets Expectations

Zona Lowell was both relieved and slightly disappointed today when she received a class schedule, map, syllabus, and school handbook that were almost identical to the ones she had at her high school in New York City. Additionally, as she went about her first day of classes, she discovered that 15- and 16-year-old kids are pretty much the same everywhere, as are teachers.

"I don't know what I was expecting to be different, exactly, but . . . everyone speaks English and seems nice, they eat in a cafeteria, we have gym class . . . It's just normal. Kind of confusing and overwhelming, but still, you know—it's just school."

Hilary Bauer and Matthew Klausner, former classmates of Ms. Lowell's, were unavailable for comment, but were reported as looking "extremely smug."

Filed, 11:08 a.m., Athens.

I was assigned a buddy to take me around the first few days, a girl who is in all my classes. She's really nice, but kind of a *lot*. Exactly the type of person who would volunteer to *be* a buddy: she's very chatty, involved in lots of activities (which she tells me about at lightning speed every time we change classes), very "on" in general. Her name is Artemis, which I had no idea was an actual name outside of *The Odyssey*, and she's pretty great about introducing me in every class. Her little speech about my being from New York City and living in Greece just for the rest of the year saves me from having to do anything at all except smile and sit down. Basically, my dream come true.

By the end of second period I've figured out that Artemis is the Tracy Flick of our grade. She's the girl who always raises her hand, always points out other kids' mistakes (or the teacher's), and is never late or skips an extra credit project or doesn't run for student government. Like the super nerdy guy who asks too many questions and makes the other kids groan, or the kid who flat-out refuses to pay attention in class and gets sent to detention every other day, every grade in every school has an Artemis. I wonder briefly if being associated with her will be bad for my street cred, but then remember I don't actually have any and get over it. After all, she is (at this point) the only person I know at all.

But as glad as I am to have someone answering my questions and making sure I don't get lost, Artemis is definitely not someone I would choose to hang out with. She's nice enough, as I said, but just . . . too *much*. I can't process her. So I'm not that distressed when she tells me she has to run to her locker after fourth period, but she'll come find me later.

As I drift into the cafeteria (easily found by following the masses on their way there), I realize it doesn't really matter that I don't have anyone to sit with. I have a cell phone to play with, a book I can pretend to read (or even *actually* read), and a million new pages of school stuff to memorize—the layout of the campus, the order of my classes, my teachers' impossible-to-pronounce names. All I have to do is get food without humiliating myself and find a place to perch and I'll be set.

I get in line and am immediately crestfallen. It's not like I expected the food to be amazing, but when I look at my choices, I don't really know what anything is. No grilled cheese sandwiches or plain pasta here; *everything* is covered with olives or weird breading or drenched in mysterious sauce. I can practically feel the people behind me growing impatient, so I step out of line with an empty tray, looking around desperately for a nice safe granola bar or potato chip section.

"Not too appetizing, is it?" a girl behind me says. I turn, not entirely sure the comment is directed at me. Sure enough, there's a pretty dark-haired girl holding a paper bag. "I hate heavy food. You want to share my PB&J?"

"I—I don't want to take your—" I start, surprised.

"Oh, I'm really not that hungry today. Had a big breakfast, so . . ." She shrugs. "Anyway, you're in my history class. I'm Lilena. Lilena Vobras. I love your earrings."

"I'm Zona. And thanks," I say, my hand instinctively going up to my right ear. The earrings are made out of soft leather that's copper on one side and bright blue suede on the other, and they're shaped like lightning bolts. I wore them for good luck. "My best friend makes them," I continue, falling into step with Lilena as she heads for a table near the windows. "My best friend at home, I mean."

By now we're standing beside a table full of kids, some

of whom I recognize from my classes. Lilena slides into an empty seat. "Do you want to sit down?" she asks me. So I do.

The other kids stop talking and look at me, but not in a suspicious, who's-the-girl-invading-our-table way. Lilena points to each person in turn, making introductions. The school population is really diverse, and this lunch table is no exception. Everyone seems friendly and totally cool with my joining them. I guess I was expecting more typical cliquey cafeteria behavior, and my shoulders relax yet another small notch.

Lilena opens her lunch bag and takes out a sandwich, an orange, and a bottle of water. She gives me half the sandwich and the orange, and when I protest she reminds me about her big breakfast. I'm so hungry that finally I just take it. I notice the two girls sitting across from me exchanging a look, but it passes so quickly that I figure it's probably nothing.

"So, you're from New York, yes?" asks a guy whose name I've already forgotten. He has an accent that I can't place.

"Yes, born and raised," I answer around a bite of peanut butter. I haven't been able to find regular peanut butter in the grocery store near our apartment—does Lilena have a secret stash? Also, I can't believe I just said "born and raised" out loud. I hate when people do that, like they have to prove they're cool enough to be from New York. Ugh. I remind myself to chew and swallow and also to breathe.

"What about you?" I ask him—Nikos! Nikos is his name!—in an attempt to recover.

A girl with a blond pixie cut across from me giggles. "Where *isn't* he from?" She pokes him in the arm. "Portugal, Arizona, Indonesia, Dubai, Greece . . ."

Nikos smiles at her. "You forgot Italy, but that was otherwise pretty good. Have you been writing a blog about me, Ashley?" I like the way he talks, and his accent makes more sense to my ears now—it isn't really from anywhere, more like *everywhere*. I wonder if he and Ashley are a couple, the way they tease each other. Nikos looks at me. "My father works for a world bank. We're on a free world tour, as my mother likes to say."

I laugh. "So you were born in Portugal?"

"Yes, but we're Greek. My mother insisted we come back to Athens, finally. That was when I was in eighth grade."

"Yeah, now we're stuck with him!" Lilena chimes in, and everyone at the table laughs. She's only nibbled around the edge of her half of the sandwich and is sort of playing with it by rolling bits of the bread into tiny balls. Oh, how I wish I were eating it instead! I try not to think about it.

"Here you are!" I hear over my shoulder. Artemis. I turn around and smile, unsure whether I should get up and go with her or what. I sort of feel like her project, but I was just starting to get to know these new kids, and it doesn't seem like they're friends with her.

To my surprise, Nikos stands up. "Do you want to sit?"

Now it's Artemis who seems torn, as her friend is waving to her from across the room.

"Oh, thanks, Nikos." She smiles. "Melody and I were going to go over a paper, actually . . . but you seem good here, Zona. Want to find me after?" I nod, and she wends her way over to her friend. Nikos sits back down.

"That was nice of you," I say to him. I can't imagine one of the guys at home being so polite; Matty's really the only civilized boy in our school as far as I'm concerned (Ben Walker doesn't count, as he's in his own category). Of course, Matt just loves to remind me and Hilary that he prides himself on being a feminist, which, according to him, means letting women stand instead of offering his seat. God, I miss that little jerk.

Nikos shrugs, looking away. "It's nothing."

The girl next to Ashley pipes up. She has a very cute, very high-pitched voice and an English accent. "We don't really hang out with Artemis outside of school, but she's fine. I mean, we don't have cliques here like in the States. No one gets chased away from the lunch table like in *Mean Girls* or that sort of thing."

I feel myself blushing, as though I'm somehow responsible for the reputation of American teens being jerks. Also because it's exactly what I'd been thinking. If I went over to a lunch table where I didn't usually sit at home, most likely no one would offer me a seat and it would be weird. But then again, I would never do that.

I'm mentally forming an idea for an article about cafeteria politics in different countries when Lilena leans over. "Yeah, I was surprised, too, at first. I got here a year ago, from Chicago. My family moves around a lot, and it really is different that way. People are just kinda friends with everyone here. It's very cool, actually."

"We read about bullying in the States and it's just so odd," the British girl adds. "Did you have that at your school?"

"Wow, uh . . . that's a pretty intense lunch topic, um . . ."

"Betony," Ashley says helpfully.

"Bethany?"

"Be*tony*," she corrects me. "Just like Bethany, but no *h*. It's a flower. No one ever gets it right, so don't feel bad."

"*Betony*," I say slowly, making sure I have it. So far it's the first tricky name that I've successfully said out loud, so I feel kind of proud of myself. (Even if it's probably a British name and not a Greek one. Still counts.) "Anyway, bullying is . . . well, it happens, yeah. Someone actually committed suicide at a school near the one I go to. People can be . . . well, they can be really mean to each other. Our school paper did a whole series of articles last year about it, actually, talking about the history of bullying, new awareness, how social media affects kids . . ."

"It just seems like things are pretty out of control in the States with that kind of thing," Ashley interjects.

"Well, you can't always believe everything you read. Journalists should be unbiased, obviously, but you can only use the information you have." I sense that I'm losing them. "I mean, Athens isn't what I expected at *all* based on what I'd read before I came here."

"Really? What did you expect?" Nikos asks.

"Honestly? I was kind of expecting war-torn Syria." I eat the last orange wedge. "Like, just empty, ravaged buildings and displaced people wandering the streets . . . columns of smoke darkening the sky . . ."

"You have a very . . . colorful way of speaking, Zona," Nikos says. I blush and duck my head. I can't tell if he's making fun of me or complimenting me.

"Oh my God, so not like that at all, right?" Ashley's eyes light up. "Athens is amazing. Best city in the world."

Lilena grins at her teasingly. "You've lived here your entire life! How would you know?"

"Because I can tell." Ashley scowls. "And I've been other places. Including New York," she adds, looking at me.

"Wait, you've lived here your whole life?" I interject. "Are you—"

"Greek?" Ashley takes a sip of water. "I know, I don't look it and my name is Ashley, right? But yeah, Greek-American mom and Greek dad. My last name is Papadimitriou. And for the record, I liked New York. So no offense. I just think Athens is better." She beams. "You'll have to come out with us sometime. I've heard you can't do *anything* cool in the States when you're our age, but here you can do everything."

"*That* at least is true," Lilena says, nodding.

"Are we supposed to be having fun? Because all I've done lately is work," Nikos says glumly.

"We just don't invite you, that's all." Betony giggles.

Nikos makes a face, like he's extremely offended. "Well, fine, then! I'll go hang out with Giorgos!" He calls out across the cafeteria to a guy at another table. "Giorgos, these girls are being terrible to me. Come save me."

Ashley and Betony are laughing. Lilena turns to me. "Giorgos is Nikos's brother—they're twins. Fraternal, obviously," she explains when she sees me looking.

Giorgos turns around, waving for his brother to join him.

Girl Witnesses Cafeteria Miracle

It was a heart-stopping moment—not unlike the discovery of the Shroud of Turin—when Zona Lowell, NYC transplant, discovered that a guy in her school is the handsomest boy she'd ever seen in her entire life.

"Sure, I fantasized that I'd move to Athens and meet a Greek god, but I didn't think that would actually happen," Ms. Lowell gushed. "How can that guy be only 15? He's, like . . . chiseled out of stone, he's so perfect. I think I'm going to faint."

Though she did not faint, Ms. Lowell did confirm that she would treasure that amazing moment when Giorgos Hadjimarkos turned around for the rest of her days on earth. And possibly beyond.

Filed, 12:08 p.m., Athens.

Lilena nudges my leg with her leg. "Stop staring, Zona. I know, he's gorgeous, right? But *weird*. You'll see." Her phone buzzes, and she checks the screen. "Oh, gotta go!

I'm meeting someone to work on a project during our free period. See you later?" She scoops up her mangled, uneaten sandwich and empty water bottle and dashes off before I can even thank her again for being so nice to me.

I sweep the remnants of my lunch into a napkin and stand up, looking around for Artemis. I feel about 60 percent sure I could figure out where our next class is, but there's no need to push myself. It's only the first day, after all.

"So, do you want to?" Betony chirps in her sweet little voice.

"Do I want to . . . ?"

"Come out with us sometime. Check out Athens," Ashley clarifies. "Here, give me your cell number and I'll text you so you have mine."

"I—oh, that'd be terrific," I say, flustered and pleased. "I mean, great. Yes." *Stop talking now, Zona.* Ashley holds out her phone so I can punch the numbers into it. This seems so weird, giving some girl my phone number, like we're going to go on a date or something. (Also, I don't remember my phone number and have to look it up. So lame.) But I'm excited at the same time—can I possibly have found a group of people to hang out with on my first day? Hil and Matty will be so proud!

I hand Ashley's phone back. "Well, I have to run to class, so . . . I'll see you guys later? Thanks, um . . . thanks for letting me eat with you."

Betony and Ashley shrug and say "No big deal" at the exact same time, which makes them burst into laughter again. I smile, still a bit hesitant to step too far into *THESE ARE MY NEW FRIENDS!* territory.

But my phone buzzes in my pocket with a text from Ashley as I walk to class, and for the second time since we arrived here, I'm starting to feel like this might be okay.

16

Ashley is true to her word and invites me to join them in the city that first weekend; I still feel nervous, even though they're so friendly, but I force myself to go. And it's fun. Not as easy as hanging out with Hilary and Matt, of course, but I didn't expect it to be.

So when Lilena offers to show me her favorite spot in Kallithea the following Tuesday after school—like Yiota, she's found a tiny coffee shop hidden down a narrow side street—I agree right away, despite the crushing amount of homework I have. It was exciting to discover that Lilena lives in the same neighborhood as Dad and I do. It makes me feel another notch less lonely.

We sit down on rickety iron chairs in the winter sunshine, happy to put our heavy backpacks down.

Local Café Run By Poorly Disguised Sorceress, Teens Surmise

Lilena Vobras, schoolmate of recently matriculated GIS sophomore Zona Lowell, was elated to share a hidden gem of the area with her new neighbor.

"Honestly, I never would've noticed this place if she hadn't pointed it out," Ms. Lowell revealed. The café itself, which has no name that the girls could ascertain, offers outdoor seating only—regardless of the weather. The ancient blue-tiled tables and mismatched chairs lend it an antique flair. But the real draw is the proprietress, Ms. Lowell explained.

"It's run by this super scary old Greek lady who refused to speak to us directly. Instead she slouched over to the table and slammed down cups of coffee and a bowl of wizened grapes—without even asking what we wanted. Then she scurried away again, muttering under her breath the entire time!"

Ms. Lowell found the dining experience to be "hilarious and fascinating." We're sure Zagat would agree.

Filed, 3:30 p.m., Athens.

"I'm pretty sure she just cast a spell on us," I whisper to Lilena as the old lady lurches back inside to what I presume is her secret witch's lair.

"She does that every time!" she hisses back. "I can't ever tell what she's saying, and Ashley never wants to come here because Betony hates coffee and the wicked witch won't give her tea."

"Can't Ashley come without Betony? Just to translate?"

Lilena giggles. "Yeah, right." Her phone buzzes, and she glances at the screen. "Did you get your quiz back in Chemistry today? Nikos wants to know."

"No, not yet, thank God. Ugh, I can't believe you've survived a whole year at GIS already." I groan, leaning back in my chair. "I don't think I'll make it to the end of one if they keep piling on the work like this. And I thought my school in New York was bad!"

"I know—it's crazy, right?" Lilena agrees, taking a sip of her coffee.

"Do you miss Chicago?" I ask, adding sugar to mine.

"Um, yeah, I guess. But I only lived there for a year, so it wasn't really . . . I don't really keep in touch with anyone from there. I like Athens better. It's warmer, that's for sure!" she adds.

"I didn't realize you moved around so much. You and Nikos . . ."

"Yeah, it's because of my mom's job. We've lived in, like, ten places since I started school, so I'm used to it by now," she says quickly. "How about you? Are you missing New York, or more excited to be in Greece? I mean, it's kind of crazy that you have this whole family you've never met before!"

"Well, I do miss New York. A lot," I explain. "It's kind of complicated . . . So, what exactly does your mom do? That must be pretty cool, getting to experience so many different cultures and—"

"Yeah, I guess," Lilena cuts in. She has a look on her face I can't quite read, but it isn't a happy one. She changes the subject back to me again. "*Your* mom must be happy to be back home. It's your mom's side, right?"

"Yes, but, um . . . my mom died. It's just me and my dad, so . . . But yeah—it's her family."

Lilena looks stricken. "Oh my God, I'm so sorry. I didn't—"

"It's okay. Of course you didn't know. Don't worry about it."

"I'm really sorry."

"Thanks." It's always such a weird and awful moment telling someone my mom is dead. They always say "I'm sorry," and I think, *Why are you sorry? It isn't your fault.* And then I always say "Thanks," which makes no sense either, but I don't know what else to say. Sometimes I wish the person would just say, "Wow, that totally sucks," so I could say, "It sure does" or "Well, I didn't know her." At least that would be honest.

"So they never visited you in New York? Your mom's . . ." Lilena starts again, trying to end the awkward moment.

I smile at her, deciding to tell the truth, and I give her a quick rundown of the deal with my family.

"So yeah," I finish, "I'm not so much excited as I am . . ."

"Completely terrified?" Lilena offers, raising an eyebrow. We both started laughing. For some reason the whole thing seems funny all of a sudden; I mean, seriously, who actually travels across the world to meet a bunch of strangers in *real life*? Why would anyone do that?!

The witchy café owner creeps over to our table and fires off a string of angry-sounding words: *"Greekgreekgreekgreekgreek!"* We pull ourselves together, but I'm left with a feeling I haven't had yet about the whole situation. Yes, it's going to be scary (and will get scarier as spring break approaches), but there's another way to look at it, too: as an adventure. A crazy one, to be sure. Maybe this was what Hil and Matty—and my dad—have been trying to tell me all along.

"Okay, but seriously," Lilena continues, "terrified makes sense. But curious, too, right? Like, did the older relatives even know you were alive before two years ago? Or that your mother had died? Or did they just find this all out?"

I've never asked these obvious questions—have avoided asking them, in fact. Definitely poor journalism. And yet. Would the answers change anything?

I don't know, but there is one person who would: Yiota.

"You want to get something to eat? Maybe some baklava?" I ask Lilena. "My treat."

"Aw, thanks," she says, "but we eat dinner really early at my house, so . . ."

"Next time," I reply, smiling. Because I know there will be a next time, and that makes me feel even less scared still. I made a friend.

And it wasn't even that hard.

17

By the end of that second week, I've nailed down how to get to my classes, ascertained that there is no way to fake it on Level-One Greek pop quizzes, shamefully stalked Giorgos all over school (just watching him walk through the halls is an incredible treat), and discovered that everyone calls the teachers "sir" and "miss" here, like we're in a British boarding school or something. (It's weird.)

I've also started being able to distinguish Greek from other languages, which sounds pretty simple but actually isn't. At an international school like GIS, kids speak every language under the sun: Arabic, Portuguese, Greek (obviously), Czech, you name it. But you only really hear people conversing in their native tongues in the cafeteria. Part of the reason things aren't so cliquey is because people sometimes sit together so they can chat in their first language, not because they're necessarily close friends. And when you don't speak *any* of those languages . . . they all glom together in a big buzz.

Lunch Table Behind
The Scenes: Insider Scoop

Newly matriculated GIS sophomore Zona Lowell has impressed our readership by quickly identifying the finer points of some of the relationships on view at her recently joined lunch table.

"Ashley and Betony are almost obsessively *best* best friends and do everything as a unit," she shares with us. "They sit together in every class, eat together, study together, talk over each other, share pens and clothes, and are basically attached at the hip." Still, the girls have welcomed Ms. Lowell into their group, and they've spent many afternoons and evenings exploring the city's attractions together.

Then there's Nikos Hadjimarkos, who is essentially the group's official Guy in the Friend Zone: the safe, beloved, go-to guy around whom it's okay to be gross or silly, and who's always there to give advice and offer flirting practice. "I get the sense that Nikos is hopelessly in love with Betony but will never tell her because Ashley wouldn't like it," Zona reveals. "I guess time will tell."

So far, Zona hasn't been able to gather much intel on Giorgos Hadjimarkos, Nikos's dashingly handsome twin brother. She hopes to have hands-on information as soon as possible.

Filed, 10:34 a.m., Athens.

As the days and then weeks and finally two months go by, I've found a place to fit in pretty comfortably, which is great—but I soon start to notice something: I have never actually seen Lilena eat. Not once.

I didn't notice at first how thin she is, because it's still chilly in Athens and everyone is wearing sweaters and pants. But when we hug good-bye after hanging out, I can feel all the bones in her back through her jacket. I've started paying more attention to her at lunch . . . and now I can't *stop* paying attention. She never puts food near her mouth without playing with it first, and she always has an excuse about why she doesn't want to eat. No one's ever mentioned her being ill. So I wonder what's really going on.

"Aren't you eating?" I ask Lilena at lunch on a Thursday. Nikos is sitting with Gorgeous Giorgos, so it's just us girls at our end of the table. I shovel a huge mouthful of food into my face, as if trying to lead by example. I don't ask her why she's not eating every day—I try to be subtle and space it out.

Lilena stands up, not looking directly at me. "Oh, I ate before, during my free," she says, gathering up her lunch bag. "I have to hit my locker, you guys. Text me later!" And she's gone.

Ashley and Betony look at each other and roll their eyes. Ashley laughs.

"That isn't funny, you guys," I point out, annoyed. "I think Lilena really has a problem, don't you? Shouldn't we—"

"Ugh. Americans always think everyone has an eating disorder," Betony scoffs. "She's just, you know . . . she doesn't like to eat. Whatever. She's fine."

"Wait til she shows you her thinspo collection," adds Ashley. Betony groans.

"Um . . . what?" I'm lost. I have no idea what that is.

"It's, like, pictures to help you stay thin. Thinspiration, get it? Thinspo for short? They're all, like, really under-weight models and girls who don't ever eat and have blogs about it or whatever. You know, to compare herself to," Betony explains.

"She's never mentioned that to me at all! That's, I mean, I . . ." I'm appalled. I guess I'd been letting myself think that Lilena just didn't *notice* she wasn't eating. The idea that she has a collection of pictures of super skinny women is horrifying to me. I've never heard of such a thing.

"Yeah, well, you only just met," Betony continues. "When she got here last year, right, she showed us the pictures after a few months, like, to see if we were into it. So she can have a partner in not eating or whatever, you know?"

"It's pretty sick," Ashley adds. "I mean, she's so skinny anyway."

"Yes, she's that skinny because she's *starving herself*," I say, standing up. I'm really upset—why are these two so blasé about this? I'd be devastated if Hilary or Matty started doing something like this. "You guys are her friends. Why don't you tell her parents or a guidance counselor or . . . ?" I trail off because I'm starting to sound like a Lifetime movie, or worse. But come on—this isn't okay.

"Yeah, I'll call her mother." Ashley laughs. "Do you know who her mother is? She's the American consul to Greece."

"So?"

"So, she's a very important and smart woman. If she thought there was something wrong, I'm sure she'd handle it. Don't go getting all Oprah, okay? Lilena'll be fine. She's always done this weird eating stuff and nothing's happened. She probably just wants attention, you know, because her parents move her around every couple of years." Betony turns to Ashley. "Remember when she first came, she used to hide people's snacks til Anais got pissed and called her out on it? That was nuts."

I've had enough. How can they be so . . . unsympathetic?

"I have to go," I say, picking up my tray.

"Zona, don't be mad," Ashley calls. "Zona!"

But I don't turn around.

I wish I could call Yiota and ask her for advice. But I've hardly seen or spoken to her since school started because she's been super busy with her courses and part-time job at one of the stores downtown. And this doesn't seem like the kind of thing I can ask about in a text message.

As I walk to my locker, I try to clear my head and think about something else. Since I started at GIS, I haven't had time to do much writing. Hilary seems to have gotten the hang of things at the *Reflector* and hasn't needed my help.

How have two months gone by without my having looked into the GIS newspaper at all?

I'm going to go find out about it right now. Why not?

I dig the boring informative pamphlets I got my first day

out of my locker and flip through them. Nothing about a school paper. There's a lit mag, but I'm not much for poems. There's a photography and art journal. Yearbook. Faculty-written school magazine. But no newspaper. How can this be? They offer AP Psychology and Russian Civ classes and have a thousand ways to earn advanced college credit, but no newspaper?!

I head to the library to ask. When I get there, I'm immediately hit by that yummy book smell. Isn't it amazing how all libraries smell the same?

At the front desk I ask Ms. Aivatos, the librarian. She smiles, types for a few seconds, and then turns her computer monitor around.

Horror, Disbelief Rocks Teen's World In Paper Scandal

It was revealed today that the so-called "school newspaper" at the Greek International School is, in fact, merely a website. "The Sheaf," a pitifully ironic moniker, is barely a newsfeed, and certainly not a paper.

"It's not a paper if it's not *paper*," said Zona Lowell, the lifelong journalism enthusiast who discovered the travesty earlier today. "All these articles are written by the same three kids, which is incredibly limit-ing—though not surprising, considering how difficult it was to even find out we have a school paper. It's only updated once a quarter! And it's in color!"

Ms. Lowell declined the offer of a brown paper bag to assuage the panic attack she was on the verge of having. "Just wait until my dad hears about this," she warned.

At this time, it is unknown whether or not her dad has, in fact, heard about it.

Filed, 1:37 p.m., Athens.

Ms. Aivatos can clearly sense my distress. She whispers to me, "If you want to talk to someone about it, try that boy there." She points out a guy sitting at one of the research tables by himself. He has a laptop open, typing furiously. "That's Alex Loushas. He works on the paper."

It's a website, not a paper, I think. I thank Ms. Aivatos and go over to the table.

"Mind if I sit?" I ask. It's easy to be outgoing when your mind is focused on the collapse of society's necessary tools.

He looks up, and I immediately notice three things about him:

1) He's wearing very cool metallic green half-rim glasses.
2) He doesn't look like anyone I've met before— I can't tell what his ethnicity is at all. His skin is darker than mine, but not really brown. His hair is jet-black with gorgeous curls, and on the long side. Very Harry Styles. His dark eyes are slightly slanted and bore right through me.
3) He doesn't seem very friendly.

Number three is troubling, and I feel the urge to run away, but I don't. Dad wouldn't, Anne Newport Royall wouldn't, and neither will I.

"I'm Zona, a new sophomore here," I say bravely. "I wanted to ask you about the paper."

His demeanor immediately shifts, to my great relief. "Oh, cool," he says. "I thought you were going to tell me you needed this table for some meeting or something. I'm Alex." He holds out a hand, and I shake it before sitting down across from him. "So, what's up? You want to write for the *Sheaf*?"

"Well, sort of . . ." I begin. "I was features editor for my school paper back home, and I was pretty surprised that there's no paper here. I mean, Ms. Aivatos showed me the website, but . . . well, a website, while ambitious and modern, isn't tactile: you can't put it in front of people's faces, you don't get ink on your fingers to remind yourself you've read something, you know? And from what I've seen, the issues aren't themed, the articles seem pretty generic—I mean, they aren't focused on the students or the concerns of the school. What's your agenda? Where are the pull quotes from the student body? Where are the special interest stories? I don't—"

"Wait, hang on. First of all, I'm not in charge of the paper, okay? I just write for it. And secondly, I agree with you about the content part. It sucks. But, you know, it's a lot cheaper to do the website. Plus, many would argue that physical papers have become obsolete."

I feel like my eyes might fall out of my head. Am I going to have to take on the "newspapers are obsolete" argument, right here in the school library?! I don't know if I have the strength today.

"Listen, Alex, I'm sure you—" And just when I'm about to get going, the bell rings.

"Dammit," Alex mutters, pressing a few keys on his laptop. "Not even close to finished."

He looks back up at me, and I realize that his eyes aren't brown, but a very dark gray. "Well, Zona, we'll have to finish this another time—I gotta get to Physics. See ya."

I mentally note that if he's in Physics already, he's either very smart or a junior. Or both. By the time I decide to ask him in a surge of boldness, he's all packed up—and just like that, he's gone.

After school I go home and look around my room; usually I have notebooks everywhere for taking notes and jotting down ideas. Here, I have pretty much nothing. I'm annoyed with myself for not writing more, for not being focused. I don't know what's stopping me; my brain still thinks in headlines and articles, but I don't *do* anything about it. Schoolwork, Athens, life, worrying about spring break (going to Crete and meeting *the others*) . . . it's getting in the way of what used to make me *me*.

And I still don't have a newspaper to work on.

18

"Do Americans still care about newspapers? I thought they were, like, dead, yeah?" Betony says.

It's the next day in study hall, and I've just described my impromptu meeting with Alex Loushas in the library. (The argument about Lilena seems to have been forgotten—at least, the girls haven't mentioned it, and I'm not going to, either.)

"What? Newspapers aren't dead!" I exclaim, outraged. This is the second time I've had to defend the legacy of the printed word in two days. What is wrong with people?!

"Why don't you make a website instead? Like a news-feed," Lilena suggests. "Isn't that what GIS has? Not that I've ever read it. I like the lit magazine, though."

"Because . . . because it's not just about instant gratification, you guys. It's about crafting a story, finding the right lead, the hook, research . . . it's about quality."

"But it's so boring." Ashley sighs. "I'm bored just talking about it right now. See? Here's me, falling asleeeee-zzzzzz . . ." Her head falls onto the table. Hilarious.

"You're totally missing the point," I say, trying to stay calm. "We're all so used to getting texts and posting pictures that we don't even look around to see how what's happening now connects to anything else. Think about plotting a story from start to—"

Betony imitates Ashley's head-dropping-onto-desk move. Lilena giggles, playing with bits of a granola bar that she is, of course, not eating. I give up.

"Fine, forget it. Go back to the live feeds of your lives. Don't reflect on history. Carry on."

"Oh, thank God," Ashley cheers. "So, what's for tonight? Anyone have a great idea?"

"What's tonight?" I ask.

Lilena smiles broadly. "Just Friday. And thank God for that—this week has been a *nightmare*. I can't believe how much homework we got in History alone."

"Let's go dancing in Gazi—we haven't gone there in ages and Zona's never been," Betony suggests. "I got these amazing new shoes at Christmas that I haven't even worn yet."

"What's Gazi?" I ask.

Nightlife Awesomeness Revealed, Anticipated

Though she's certainly done her fair share of exploring in her adopted city, newcomer Zona Lowell was thus far unexposed to the exciting possibilities of Athenian nightlife. Today, that all changed.

"Gazi is a really trendy neighborhood with clubs and bars," explained classmate Lilena Vobras. "When it's warm they set up couches and tables outside the cafés, so it's like the whole area is a huge fancy living room. And then the dance clubs are open all night, and they each have a DJ and usually live performers, too. It's awesome."

Ms. Lowell, accustomed to the strict policies of NYC establishments, expressed her concern that she would need a fake ID to participate in the festivities. But Ashley Papadimitriou, classmate and apparent nightclub expert, assured Ms. Lowell that her fears were unfounded. "Just say you're 18 if anyone asks—which they won't," she instructed.

"It's kind of weird, the freedom teenagers have here—to stay out all night, buy alcohol . . . I don't know. I can't really get used to it," Ms. Lowell concluded. "It's one of the biggest cultural differences I've noticed so far, the way younger people are trusted more, I guess, to behave responsibly."

Ms. Lowell is looking forward to hitting the town and getting crazy.

Filed, 1:02 p.m., Athens.

"I have no idea what I own that'd be right for a club, since I've never actually been to one," I admit.

"Really? Well, I'm sure you have something, or you can borrow from me," Lilena says. "We can find out online which DJs are playing where and go to a few places. I can't believe you've never been to a club!"

"Well, I wasn't really into that kind of stuff back home. I mean, I like dancing. But I don't have an ID or . . . But my friend Matty, he goes to tons of clubs," I offer, trying to bump my cool factor back up a notch.

"That's your gay friend?" Betony asks.

"Well, yes, but I mean, he's just my friend. *And* he's gay. Along with being a lot of other—"

"Right, so . . . your gay friend," Ashley says.

"Guys, come on. Don't be obnoxious," Lilena says

quietly. I smile to let her know I appreciate her chiming in on my behalf; Ashley rolls her eyes at Betony. I decide it's not worth making this a big deal.

"Sure, fine. My gay friend," I say. "So . . . ?" I'm not sure where Ashley is going with this.

"It's just interesting that he's, you know, open about it. No one here is, really. There are gay kids, obviously, but no one talks about it. Ever," Ashley continues. "Greece is more traditional."

"That's ironic," I quip, trying for a bit of levity.

"Why is it ironic?" Betony asks.

"Um, Greek history? Haven't you ever . . . ? Oh, never mind." Sometimes I wonder what would've happened if I'd stuck with Artemis, my first-week buddy, this whole time. She kind of annoyed me, but she's smart and says what she thinks without worrying about the consequences. Too late now. And I like these girls well enough, I suppose. "Anyway, I know Matt struggles with that—not with being gay, but with the fact that he's one of few guys at school who's open about it. I'm sure he'd like to have other guys to talk to about stuff. Not just me and Hilary."

"Well, it's really sweet that you're supportive," Betony says. I don't think she's trying to be condescending, so I don't say anything in response.

"So, what do you think, meet at eleven?" Lilena suggests, changing the subject. She stands up from the table to gather her things.

"Oh, don't you want to go to dinner first?" Ashley asks pointedly. Lilena looks away.

"I'm going to eat with my parents," she says. "So, I'll text you guys later about what you're wearing and where to meet. Glad you're coming, Zona!" And she's off.

I don't get Ashley when she baits Lilena like that, I really don't. Cry for help? Anyone? Ashley's so proud of how there are no "mean girls" at GIS, but this seems a lot like bullying to me. Maybe I *am* being uber-American and overly sensitive, but . . . well, I've already made my thoughts clear about the Lilena situation and gotten nowhere.

So I let it go. Again.

Instead I ask Betony about her new shoes and wish I could figure out what I'm doing here, so far away from my real life.

19

Gazi, which is not too far from where I live in Athens, is just as popular and trendy as the girls promised. There are nightclubs, bars, and cafés one after the other along a few long streets, plus people milling around in groups as they bounce from place to place. Music pulses in the night air, and the sky is bright with neon lights.

After making sure we're all straight on our "club names"—I was assigned Zoe by Ashley (or should I say, Anne)—we head into a club in the middle of the strip. Just like they said, we have no trouble getting in, though there's a pretty steep cover charge of twelve euros per person. And then it's lights and people and smoke and music that's a thousand times louder than it seemed from the street. And it's fun—a bit overwhelming, but really fun.

We dance and drink Red Bull with vodka (only one for me, so I have something to hold) and flirt with some random guys trying to dance with us. I'm pretty sure I've sweated off all the eyeliner that Lilena painstakingly applied on the train ride over, and I can feel the bass from the speakers down to my toes.

Suddenly I realize I have to pee—like, now. I shout my intentions to Lilena, who is pretty tipsy and dancing exuberantly next to me. She grins and goes back to bopping up and down, so I squeeze my way through the crowd and *just* make it to the facilities before it's too late.

When I come back, my friends have vanished.

I shove my way through writhing, grinding people in the general direction of the door, trying not to breathe in too deeply. The air reeks of cigarette smoke and various colognes. A hand snakes out and grasps the side of my waist, trying to pull me into the melee; I wriggle away, still scanning the room for my group. So *this* is why girls go to the bathroom together—not for moral support, but so they won't end up all alone surrounded by drunk people. I slide my phone out of my pocket. Nothing. Should I be worried, or pissed off? And, more importantly, where did they all go?

I spot a very intensely spiked hairdo and think I've finally located Nikos, so I shove toward the bar. The hair disappears and is replaced by a man who may in fact be wearing all the cologne in this whole place; I feel slightly guilty now for assuming anyone else here contributed to the stench. He isn't bad-looking, but he seems sleazy and is definitely way older than I am, both in real life *and* the age I'm pretending to be tonight.

He blocks my path. "Sorry, just looking for my friends, 'scuse me," I mumble, trying to get past him.

"Who would leave such a beautiful girl all alone?" he says, grinning. He has perfect, weirdly shiny white teeth. I'm a little nervous he might bite me, actually. "I'm Stavros. We'll have a drink, yes?"

"Oh, that's nice, but my friends—"

"Champagne for you, yes?" He yells to the bartender, who starts bustling around with glasses. Stavros takes out a pack of cigarettes, offers one to me and, when I shake my head, sticks one between his lips and lights up.

Common Sense Tested In The Face Of Free Drinks

Zona Lowell, 15 and presumably not an idiot, faced a conundrum this evening. Finding herself totally deserted in a dance club, she finally cracked the "free drink" code that she had heretofore only seen other girls taking advantage of: look lost + be a girl = get a drink. But whether or not to accept the offer was not as simple.

"Look, I didn't want to be rude and just assume the guy was planning to roofie me, you know? And it would be stupid to turn down free champagne," Lowell commented. "On the other hand, I'm pretty sure my dad would be very upset if I showed up three days from now in a field."

Filed, 1:04 a.m., Athens.

I look around again, trying to spot anyone I know. It's weird—if Ashley or Betony were with me, I'd feel so cool that this guy wanted to buy me champagne. Not that I'd ever hook up with him—come on—but it's still flattering and I know they'd be jealous. But being by myself, it's way less cool. I don't want him to think I'm lame, though, so when Stavros hands me a glass, I take it.

I look at the fizzing liquid, trying to tell if there's anything in there that shouldn't be. Can't tell. Honestly, how have they not invented something that tells you if your drink's been tampered with? Or maybe they have and they're just withholding it from high school kids, like the morning-after pill. Now *that* would be an interesting article, I muse, forgetting where I am for a moment.

"Aren't you going to taste? It's delicious," Stavros purrs, taking a swig from his glass. Okay, that's definitely a sketchy sign, right? Like a pushy, peer pressure-y thing to say? I think I'm ready to leave.

"Really, I should go find—" He steps in front of me as I move toward the door.

"You won't have a drink with me? This hurts my feelings," he says, clinking his glass against mine. So now if I don't taste it, this will be even more awkward. I hesitate, fidgeting with the bracelets Lilena lent me. *But if I do taste it, I could end up raped and murdered in a foreign country,* I think. Awkward is better than murdered, certainly, but if he's actually just flirting with me then I'm being rude, and—

"*There* you are!" A man's voice, thick with a French accent, breaks through my reverie. "I've been looking everywhere for you!"

I look up from my glass at a tall guy, at least thirty (I think? I freely admit that everyone older than twenty looks about forty to me), who has the darkest, smoothest skin—it's almost a true black, like Lupita Nyong'o's. He has big brown eyes, and they are peering into mine almost imploringly, like he's trying to tell me something.

I instantly trust him. Which is maybe foolhardy . . . but I don't think so.

"Oh, hey!" I shout over the music. Okay, I'm stumped. What now?

"You know this man?" Stavros asks, miffed. "You want I will ask him to leave?"

The black guy laughs, like he and I are in on some big joke. "Of course she knows me. She's my cousin. Come on, everyone is waiting for you," he hollers over the music, taking the glass of possibly roofied champagne out of my hand and putting it on the bar rail. My brain is racing.

Stavros sneers, gazing at him skeptically. "Your cousin?"

"That's what I said." The French accent makes the guy's reply sound sophisticated and menacing at the same time.

"This is your *cousin*? This man?" Stavros isn't giving up.

"I'm adopted," I say, looking him straight in the eye.

My "cousin" cough-laughs, and Stavros scowls.

"Thanks for the drink!" I call over my shoulder as my savior (kidnapper?) grabs my arm and steers me past the crowd and out the door.

All the lights in the city are on now. It's beautiful, and only a little cold.

The second we're on the sidewalk, past the throng of people still lining up to get inside, he drops my arm and backs up. I rub my bare arms in the night air, wishing I had brought a coat even though Betony insisted there'd be nowhere to leave it.

"Are you all right?" he asks.

I nod, feeling a massive sense of relief. I may not actually have been in danger, but now I see that I definitely *could* have been. The fact that I'm still not sure tells me I'm lucky this guy stepped in.

"Yeah, I'm okay," I say, smoothing my hair off my sweaty face. "I . . . Thank you so much, that was so nice of you. That guy wouldn't let me leave, and I didn't want to be—"

"I figured," my savior (pretty sure by this point) says, nodding. "I was about to leave myself when I saw you. You looked quite frightened. I'm glad you played along. I'm Andrew, by the way."

"I'm, uh . . ." Crap. Am I supposed to tell him my fake club name? He just did a really awesome thing for me, so maybe my real name?

"It's fine." Andrew smiles kindly. "You don't have to tell me. Seriously, I just wanted to make sure you were all right. Do you have a way to get back to where you're staying? Do you need money for a taxi?"

"I . . . um, my friends were . . ." I don't know what to say.

Andrew has been so nice to me, and now I just feel like an idiot. "You're so sweet to offer. I mean, you must think I'm really stupid. I actually am here with people, they just—"

"ZOE!" Ashley bounds up behind me, just as exuberant and tipsy as when I last saw her. Which seems like it was hours ago, but was probably only thirty minutes. She takes a drag off her cigarette. "Where have you been? We've been looking everywhere! Uh, hi?" She looks from me to Andrew. "I'm Anne. Do you need something?"

"This is Andrew," I say, embarrassed by her rudeness. "I don't really know how hard you were looking for me since you're outside, *Anne*."

"Well, we couldn't find you, so we thought you came out to get cigarettes or something. We were waiting for you."

"I don't—"

"So, yeah, Betony—I mean, Beth—knows another club that has some good bands tonight, and we're gonna go there. So, um . . . Andrew, do you want to come with us, or . . . ?"

"I think I'm going to call it a night, thanks. Have fun, girls. Be careful, okay?" Andrew directs this last line to me.

"Wait, are you sure? Because I want to thank you for—"

"*Zo*, he said he's going home. We don't want to keep him." Ashley is dragging me off. Not sure why I'm letting her. I kind of want to punch her, actually. "Nice meeting you, Andrew! Bye!"

Andrew gives a little wave, and I feel stupider than ever.

"Thank you again!" I call to him. And then he's gone.

Lilena is waiting for us with Betony and Nikos by a fountain. "Where have you been?! I am *freezing*!" she says, teeth chattering. My first thought is that if she weren't so skinny, she wouldn't be so cold. But of course I keep that to myself.

"Um, Zona found some old guy to hang with, apparently. You weren't actually going to hook up with him, were you? He was, like, forty! Did he at least buy you a drink?" Ashley says, laughing. Now I *really* want to punch her.

"No, actually, he was—"

"Girls, come on. I'm bored," Nikos whines, putting out his cigarette. "Let's go already, huh?"

I look at these people, my friends—my sort-of friends—and I wish so much that I were home with Hil and Matty. Hell, I actually wouldn't mind being home with my dad right now. That sounds pretty great, to be honest. I look at my phone and realize it's two A.M. already.

"You know what, guys? I'm gonna head home. I'll see you later, okay?" I start to head back to the street to flag down a cab. I think it's okay to splurge on one this late at night. I can see Betony looking at Nikos and shrugging. Lilena follows me, a bit unsteady on her high heels.

"Hey, are you okay? I really thought you were coming outside—we didn't mean to ditch you, I swear," she says. "Zona?" She looks worried, like I'm mad at her.

"It was really loud in there. Don't worry about it," I say, scanning the street for an available taxi.

"Listen, if you liked that guy—"

"No, no, it's fine." I turn to her and smile. "I'm just really tired." I'm not really mad. More like homesick.

"Okay, well . . . I hope you had a good time, at least. We'll talk soon, 'kay?" She gives me a big hug, then plants a kiss on each of my cheeks and totters away.

"Sure thing," I reply to myself.

20

Getting a cab proves to be much harder in Athens than in New York. I finally give up trying, figuring it'll be easier to just walk to the Metro. I don't feel unsafe anymore—I'm surrounded by people. On weekends, people stay out all night, straight into breakfast. So everything around is open and well lit.

I sit down to wait for the train, wishing I had a book or newspaper to read. I take my phone out to see if I have enough battery to play Angry Birds. I let my mind wander, thinking again about Andrew and how you never know who you might meet when you least expect it.

Then, for the second time that night, I hear an unfamiliar voice over my shoulder.

"Hey. You go to GIS, right? We talked in the library?" I look up and see Alex, the guy who insisted that a website was as good as a physical paper.

"Zona," I say, scooting over so he can sit. "Alex, right?"

"Yeah. What are you up to? Why are you all by yourself?"

"Oh, I was at a club with some friends from school," I say, trying to sound nonchalant. "I just got tired. Still not used to the super late nights, I guess."

He takes a long sip from a bottle of water. "You want some?"

I shake my head. "I'm good, thanks. So, how about you?"

He slides the bottle back into his backpack, then takes his glasses off and polishes them on his shirt. "It's going to sound incredibly lame, probably. I just like to take pictures at night sometimes." He takes a fancy-looking digital camera—the kind with an attached lens—out of his bag and passes it to me. "There are some really cool graffiti murals around here, and some abandoned train tracks . . ."

I toggle through the pictures, and they're really good. I can see why he likes taking them at night, with the hazy colored lights from the clubs blending into shadows at the edges of the frame.

"I don't think photography is lame at all. You're obviously really good," I say, handing the camera back.

"I just meant, you know, guy wandering with a camera, trying to look cool. Bit of a cliché, right?"

I think it's pretty interesting how self-aware this guy is. He seems a lot more relaxed than he did the first time we met. And *I* suddenly feel . . . a lot less relaxed.

I try very hard not to think about the guy I know in New York who loves carrying a camera around, even if it is a cliché. Who also happens to have gorgeous eyes and an easygoing way about him. I will not think about that at all. Because it would be too . . . coincidental. I mean, actually meeting a Greek Ben Walker? Things like that never happen to me. Besides—I'm on a quest to conquer Giorgos the Glorious, lest we forget.

The train pulls into the station and I look up. "Ah, finally," I say, waiting for Alex to join me as I head toward the doors.

"I'm going the other way," he says, hooking a thumb at the tracks behind him.

Is that regret I'm picking up in his voice? I think.

Maybe I'm reading into this.

"I was serious about that website, by the way. I think we can do so much better!" I call from the mostly empty train car. The doors snap shut. Alex waves from the platform. Then my train zips out of the station and I can't see him anymore.

This Just In: Man Doesn't Leave Living Room For Two Months Straight, Eats Only Crackers And Coffee, Survives

Upon returning home in the wee hours of the morning, Zona Lowell, 15, discovered her father half-asleep at his desk, surrounded by mugs.

David Lowell, old, has re- cently moved on from sifting through mountains of documents to prepping interview questions and becoming a living, mostly breathing caffeine experiment.

"You went to Gazi?" Yiota asks on the phone the next morning—well, afternoon, technically. "Did you love it? I'm so sad to never see you for so long. I have only been working all the time. I want to go dancing, too!"

I laugh. "It was . . . interesting. No, it was really fun. Just got a little weird at the end."

"You are okay, yes?" Yiota says, sounding worried.

"Yes, I'm totally fine. It was kind of cool, actually; this guy Andrew rescued me from—" I hear shouting on Yiota's end of the line.

"I am so sorry, Zona, that is my boss yelling, and I have to go back inside. Ugh, I miss our days together! Soon spring break will be here, though, yes? Crete will be so . . ." She mutters something in Greek under her breath. She sounds annoyed. "Sorry again—I'll text you later!"

Well, it was nice to hear her voice for a minute, even if we didn't really get to catch up. Her mention of Crete makes me think of all the questions I still need answers to.

I stretch out on my bed, still tired after staying up so late. Tony pads into my room with his leash in his mouth. I guess Dad is still knocked out, which is good. I'm used to his disappearing into his work, but I don't think it's ever been this intense—maybe because here he's at the mercy of a translator, so he has to get everything ready before he starts interviewing instead of feeling things out as he goes along. Either way, he definitely needs to sleep and recharge.

Despite worrying about him, I'm also proud. How lucky am I to have such a cool dad, who treats me like an equal and trusts me enough to focus on his work instead of micromanaging my life like Hilary's parents do? Of course, she doesn't have to drag them to bed, but it's a small price to pay.

"C'mon, Tone," I say, clipping on his leash. "Let's see what's happening in Athens today, shall we?"

For the first time since I arrived here, I reach for something besides my keys and cell phone when heading out for a walk: I grab a notebook and pen.

I haven't felt the urge to write—or even just write something *down*—in so long . . . but it feels comforting to have the tools of my trade with me anyway. Just in case.

21

"So, tomorrow is my birthday. My sixteenth birthday. My sweet sixteen? A day I thought would have a great deal of significance, or at least warrant some kind of small gathering?" I mention casually to Dad over dinner—sandwiches in the living room—on a Thursday night in late March. I can't believe how quickly the time is passing here, but suddenly it's almost spring, with spring break (and Crete) looming ever closer.

Dad doesn't look up from his notes.

"Yes, definitely . . . September 2009," he mumbles. He makes a squiggly mark on the top page, then throws it on top of about sixty similarly marked pieces of paper on the floor.

"Nope. Not even close. But good chatting with you." I grab my book and head out to the terrace to text my GIS friends.

Father unmoved by birthday imminence. Want to do something tomorrow eve?

And everyone does. In fact, they seem more excited than I do.

Ashley says she has a great idea that will be very, very Greek. I'm intrigued and a little nervous, but I go with it. Why not?

Don't forget to bring the chocolates tomorrow! she adds.

Chocolates? What do you mean? *Um, shouldn't someone be bringing me a cake? With sixteen candles and one to grow on?!*

My phone rings. "Zona!" Ashley exclaims the moment I answer. "You have to bring chocolates, sweets, whatever you like, for the whole class. It's how we do it here—the person whose birthday it is brings treats." Ashley sounds incredulous. Apparently I've been missing some vital information. "People have been bringing things in all year, almost every day for birthdays or name days; didn't you notice? I know you ate some!"

"Yes, but . . . I guess I just thought they were being nice?"

"Nope. I mean, maybe, but it's your turn to be nice now. Don't forget!" And she hangs up.

Greek People Do Things Backward, Result Is Lots Of Candy

Today was a landmark event for tradition enthusiasts everywhere, when it came to light that Greek people do not give birthday girls cake on their birthdays; instead, birthday girls must bring cake to the masses. Specifically, chocolates or small cakes are shared with classmates or coworkers. This happens both on actual days of birth and on name days, otherwise known as saints' days. (Greek names are associated with specific saints, and almost every day of the year is devoted to a saint.) This means that free chocolates are on offer pretty much every single day if you know where to look. Plus, people get to celebrate their existences not once a year but twice, which, according to our on-the-ground correspondent Zona Lowell, is "a pretty sweet deal. No pun intended."

In a related story, not all names have their own special day, but there is a collective group name day called Aghion Pándon. To no one's surprise, "Zona"—an unusual moniker— gets relegated to group day. Ms. Lowell declined to comment.

Filed, 7:14 p.m., Athens.

The next morning, after giving away my meager savings to my entire class in the form of chocolates, I float through school on a wave of well-wishes and go home for a lovely dinner with my dad. He has not only left his notes-laden desk to prepare said meal, which is being served on real plates *with* silverware and eaten at the table, but he even showered and dressed to eat! Tony spends the meal happily sitting on my feet. Dad and I share a celebratory glass of raki (an extra-distilled wine from Crete that he loves; I think it tastes like rubbing alcohol, but I have a few sips anyway to be festive), yummy cake from the decadent bakery down the street, and our first real conversation in what seems like forever.

"So. How's school?" he asks through a mouthful of chocolate icing.

"Oh, I dropped out two months ago. I joined a gang and we spend our days looting and pillaging."

"Hardy har," he scowls. "Ugh, Ace. I'm sorry—I know I've gone AWOL on you. But I do want to know everything you've been up to. I just—"

"Dad, it's fine. I'm used to being neglected. You can repent by leaving me your fortune in your will." I sigh heavily, leaning back in my chair, trying to look forlorn.

"Young Writer Abandons the Pen, Takes Up Acting?" he says dryly.

"Actually," I say, cutting myself another slice of cake, "I wanted to talk to you about that. Seriously, I mean."

"Why, what's up?" Dad leans closer. "You know, if you want to do something other than write, I'd support you no matter what, right?"

"Yeah, I know—it's not that. It's more like . . . it's not that I don't *want* to write. I still think about it all the time. Just, since I've been here, I haven't had the urge to sit down and *do it*. And I don't know what that means."

"Zona, you've had a lot going on. You know, back home that was your thing and it came very naturally to you. But part of being a journalist is knowing when you're objectively reporting on a situation and when you're inside the story; sometimes that makes it a better story, and sometimes it makes it not your story to tell. I'm experiencing that myself, with this piece. It's hard to frame something so personal—do I include my experiences? Do I not?"

"But you're doing it," I interject. "You sit down every day and work. I just sort of . . . I don't know."

"Yes, but I've been doing this for a long, long time. Believe me, kid, when I was your age I didn't do a damn thing." Dad tips his head to the side and gives me his lopsided Dad smile. "If you need to just experience things and not write about them for a while, that's okay. The writing will still be there—maybe you'll discover a different kind of storytelling that inspires you. Maybe not. But obviously your brain is busy with just . . . figuring things out. And that's great. I'm really proud of how well you've adjusted to being here. Not that I ever doubted a daughter of mine, of course!"

I laugh, but it feels halfhearted. I want to believe what he's saying, but it's hard to let go of the feeling that I'm slacking off somehow. Even though I know that's kind of silly; I'm a fifteen-—wait, sixteen-!—year-old girl who writes articles, not a real reporter. It's not my job, or even an extracurricular activity anymore. But still . . .

"I think it's time for some *presents*," Dad says, tossing his fork onto his empty plate. He gets up and retrieves two wrapped boxes from under his chair, a medium-size flat box and a second tiny box. He hands them to me, singing off-key: "Happy birthday, dear Zona . . ."

Two presents. I have no idea what they could be; usually Dad takes me to a store and lets me pick out something I can't afford to splurge on myself, or we go to an exhibit or a show or something. This is new.

"Well, it's not every day my favorite daughter turns

144

sixteen, is it?" He smiles and I grin back. "These are both things I've been saving for you for a long time. Open that one first."

I rip into the bigger one as directed, and under the paper is a shiny gray leather box, plain but pretty, like from the Container Store or something. Inside are clippings from newspapers. Old newspapers. As I sift through them, I realize they're front pages from newspapers all over the United States and the world . . . all from the day I was born. March 28, 1998.

"I had a whole network collect those for me, all your biggest fans," Dad brags, and I imagine all his colleagues and sources finding these and sending them to Dad in the weeks after my birth, and maybe even years later.

"Dad, it's . . . *perfect.* Thank you so much." I wipe tears away with the back of my hand, a little embarrassed. Dad pushes the smaller box toward me, obviously pleased by my reaction.

I tear the paper off, and it's a jewelry box. Inside is a simple gold band. I don't have to examine it to know that there are initials engraved on the inside: *DL+HM*. It was my mother's.

"You don't have to wear it if you don't want to," he says hurriedly. "Or you can. Or you could wear it on a necklace . . . I just thought you'd like to have it. To keep with your things, I mean, instead of with hers. Since, you know. We're here now and everything."

I don't know what to say. Despite being here and getting to know my cousin, I haven't exactly developed this grand connection to my mother. I still don't know her. I'm still not particularly jazzed about meeting the rest of the family. But I know what this gift means to my *dad*, and that's the most important thing. I put the ring back in the little box and get up to hug him. "Thanks, Dad—for everything. I'll keep them all together. Memories from both families, right?"

He looks relieved, and I know I've said the right thing. We clear the dishes and I get dressed to go out with my friends.

My cell rings and I pick it up without looking at the screen, assuming it's Lilena calling for an outfit consultation.

"HAPPY SWEET SIXTEEN!!!!!!!" I hear on the other end of the line. It's Hilary and Matt, and I'm totally surprised. I got hilarious cards from both of them in the mail already, and we usually have Skype chats on (USA) Sunday mornings if we can. "You guys!" I say. "Where are you? Isn't it, like, one P.M. or something?"

"We're in the computer lab at school," Hil says. "You didn't think we'd miss calling on your actual birthday, did you?"

"No, of course not!" I say, trying to put on mascara and balance the phone with my shoulder at the same time. "I just didn't think you'd call now. I miss you guys."

"What're you doing for the big event?" Matty asks. "Dressing up in a toga and eating fancy yogurt with John Stamos?" Hilary laughs.

"Yeah, exactly," I reply sardonically. "How'd you ever guess? No, I ate with Dad—I have to show you what he gave me, it's amazing—and now I'm going with my GIS friends somewhere, but I don't know where it's going to be."

"Oooh, is Gorgeous Giorgos going to be there? Maybe that'll be your *real* gift," Hilary coos. (Yes, I have surreptitiously taken pictures of him and sent them to my friends. That's called undercover work, thank you very much.)

"Oh my God, I think I'd age twenty years instead of one if he actually spoke to me," I say, adding another coat of mascara. "Great, now I'm panicking." I sit down heavily on my bed.

"Oh, cut it out. Guys like confidence. Just be yourself and say what's on your mind," Matt advises. "Trust me. That's what I did with Scott and now we hang out all the time."

"*Literally* all the time," Hilary adds. "Not that I've ever met this guy, by the—"

"Now, let's not go misusing the word 'literally' just to make a point," I scold her. "Matty, stop neglecting Hilary. Hilary, you should be focusing on the *Reflector*, anyway. You haven't told me what's—"

"And . . . she's off!" Matt interrupts. "It's your birthday, woman. Go out. Have a drink. Kiss a guy. *Be* the story for a change, huh?"

"Ha, funny—that's what Dad said," I say thoughtfully.

"About Giorgos?!" Hilary squeaks.

"No, about writing. Because, you guys, I haven't written a thing since I got here. I'm sort of . . . I don't know. I just want to at least know things are going smoothly back home!"

"I'll send you the new issue later," Hilary promises. "But Matty's right. And so's your dad—go be in the story!"

After we hang up, I audition all my clothes as potential birthday going-out outfits before deciding on the very first thing I tried on. I get a text with directions from Lilena, say good-bye to Dad, and head out for a birthday adventure.

22

A Night At The Bouzoukia:
Teens Fête Friend, Greek-Style

Tonight's Sweet Sixteen celebration started at a local *bouzoukia*, which turned out to be an intimate venue featuring traditional Greek musicians, at least one of whom plays a *bouzouki*, an instrument similar to a mandolin.

Birthday girl Zona Lowell's GIS friends surprised her by pooling their resources to procure a table reservation and a ready supply of roses to throw at the stage. Ms. Lowell was amazed once again to discover that the group's underage status had no effect on their being welcomed or served at the venue, and that the music—while unfamiliar—was fun and catchy. Proving typical of Greek nightlife, the crowd was very into the experience, and even a somewhat reluctant Ms. Lowell was dragged into a circle of dancers.

Also of note is the attitude of Greek teens to alcohol, which is generally blasé. "It's so different from New York, where it's such a thing, you know?" Ms. Lowell remarked. "Who can get it, how much, etc. I'm not really into drinking myself, but it's still always a concern when it comes to making plans. Here no one really cares, so kids don't worry about fake IDs. They rarely get drunk or out of control. There's simply no reason to."

Lilena Vobras, a recent Chicago transplant and friend of Ms. Lowell's, agreed with these sentiments, stating for the record, "I mean, a six-year-old can buy a bottle of whiskey from a street kiosk here. It's just not a big deal at all, so kids don't really abuse it, you know? They're just relaxed. It's a lot less pressure to be . . . cool, somehow, because of that. Totally different from my old school, for sure."

Things took an unfortunate and very messy turn when some extremely drunk Australians (who did not get the "relax and don't overdo it" memo) started smashing dishes and yelling *"Ópa!"* This to the great displeasure of the venue's proprietors, who thought everyone knew that the custom of smashing plates while screaming is, frankly, antediluvian.

Filed, 9:07 p.m., Athens.

After we escape the mania of plate-throwing Australian tourists, laughing like loons all the way down the street, I pause for a second to really feel the evening. Here I am on a pretty big birthday, outside without a coat, surrounded by people I don't know that well, really, and they've all gotten together to show me a great time. I feel kind of, well, *special*—which, I suppose, is how you're supposed to feel on your sixteenth birthday.

And just when I think it couldn't get any better unless Hilary and Matt suddenly appeared, Nikos says, "Come on, let's go down to the marina. Giorgos is there with some people for drinks." And then the five of us are piling into a taxi and speeding toward the hottest guy I have ever seen, who I've been ogling for three straight months. And it's *my birthday.* I mean, you can't make this stuff up.

Maybe I should be up-front about my past experiences with guys: they're pretty lame. I've hooked up a few times, but nothing too exciting. My first kiss was at that same interschool dance where Hilary and I first became friends with Matt. It was awkward and I never saw the guy again. The three of us snuck into a couple of upperclassman parties last year—not my idea, of course—and at one of them I got kind of drunk (the first and only time I've had more than a couple of beers) and made out with a guy who tried to hang out with me again after that, but I freaked out that he wanted to be my boyfriend. I barely even remembered making out with him. Not my best display of maturity, I have to admit. Then there was one random but actually very nice kiss with Hilary's cousin when I stayed with her for a few weeks when my dad was out of town on assignment.

And . . . yeah. That's it.

But tonight, the universe is clearly sending me a signal: I'm in a strange land, I see this gorgeous guy across a crowded cafeteria on my first day of school, and now we are having our first real meeting on my *special night*?! Come on.

I still haven't figured out why the girls think Giorgos is so weird. It's true that he kind of keeps to himself, and reads by himself a lot . . . but so do I! Maybe we're meant for each other.

In the cab, everyone is asking me what I thought of the *bouzoukia*. From the front seat Nikos says, "You know, it interests me very much that you came here to see family,

151

but you never mention them. I mean, is it different, staying with your Greek family, or like the same as in New York?"

Huh. I was much happier thinking about Giorgos.

"Well, I'm not actually . . . So, there's Yiota, my cousin. I told you guys about her. But I've never, um . . . I haven't met anyone else in my family." I exchange a glance with Lilena, who looks at me questioningly.

Ashley gasps. "Seriously? But I thought—"

"Yet," I go on quickly. "I haven't met them yet—they live in Crete. So I'm going there for spring break."

"You don't sound very excited," Betony chirps.

I so do not feel like going into the whole dead mom saga, especially since this is actually the anniversary of said tragic event.

Lilena comes to my rescue, saying, "You guys, Zona doesn't want to talk about this stuff. It's a party! Let's—"

The cab screeches to a halt at the curb outside the marina. Saved. I squeeze Lilena's hand gratefully as we're clambering out of the backseat. She squeezes back.

Once we get out of the cab, I sneakily reapply my lip gloss, try to remember Matty's tips for talking to guys and being myself, and stroll onto the scene looking extremely casual. Or in a way that I think looks really casual. Same thing, right?

And there he is, sitting with a few other people at a table. I recognize one girl, a senior with long dreadlocks and an eyebrow ring, but the others I've never seen before. One of them looks about forty, actually. They have many empty coffee cups and an overflowing ashtray on the table, and they're all smoking and not talking to one another. Giorgos is underlining something in a very old paperback book. Nikos claps his brother on the back and Giorgos looks up, smiling.

"Greekgreekgreekgreekgreek," he says, which I assume means, *Oh, Zona is here? Fantastic! Perhaps I'll take her for a romantic walk along the water!*

He gets up and joins our group, and I think for a second I might just tip over into the water and never be heard from again.

"Hi, I'm Giorgos," he says to me. His voice is really deep and growly. He kisses the other girls on both cheeks, then returns to me. *"Chronia polla."* I'm pretty sure that means "happy birthday" in Greek, but I choose to believe it actually translates to *Zona, I have been stalking you, too. I didn't approach you earlier because you are so beautiful and I wasn't sure you were real.*

"Efcharisto," I say, ambitiously using a Greek word. "We were just at a *bouzoukia*. There were—"

"Giorgos, maybe you and Zona should go get some ice cream or something. She loves ice cream, don't you, Zona?" Ashley says, not very subtly. Also not so subtle is Betony tugging on her sleeve and giggling. Lilena nudges me, and Nikos rolls his eyes at all of us. Giorgos doesn't seem to notice. He's staring into the distance and rocking back and forth on his toes. I wonder if he's high. Do people smoke a lot of weed in Greece?

"Uh . . . yes, I do love ice cream. Especially outside, at night, after eating half a cake earlier." I smile broadly. Hey, if nothing else, I can take a cue.

Giorgos shrugs and starts walking toward a little gelato stand. Shooting a panicked/elated look at the girls, I follow him.

"We'll get a table!" Lilena calls after us.

"So, um, are those your friends over there? I think I recognize one of them from school."

No response.

I don't give up. "So, you and Nikos have lived a lot of places, right? That must be so fascinating, culturally . . . sociologically. Have you ever—"

"What flavor do you like?" he asks me in his gravelly voice.

"Whatever you're having is great. I can be incredibly mercurial when it comes to ice cream." Oh no. The SAT words are sneaking out; English isn't even this guy's first language—he probably has no idea what I'm saying.

He orders two vanilla cones and looks around the marina again. Then he breathes in deeply.

"The air is so pungent here, isn't it?" I say chirpily. "Salt and something floral . . . I love it, don't you?" *Jesus H, Zona. What are you* talking *about?*

The counter boy gives him the cones, but Giorgos doesn't hand me one.

Should I ask for it? Did he forget he's holding it?

"So, I know Nikos pretty well, but you and I haven't, um . . . I mean, I see you're a big reader. What are you reading?"

He says nothing, but looks at me steadily and licks one of the cones. I try not to think about his tongue and instead look up at his eyes. Mistake. They are so sparkly, I feel like I'm being sucked into a vortex. Even his shaggy Justin Bieber haircut is adorable instead of lame. I can't look away.

Say something.

"I'm a writer. I mean, I was, in New York, which is where I'm from. You probably knew that—or not. Um. I probably don't sound like much of a writer right now, huh?"

"You talk a lot, do you know that?" Giorgos remarks calmly. His jaw, it's so well-cut, like he was drawn with a felt-tip marker. When he speaks it's almost as mesmerizing as when he's not speaking. "You should try to spend more time being quiet, I think so, yes?"

He doesn't seem to be insulting me, really; it's more like he's trying to figure me out. Though frankly I'd be happy to listen to him insult me all day long. I just want him to keep saying things. I'd like it even more if he said things and then put his hands . . . anywhere.

He licks his ice cream very slowly, thoughtfully. I may actually pass out.

"It's good, you know, to just *be*, Zona. Can you just *be*?"

I have no idea what that means. It sounds like the kind

of thing a yogi or a hipster would say. Do they have either of those in Greece? I try to focus on Giorgos's pink tongue, once again gliding smoothly over the cool, white . . .

Then, slowly—so slowly that I'm mesmerized and don't even realize what is about to occur—the hand holding the second ice cream comes up, up . . . over my head . . . and then down. I don't stop him because I can't believe it's actually happening.

Giorgos places the cone—cold side down—on the top of my head, delicately but firmly. Then he tilts his head to the side like a bird and gazes at me.

"What the—are you—why would you *do* that!?" I sputter in disbelief, snatching the cone off. The ice cream, unfortunately, stays put.

You might never have thought about what it would feel like to have ice cream all over your head—I certainly hadn't. Answer: it's freaking cold!

"I can't . . . I can't believe . . ." I grind to a halt.

He's still just staring at me. Is this guy nuts or what?

Suddenly, I start laughing. Everyone is staring at me, and I can't stop laughing. The ice cream is melting, dripping down the side of my face and all over my hands as I try to wipe it off, and it's cold, and sticky, and I'm *still* laughing, so hard I think my insides are going to burst.

"See?" Giorgos says calmly. He swallows the last of his cone. "It's okay. Just be. Just like that."

He goes over to the counter, then hands a bunch of

napkins to me. I start to wipe my hair, but it's a disaster there's no help for. I'll have to shower to get this mess out.

"I don't think having an ice cream cone on your head is the key to the universe. In fact, I'm not sure why I'm laughing instead of punching you right now," I say, balling up the soggy napkins.

"It's because you're not thinking about meaningless stuff, that's why. You're chilled out."

"Oh, I'm definitely *chilled out.*"

"That *is* the key to the universe, Zona." Giorgos takes his cigarettes out of his pocket and shakes one out. "You want?"

"Thanks, but I don't smoke. Also, I'm covered with ice cream, so I'm pretty sure I need to go home. But thanks for the life lesson, Giorgos. It was . . . real."

"You're okay, Zona." He nods, inhaling smoke as he lights up. "I like you."

I extricate a knit hat from my bag and shove it over my disgusting hair. At the table, the girls are cracking up, but not in a mean way—more a "We tried to tell you!" way— and Nikos is shaking his head. Giorgos is still smoking by the water, looking into the distance, rocking back and forth again.

I thank the others for an amazing and totally unique Sweet Sixteen experience. I promise to hug them properly when I'm not, you know, covered with vanilla ice cream.

. . .

Obituary: Death Of First Official Greek Crush Confirmed

It was with a heavy heart this evening that Zona Lowell, 16, said good-bye to her love for Giorgos Hadjimarkos on the pier in Floisvos. Following months of stalking him around school while imagining shared conversations and cozy makeout parties, Zona had no choice but to admit that theirs was a relationship that could never be.

"I've obviously heard that boys flirt by doing weird things," Ms. Lowell explained, "but this wasn't like that at all. He really is just . . . odd. I mean, he put ice cream on my head. Plus he's a smoker—nail in the proverbial coffin."

We applaud Ms. Lowell for keeping her chin up during this dark time and hope she finds another object for her affections soon.

Filed, 11:23 p.m., Athens.

23

I follow Lilena's directions to the nearest train, not wanting to pay the fare for a cab by myself. I'm very sticky but mostly bemused; it's always nice to solve a mystery, I suppose. And who was I kidding, anyway? Giorgos was no more interested in me than Ben Walker ever was.

I resolve not to get depressed about dumb guys on my birthday—after all, the day isn't over yet! I look up at the beautiful night sky, lit by stars and the glow of lights from the marina.

Pretty nice place to spend a birthday.

As I approach the station I see a familiar pair of metallic green glasses sitting next to a camera bag on a bench. They look just like Alex's, but I don't see him. How weird. I turn back around and spot him perched on a low wall, camera against his face. I'm tempted to run—do I really need to be seen by anyone else I know with ice cream all over my head?—but it's such a funny coincidence, running into him again at a random train station, that I feel like I have to say hi.

I yank the hat farther down to make sure my disgusting hair is covered, then wait until I'm sure he isn't about to take a picture and step into the frame.

"Hi again," I say.

He pulls the camera away from his face. "Miss *New York Times*! Are you stalking me or something?" he says, hopping down.

"I could ask you the same thing." I grin. It's the first time I've seen him without his glasses on, and he looks awfully cute. *This night gets more and more interesting*, I think.

"You caught me," he says, walking over to the bench. He puts his specs on, wiggling his nose to get them situated right. "I like to shoot without them sometimes, just to mix things up; I let the camera do the focusing instead of my eyes. I dunno—just an experiment." He shrugs.

"Clever," I say. "I don't know much about the actual art of photography, honestly. But I like the idea of it."

"Thanks," he replies, smiling. "I guess I'll find out when I go through them. Getting good pics at night is hard anyway, so I'm just making it harder on myself. You know—for fun."

We both laugh, and he picks up his bag. "What are you doing over here? And what's with the hat? It's not that cold."

My hand flies up to my head. "Oh, I was with some friends celebrating my birthday at the marina. We went to a *bouzoukia* first, which I'd never been to before."

"Oh, nice!" he says excitedly. "Did you dance and throw roses and everything? Happy birthday, by the way."

"Thanks!" I can tell that I'm blushing, because my cheeks feel warm. "Yes, we did the whole *bouzoukia* thing. It was pretty awesome. And the hat . . ." I pause, trying to think how much to share. "It's kind of a long story."

"Really? Now I want to hear it—no one's ever told me a long story about a hat before, I don't think. Wanna grab a bite or a drink or something?" he offers. "Unless you're all birthdayed out, that is."

"As long as it isn't ice cream and you don't make me take my hat off, I'd love to."

Teen Has Impromptu Date; Cannot Believe It Is Actually Happening

Very early Saturday morning, GIS Sophomore Zona Lowell found herself on what seemed to be her first real date—ever—with junior Alex Loushas, also 16. "I'm not even really sure how it happened," Ms. Lowell was overheard explaining to a schoolmate on the phone the next day. "One second I'm heading for the train with ice cream–covered hair, and the next he's describing where he grew up in Egypt and telling me he's only a quarter Greek but his parents really wanted to live in Athens. Apparently he's always gone to American schools, which is why he has no discernible accent. He asked if I've been to all these places around the city where he likes to take pictures, what I got for my birthday, and about my dad's work. Just joking around and . . . flirting. I mean, really flirting. Not just being nice."

It has been confirmed at this time that Mr. Loushas, who

Alex insists on waiting for the train with me even though he isn't taking it himself—he rode his bike. I mention how nice it is to be able to take the train so late at night and not really worry about walking alone, like I would in New York. (Who am I kidding? I wouldn't in a million years be out at almost two in the morning in New York, alone or otherwise.)

"Athens is a special place," Alex says. "A lot of people have the wrong idea about it. Don't get me wrong—there are problems, obviously. But I like living somewhere where people feel safe at night. Especially pretty girls." He smiles.

Wait. He means me, right? Maybe he's just, uh . . .

"I—"

"Pretty girls with ice cream stuck in their hair, I mean," he adds quickly, cutting me off. Then he leans down and kisses me softly on the lips, just as the train blasts into the station.

Giorgos? Giorgos *who*?!

Best. Birthday. Ever.

24

"Zona. This is supposed to be the fun part. You're just flirting. He obviously likes you. He kissed you. He texted you. That's *fun*. *Right?*" Lilena is chastising me over coffee at our usual café on Sunday afternoon (forty hours and sixteen texts after The Kiss).

I've been driving her—and myself—completely crazy since Friday night. Well, Saturday morning, if I'm being accurate.

Liking Alex feels different from liking Ben. Ben was sort of . . . further away. And Giorgos was even more of a fantasy. It didn't feel scary to like him like this does. This feels like I want to cry and laugh at the same time. I barely know Alex—we aren't even Facebook friends!—but when he kissed me, it was the first kiss I've ever had that felt . . . the way it's *supposed* to feel. I can't explain it any other way. I can't prove it with background information or witnesses. I just know it's true.

But now my imagination has been running rampant and

leaving my rational self behind. I spent most of Saturday imagining us making out for hours instead of doing my homework. How he'd tell me things he's never told anyone else and maybe I'd meet his parents.

And just a split second later, while that happy feeling was still swishing around in my brain, I immediately panicked that he would never call me and it was just a kiss that didn't mean anything.

Then I thought: what if he *did* call me and then he didn't think any of the things I like are cool and he never talked to me again and it hurt so much that I couldn't even feel *anything* after a while? And then what? How would I sit there in school knowing Alex wouldn't talk to me or look at me if I ran into him in the hall or the caf? What if he started flirting with someone else?

Of course, none of this had even *happened*. I was being completely nuts. But I couldn't stop myself; it was like I had a little hamster on a wheel inside my head and he was just running and running and wouldn't stop.

Finally, on Saturday afternoon, when I was in the middle of yet another bonkers meltdown, my phone buzzed . . . and it was *him*.

Last night was a really nice surprise, Miss New York Times. See you Monday.

I actually shrieked out loud in my bedroom when I saw it. Loudly enough that Tony, who looked embarrassed for both of us, sneezed at me and left the room.

I was happy for all of ten minutes before the hamster

wheel started spinning again. *What if I texted back the wrong thing? What if he was just being nice? What if . . .*

Hilary wasn't answering her phone. I couldn't pull it together to write her a coherent e-mail. So I called Lilena, who at first was super excited to hear about my post-birthday adventure . . . and now may or may not want to throw me into the sea.

"I don't know," I tell her now, fiddling with one of the grapes brought over, as always, by the scary lady. "I'm nervous I'll do something that will make him stop liking me before he even gets to really, really like me."

"You know you sound insane, right? I mean, what could you possibly do?" Lilena adds another packet of calorie-free sweetener to her coffee. Her wrists are so thin poking out of her long-sleeved shirt that it hurts to look at them. But I try not to think about it.

"Say something. Or *not* say something. Or, I don't know, be inscrutable or laconic or overtly flirtatious or . . . something!"

"I don't know what 'laconic' means. Does it mean *crazy*? Because that's how you sound right now," Lilena asks, grinning crookedly at me, her poor, totally smitten friend.

I sigh. "It means quiet or not talkative."

She bursts out laughing. "I don't think that's ever going to be your problem, Zona!"

I throw a grape at her and the owner starts banging pans together for no reason. "I just don't want to mess it up. It's so perfect right now," I groan hopelessly.

"But you've only hung out one time. Well, like one and a half, I guess. He's just a guy. I mean, are you always like this about guys?"

I think about that for a second. "No, actually." I sip my coffee. "I guess maybe it's because Alex is the first guy who's ever been someone I might actually . . . date. All the other guys I've liked have been . . . unreachable. You know what I mean?"

Lilena looks thoughtful. "Well, just see what happens. See if you even really like him that much—get to know him better."

"You're right. I know you are. That's what I'd tell myself if I weren't, you know, me. I know in the rational part of my mind that I'm being ridiculous. We hung out once. That's nothing. But, I don't know, I just can't stop myself!"

"Well, it's always easier to see something from the outside," she says comfortingly.

"Have you dated anyone at GIS?" I ask.

"Nah," she says, looking away. I know she's going to change the subject back to me like she always does.

"What about at your old school?" I try again, hoping she'll open up, even a little bit.

"Nope. I was only there for a year, and the guys were so lame . . . This Alex situation is good, though. Maybe someday I'll meet a cute boy on a train platform and you can give me advice."

I think about giving her some advice—some *real*

166

advice—but I bite my tongue, remembering Ashley and Betony. Better to leave it alone. "Well, technically we met in the library," I remind her. "So, what are you doing for spring break?"

"Probably nothing. We're supposed to go to one of the islands, but I'm sure it'll get canceled. I'll probably ask if I can go visit my friend in Switzerland—we lived there before Chicago—and my mom will say yes, but then change her mind because of security risks. So . . . nothing."

"Want to go to Crete and pretend to be me?" I ask, only half joking.

"Have you talked to your cousin yet? About what the family knows and stuff?" Lilena asks.

"No, she's been so busy. I didn't want to ask her in a text," I reply. "Thanks, by the way, for changing the subject in the cab the other night. It's not that I want to keep it a big mysterious secret, it's just . . ."

"Private. I totally get it. Ashley and Bet can be pushy, but it's not mean-spirited. They just like to know what's going on, you know?"

"Oh, totally," I assure her. "Anyway, I don't know when I'm going to be able to talk to Yiota—really talk, I mean. It may have to be on the boat ride there!"

"Well, I bet she'll have good guy advice for you, too," Lilena says, grinning. "Or maybe she'll know a cure for boy-craziness. Like a lobotomy."

"Hey!" I laugh, tossing another grape at her. It hits her

in the forehead, and she lobs one back at me. We start laughing like lunatics, and the proprietress is *not* pleased. I have a feeling we just lost our grape privileges. Oops.

Breaking: Teen Reacts To Attention From New Crush

The week since Zona Lowell's and Alex Loushas's meet-cute in a Metro station has been, to quote Ms. Lowell, "completely nuts."

Due to the extraordinary amount of homework the sophomore student has received, she has been unable to do anything but sleep, eat, study . . . and exchange text messages with Mr. Loushas, 16. Even time to update Ms. Lowell's best friend, Hilary Bauer, has been unattainable.

Despite fears that he would act like a total douchebag in the aftermath of their spontaneous date/kiss, Mr. Loushas has proven to be quite a gentleman. Witnesses report that he "waved and smiled at [Zona] in the cafeteria on Monday, in front of all his friends. Plus he came over to [her] after he finished eating and said hi to [her] friends. It was just . . . easy."

On Wednesday Mr. Loushas was reported to have walked Ms. Lowell to her train after school, where playful arguing about the state of journalism ensued, plus more kissing.

Ms. Lowell remarked that she was "so swept up in the moment that I [sic] didn't even think to be shy or embarrassed because other people were around. It was really amazing. He is such a good kisser!"

No actual plans to hang out have been made as of this printing, but Ms. Lowell (when not driving herself insane) remains hopeful.

Filed, 3:42 p.m., Athens.

25

Wednesday night around ten P.M., my time, I finally get Hilary on Skype to tell her about my birthday and The Kiss and everything that's happened since, and I can barely get the words out fast enough.

"Ugh, I can't believe he did that! Why, Giorgos, why?!" she says, giggling. "But this Alex sounds *very* promising . . ."

"I'm making myself bonkers, though, Hil. I can't calm down and just see what happens."

"Well, that's because you're a type A overachiever. We know this," she says seriously, then smiles. "Honestly, though—I'm so jealous. Forget the cute guy part—I'd just like to be able to go out in the city and not feel like a dumb little kid all the time." She groans, shaking her head. "I tried to go out in the East Village last weekend with Sara and Keri and we got *completely* shut down. It was pathetic. I mean, Matty has been going to all these cool places, and I know he's with Scott and his friends and it's not really my scene, but . . . I miss him. I wish he'd invite me even once,

169

you know?" She picks up a sketch pad and starts doodling with a gel pen; I feel bad that she's upset, but I can't help but smile at the familiarity of seeing her distractedly drawing while she talks.

"I just feel like, you know, it's great that he's hanging out with this guy, or dating him, or whatever," she goes on, "but I'm still here, and I'm not dating anyone, and I just feel like I'm less important now. Everything is about Scott, and Scott's friends, and doing gay stuff with them. And yeah, I have other things to do, but I feel like he doesn't think I'm as cool anymore or something."

I pull the laptop closer to me, wishing I could actually be in the same room—on the same continent—as Hil and give her a reassuring hug. "I totally get it. And of course he cares. But it's his first crush, you know? On someone who might actually like him back, I mean. He's excited." As I say the words, I realize how well I understand them. "You know how hard it's been for him. And he knows we think it's kind of a bad idea because of the age thing. I think he really wants this experience. I would be hurt, too, I'm not saying I wouldn't. I just—"

"At least if you were here I wouldn't feel completely ditched. *We'd* still be together."

"Well, maybe you need to hang out with some other people for a while. Let Matt notice you're not so available, either."

Hilary half laughs. "It sounds like we're talking about some guy I'm dating instead of Matty."

"Nah. He's too short for you." I sigh with relief when she smiles at my lame joke. "Honestly, I think he needs this right now. And even though you're pissed, I know you're happy for him."

Hilary sighs. "I know. I *am* happy. I just . . . I feel lonely and I hate sounding so jealous and bitter. But I *am* a little bit. I'd like to have some guy to gush about, too, you know?"

"Yeah." My phone buzzes with a text; I glance down and see it's from Alex.

"Do you have to go?" she asks. I shove the phone under my books.

"No, it's nothing," I say quickly. Inside, of course, I'm aching to look and see what he wrote. Is it something cute? Something about homework? A text he meant to send to someone else? But I don't want Hilary to think I'm ditching her for a guy, too. "I, um . . . well, yeah, I think Matt just needs to have this for a bit. You have lots of friends you can hang out with til the novelty of Scott wears off. And lots to do—how's the paper? Have you been painting? Tell me—"

Hilary looks away from the computer in the direction of her door, then back. "It's my mom. She got home from work early for once and wants to eat with me. It's a miracle. Anyway, I have to go. Love you. E-mail me later, okay?"

And then the screen goes blank.

I snatch my phone, and when I read Alex's text I can't wipe a silly grin off my face. It's not anything particularly brilliant, but it's from him and it's about a private joke from the night we went out. And I've never gotten texts like this from a guy before.

I write back—an artfully composed message, of course. I haven't spent so much time or care writing anything since I got to Greece. *Who am I becoming?*

I go back to studying for a while, and then check on Dad, who is elbow-deep in notes as usual. Then I call Lilena.

"It's been over an hour. Why hasn't he texted back?" I blurt as soon as she picks up.

"Oh, no, you don't—I'm not having this conversation again. Did you do the Chemistry homework yet?"

"But—"

"Chemistry," Lilena says firmly. "Let's go over the take-home quiz."

So we do, though I'm distracted the entire time. *I hope Lilena meets a guy she likes soon,* I think, *so I can refuse to indulge* her *when* she's *losing it. Fair is fair.*

But it's fun, even with my crazy panicking—especially when I get another text from Alex in the middle of explaining my answer to a tricky question about chemical bonds. Because there is a boy, and I like him, and he seems to like me.

And I want him to kiss me again.

26

My flight to Greece in December, my first day at GIS . . . they both appeared on the calendar before I was even close to ready. And now, again, I feel unprepared.

Spring break is here—two whole weeks of it—and for the first time in my life, I'm wishing for less vacation and more school.

And not *just* because of Alex, by the way. He hasn't become a boyfriend or anything, but he is definitely a *something*. Not a defined something, but there has been some more kissing, which is fine by me.

Studying for exams over break is going to be awful, and being away from Dad is, too. I'll miss my new friends, especially Lilena; Yiota told me that Wi-Fi can be spotty on Crete, so I might not get to talk to Hil or Matty much, either. But nothing is as daunting as the real crux of the Easter plans: meeting my mom's entire family.

Dad has refused to budge an inch on his position and is forcing me to go. Without him. Specifically to a tiny village high on a hill outside of a bigger town called Heraklion, where the Marousopoulou clan has lived for generations.

Yiota and I finally snatched an hour for lunch one weekend before the trip, and she gave me a general rundown of who I'm going to be meeting and what it'll be like, but I honestly haven't taken in the details as well as I—Zona the person *or* Zona the reporter, for that matter—should have.

First of all, who can remember the names of seven thousand cousins she's never even seen? And second, I can't stop thinking about my childhood and growing up without a big family, and there's this dark cloud of fear and anger that is swarming around everything.

Of course, I'm trying to keep an open mind. (Sort of.)

There are a few ways to get to Crete from Athens. A quick hour-long plane ride straight to Heraklion Airport is one of them, but I've been told I absolutely *must* experience the overnight ferry (which I feel seasick just hearing about). Apparently it's an all-night party where no one sleeps in the berths they paid for—they just stay up drinking and playing music and gossiping. So that's the plan.

Overnight Ferry Party Ideal Venue For Asking Hard Questions

Zona Lowell, 16, embarked today on a journey unlike any she'd ever attempted: waiting for her on the isle of Crete was her family, none of whom she'd ever met or even spoken to.

Accompanied by her cousin, the young woman responsible for this reunion, Ms. Lowell felt she needed some questions answered before she could press onward.

Yiota Marousopoulou, 20, did not hesitate to offer up said answers, though in some cases they were incomplete ones. "The truth is, we did not ever talk about Hélenè when I grew up," she explained. "When I asked my mother about her, she didn't want my father and my uncles to know. When we talk about it again, I think they have always known that she was gone when there were no more letters. But they didn't want to believe it was true, so they didn't try to find out. You understand?"

Ms. Marousopoulou continued, explaining that her grandfather was a very strict man and refused to let her grandmother open Hélenè's letters. After he died, it was too late—there was "no Internet then, and the older people didn't speak English very much. And they were angry, and they had to blame someone. And so time passed, and they just . . . pretended. And hoped."

Ms. Lowell now had some answers, but just as many new questions. We will do our best to cover the story as it continues to unfold.

Filed, 10:38 p.m., somewhere out at sea.

When we get off the ferry, all the passengers start heading for their cars or the bus station a few blocks away. The dock is long and covered with stray cats. Before I have a chance to suggest rescuing them all, Yiota's cell phone rings. She looks around and then points excitedly. "Over there!" she exclaims, and then she's off, wending through the huge crowd of people, dragging her bag.

Beside an old, pale blue car stands a couple in their late fifties holding hands; she's wearing a shapeless patterned shirtdress and he's in a black ribbed tank top and olive-green pants. He has a bushy black beard and lots of bushy black hair—both on his head and his shoulders. The woman has one pair of glasses on her face and a second hanging from a chain around her neck, and a huge, gleaming smile. Yiota practically leaps into her arms, the man folds himself around Yiota and the woman, and they have a giant group hug.

I stand nearby, a bit embarrassed—the Lowells aren't big on PDAs—but everyone around me is hugging, too, and no one seems the least bit uncomfortable about the displays of affection. Even the men are hugging and kissing one another hello.

Finally the woman spots me and exclaims, "*Éla!* Zona, let me see you!" She holds me at arm's length, and I can see her eyes are wet with tears. "Oh, you look just like Hélenè." She kisses me on both cheeks. She turns to the man, who is piling things in the car. *"Greekgreekgreekgreekgreek Hélenè, nay?"* She looks back at me, beaming. "Just like her, I can't believe it."

"Yes, yes, okay," the man mumbles. Yiota tugs on his arm and says something in Greek. He stands up and faces me. "We go now."

"Baba!" Yiota hisses. She turns to me. "Zona, these are my parents, your *thia* and *thios*, yes? Angela and Labis. He was your mother's brother, okay?"

"Um, *kalimera*," I say. Labis looks less than thrilled to make my acquaintance. I shift uncomfortably from foot to foot, wondering if I should say something else as the silence drags on.

"Ay, Zona, it is a blessing, a blessing to have you here, and for Easter! Come, come here!" exclaims Angela, sweeping me into her arms again. She kisses me on both cheeks and squeezes my shoulders. "Just like your mother. Ay, come on, girls, get in the car before Labis leaves us here, eh?"

My uncle—my *thios*—is already in the car. We slide inside and Yiota leans over to me and whispers, "He is the oldest brother, I think I told you. Still a little angry, after all this time . . . but don't worry. He is wonderful when you know him, I promise. And my mother, she knew your mother well—my parents were married very young and Hélenè was a girl still."

I smile at Yiota, but the truth is my insides are churning. Is this what my spring break is going to be like? Winning over these people I don't know, convincing them not to be mad at me because of what my mom did almost seventeen years ago? Because I can think of a lot more fun things I could be doing instead, like chopping down trees for firewood or pulling a dogsled through the snow.

I resolve to be strong. After all, I've only just arrived.

We drive up a hill that seems to go on forever, and the road is right on the edge of a cliff, which is terrifying and exhilarating at the same time. Yiota and her mother are talking a mile a minute in Greek, so I zone out and take in the scenery.

It's absolutely incredible. Everything is vivid green and purple and yellow, and the road we're on is so high above

177

the ground, it's almost like we're in a plane. There are groves of silvery-green trees in dozens of neat rows down below, and just miles and miles of fields. I don't think I've ever seen so much empty space before. Here and there are little pockets of houses tucked into the side of the mountain, all white with delicate roofs the color of terra-cotta pots, but for the most part it's open land.

We get to the very top of the road and stop in front of an enormous, strangely shaped white house with an orange tile roof and a bright blue door. In front and right up to the front door are amazing flowering cacti and all kinds of trees growing fruits I can't identify. Along one side is a big wooden structure with grapes hanging off of it, and I have a feeling they aren't the fake ones they sell at Pottery Barn. On the other side is a garage filled with cars, and there are others parked up on the sidewalk as well as a few mopeds.

Yiota confirms that the whole family lives together, either in this "complex," as she calls it, or down the street, because they ran out of ways to add on to the original main building.

I suddenly realize I'm about to be surrounded by *lots* of people—people I don't know who all want to know me, who all knew my mother, who don't want to know my father—and I am not ready.

I feel sick.

"Um," I whisper to Yiota, not wanting her parents to hear and be offended, "I don't think I can do this. I didn't know everyone would be—"

But it's too late. The door flies open and a sea of people bursts into the street. No one's worried about cars hitting them, or my taking my stuff inside and getting settled, or whether any neighbors will be disturbed by the intense volume of everyone talking all at once. Some are smiling, some are shouting, some are little kids who only seem interested in chasing one another, some are clutching platters of food, everyone is speaking Greek . . . and one woman has a face that looks just like the faded pictures of my mother from the blue box, only much older.

And I know it's my grandmother.

And she's crying.

And then she opens her arms to me, and it's like no one else is there but us.

27

It's about three thirty in the morning. I'm lying on an air mattress in Yiota's old room next to her bed, and I'm so tired I can't sleep. Too many thoughts are whizzing through my brain. The insane amount of noise and food and laughter and yelling and just . . . *people*. People who, I realized as I was introduced to each one, actually do *look* like me. Some a lot, some just a little, but still, people I'm related to.

In some ways I feel like I've betrayed my dad by coming here, even though it was his idea. And also like I've betrayed myself, because I always said I didn't care about my Greek family, and now I've met them and I don't know *what* to think. I'm mostly just overwhelmed and excited and scared.

And a little deaf, maybe.

Everything was just raised to the highest *level* all day— meeting every person in the room, trying to gauge what they thought about the reunion, constantly being handed a new plate piled with food, a tiny glass of raki, a piece of cake . . . so many names and faces and mixing them all up and the endless laughing and crying and arguing and everything that makes a large group of people a family, I guess. I just never had anything to compare it to before.

Yiota took great pride in leading me around by the hand; I was adrift in a sea of strangers and a million feelings. My grandmother—my *yia-yia*—seemed to be hit the hardest by the whole thing. Of course, some of the people there (my cousins, mostly) were children or not born yet when my mother ran off with my dad, so they were just there because they're part of the family. But my uncles, my grandmother . . . I still feel like I need more information.

I wanted to sit with her especially, talk to her, try to understand how this round little woman with long silvery hair in a braid, who laughed and teased everyone around her (in Greek, of course, but I could tell), who insisted I eat and eat and eat some more in her broken English, who kept reaching over to touch my hand, my shoulder, my face, as though she couldn't believe I was really there . . . how this same woman could have sent all her daughter's letters back and never tried to find her.

When the party finally broke up, I followed Yiota up to her room, exhausted and ready to collapse.

"So? What did you think? Can you believe *Yia-Yia*, isn't she beautiful? Did you talk to *Thios* Theseus? He is my favorite—so silly and crazy. And aren't the little ones so cute? And Melina, you will get to spend time with her, she is so sweet and fun . . . And you must not worry about my father, okay? He is very kind, but still, I don't know—confused?—about all these things . . . Oh, Zona, I'm so happy you are here, finally here with all of us!" Yiota gushed the second the door closed behind us.

I sat on her desk chair. "It's . . . kind of overwhelming." Her face fell, and I rushed to clarify. "Not bad—it's amazing. It's just so *much*. All at once, you know? I'm kind of taking it all in. And I'm really, really glad you're here with me. I'd be lost without you."

Yiota smiled, her dark eyes sparkling. "Oh, I'm so glad! I knew it would all be okay."

I smiled back, fighting to keep my eyes from fluttering shut.

"Oh! You must be so tired—we'll go to sleep. I just have to call Nik and I'll be right back." She went to the door, cell phone in hand, already scrolling to her boyfriend's number. "Should you call Alex?" she asked coyly.

I yawned. "No, no. He's not . . . I mean, that would be weird. I'll text him in a few days, maybe."

"Okay, okay. Just asking," she said, closing the door behind her.

And now here I am, wide awake in the dark, Yiota snoring softly beside me. *Well, so what if I'm tired tomorrow,* I think, flipping over my pillow for the hundredth time. *I'm on vacation.*

Greeks Don't Want To Share Easter, Insist On Their Own

While the world generally acknowledges Easter as designated by the Roman Catholic Church, the Greek Orthodoxy celebrates its own Easter, which may or may not fall on the same date. On the island of Crete, Easter festivities last up to a month, culminating in a massive celebration including some unusual traditions. For a neophyte, the holiday can be exciting and confusing.

"Well, technically I'm Greek Orthodox because of my mom, but my dad was raised Jewish. We never celebrated anything, though. So I really have no idea what to expect," commented Zona Lowell, visitor. "Apparently they pour rosewater in the street and light lots of stuff on fire . . . It sounds pretty intense."

The Heraklion community looks forward to hosting Ms. Lowell's first Greek Easter and, if possible, totally blowing her mind with how awesome it is.

Filed, 2:37 p.m., Heraklion.

Before the holiday even arrives, there are weeks of fasting during Lent, which is what my family is in the middle of now. It's a very complicated system where certain foods get eliminated on specific days until you're basically eating a vegan diet, with the exception of shellfish, which for some reason is always allowed. Despite the restrictions, there seems to be a never-ending parade of things to eat—fresh everything, some of which comes from *Yia-Yia*'s backyard and most of which comes from the market in town where they shop every day.

Compared to Athens, Cretan cuisine is heaven. I don't even care that I can't taste the amazing-looking cheeses and other off-limits items until Easter—I'm so filled with fresh vegetables and fruit and delicious warm bread that I can hardly move.

I spend the first whole day exploring the house and surrounding gardens with the littlest cousins, who speak tentative English in their tiny voices and want me to meet all their toys and see their favorite hiding places. Yiota explains that some of them are actually her nieces and nephews, whose parents are in Athens and can't come up until the holiday. There are a few boy cousins who look like they're probably in middle school and refuse to do anything but play video games all day, ignoring the rest of us. And then there are the moments I spend sitting with *Yia-Yia*, who will come looking for me and press my hand into hers and smile and try to make me eat more.

Although I'm staying in Yiota's family's section of the Marousopoulou complex, it's my *thios* Theseus—the third brother—who I gravitate toward, just as Yiota predicted. He's like a Greek Willy Wonka (the Gene Wilder variety, not Johnny Depp, complete with fluffy reddish hair), always trying to sound mysterious. Also, he wears a *lot* of purple. Apparently he used to be a chemical engineer *and* a nightclub singer (which I can actually sort of picture), and he lived in the United States for over ten years, which is why his English is so good. He's obsessed with Elvis, old cars, and being right.

I liked him immediately when I met him at that first overwhelming family gathering, even though we only spoke for a second. Plus, I like saying "*Thios* Theseus." The writer in me can't help but love a nice dose of alliteration.

His wife—actually, his second wife, Ioanna—is a lot younger than he is, and she doesn't speak much English at all, but seems very nice. Their only daughter, Melina, is fourteen and a freshman at the local high school. I'm relieved that there's another person about my age to hang out with. I love Yiota, of course, but I know she has friends here that she hardly ever gets to see, and I totally get that. Melina seems quiet at first and then suddenly transforms into her dad—loud and a bit nuts—and then back again, like a hermit crab going in and out of its shell. She is obsessed with America, motorbikes, and boys.

We're going to get along famously.

On the third morning, after breakfast (everyone eats meals together in the huge main house), *Thios* Theseus says he wants to give me a tour of Heraklion and the surrounding area.

"We have everything here, you know," he tells me proudly. "Hip-hop, rap, kids with Mohawks. Just like New York, right?"

This may be the most astute description of New York I've ever heard.

We get in the car, me in the front so I can see and Melina in the back.

Remember what I said about insane Greek drivers? Not only does *Thios* Theseus *love* to go fast, he also loves to stop every other driver on the road to yell at them. For a

185

while I think he just knows everybody driving by, but the angry looks from the other drivers reveal that he's actually telling them off. Oh, how I wish I knew what he was saying.

As we drive, he explains everything—and I mean *everything*. Every bend in the road, why it was planned that way, every house, who owns it, every tree, how it grows, and everything each of those things reminds him of. It's dizzying and fascinating. All this, by the way, as we whiz up and down hills that have sheer drops you can't even see to the bottom of . . . and no guardrails.

Some of the roadsides have white crosses stuck in the ground—not one or two, but dozens. When I ask about them, Theseus sneers, "These are marks of terrible drivers who pay no attention. Ignore those. Ignore!"

In between wishing I were wearing a just-in-case helmet and marveling at the fact that figs start out as plump green globes before they get dried and packaged by Sun-Maid, I sneak a peek back at Melina. "*Éla*, don't look at her, Zona! Her you can see later. Now, look at these trees. These are our olives—did Ioanna give you a bar of our soap? That is made after the oil is finished. You won't find soap like that in New York, let me tell you. So these trees, they were hand-planted, row after row—yes, do you believe it? Because they had to be brought from—*Éla!*"

He screeches to a halt next to a field where three men are working. I give Melina a questioning look and she shrugs, clueless but resigned to her dad's ways. Theseus is getting his cell phone out.

"Look, girls, you see this? This is a disgrace. They are stealing this man's artichokes! You know how you plant artichokes, yes? So you put each plant in the hole, but you can cut it in half, each one, yes? And then resell the plant because it will regenerate. These men are stealing half artichoke plants!"

"Baba, you don't know that—maybe they work for the owner," Melina says quickly, clearly wanting to stop him from getting too crazy. See? Dads and daughters: the same everywhere. "Maybe one of them *is* the owner!"

"Melina, *agapi mou,* no. Trust me—they are stealing. I know the owner, and he would not have people here now, not this time of year! But I'm going to take a picture"—he clicks away at the red pickup truck next to the field—"and when he says something I will say, 'Here is the truck of the men who stole from you!'"

"Why don't you tell him now?" I ask.

"Well, it isn't my business *now,*" he says, like that should've been obvious. Melina's scrunched down in the backseat, hiding. This is hilarious; I wish I were recording the whole thing. "But when he harvests and comes to the village complaining," Theseus continues, "I will say to him, '*Éla!* Mystery solved!'"

And we're off again, skidding around the cliff, Melina shaking her head all the way.

"Now, Zona, you have a driver's license, yes?"

"No, actually."

"How can this be? How old are you? Melina can't wait to get her license, she made me promise to take her out in my Fiat . . . my car—I wouldn't let Ioanna drive it, but for my little Melina . . . ah, who could say no to her, am I right?" He gazes warmly into the rearview mirror. "I rebuilt that car piece by piece, Zona. It took years, you wouldn't believe. The mechanics, they are morons, seriously. This car is almost forty years old, still perfect. I know what is wrong with it, I tell them every time, but they don't have the right parts to fix it. It's maddening. What were we talking about?"

I stifle a laugh. "Drivers' licenses. I'm sixteen, but kids don't really bother in the city—in Manhattan, I mean—because we take the train everywhere. My dad has a car, like if he needs to travel for work, but I just never bothered to learn. Why, you want to teach me?"

"Ha!" Theseus slams on the brakes. "You think you could handle it, baaaaay-beh?" He says that last part in an Elvis voice, which, I have to admit, is totally dead-on. "I don't know if you could keep up—maybe I'll consider it."

"She was just kidding with you, Baba," Melina chimes in.

"Look, girls, look! Zona, you look especially—see that bus, the one that just passes? I will tell you now how to get to town on your own."

Bus System Only Slightly More Confusing Than Traversing Giant Hedge Maze In The Dark, Sources Say

It was during a genial afternoon drive with her newfound relatives that Zona Lowell, 16, became aware of yet another hiccup in the Greek transportation system's schematics. "The Metro may have the most gormless security parameters ever, but at least it runs well," she opined. "The bus system on Crete sounds completely nonsensical!"

Her uncle Theseus undertook the task of explaining the bus's schedule, but was met with resistance. "It's very simple," he insisted. "If you want to get to town, you take the number 7. Not the number 1 or the 5, those go to other towns, which you should go to them and explore also. But for here, the 7, *nay*? So. It stops outside our house every day at seven thirty A.M. and five thirty P.M. Well, maybe seven fifteen, seven forty-five . . . You just be ready and it will come at some point, yes? And that takes you to town. To come back you wait at the McDonald's or maybe the parking lot by the hotel at six, six thirty, and then you will be back. So easy, yes?"

Ms. Lowell's cousin, Melina Marousopoulou, 14, did not care to comment, as she was still very busy filing a report on a gang of alleged artichoke thieves.

Filed, 12:48 p.m., Heraklion.

"Wait, but . . . what about other times?" I ask incredulously. "The bus only runs twice a day?" Town is not exactly within walking distance.

"No, of course not only twice a day, only twice a day outside our *house*. Now, if you want it at other times, you walk over to the airport or the other stop down by the

189

market—remember where that moron was sitting instead of going at the little tunnel?—and you take the number 1 bus. That will drop you at the McDonald's, right past it, and then you catch a number 5 to Rethymnon, or you can stay on it—the number 1—and go to the hotel in the middle of town."

"What's Rethymnon?"

"It's another town, a very big one by the coast, you should go and walk around, have a coffee, look at everything . . ."

"Oh. But it's a different town? Not the number 1 bus to get to Heraklion?"

Theseus heaves an enormous sigh. *Oh, dear.* "No, Zona, honey, you are not listening. Okay, the number 7 bus—this is so simple!—you take that from our house at seven thirty A.M., yes? *Or* if you miss that, you take the number 1 to the McDonald's, just past it, and *there* you walk a few blocks and that is where the other buses are, to go to Rethymnon, Chania, wherever you want to go. Melina, you tell her."

Melina sighs, exactly like her dad. "I am not getting involved with this—Baba, you're confusing her." She leans over my shoulder. "He's making it confusing. I'll explain it later."

"I am confusing?" Theseus roars. "Who told *you* how to go, I'd like to know? *I am confusing,* my own daughter says to me."

"My mother told me," Melina whispers in my ear. I giggle.

"Girls, why is this so hard for you? Zona, you just told me you take the train everywhere. So, this is a bus. Same thing."

"But . . . Is there a map I could maybe—"

"A map?!" he scoffs. "Listen, listen, you don't need a map, right? I just told you how to do it!" Theseus slows the car as we approach a big square building. He rubs a hand over his eyes like we've exhausted him.

Melina groans. "Can we get lunch, Baba, *please*?"

Theseus makes a sharp turn, almost taking out a stray dog and what's left of my sanity. "For you, my heart, we can do anything. So, now to Heraklion!"

28

The town of Heraklion is different from the green country village I had expected. The air smells like the sea, there's a fine layer of sand spread along the gutters, and people stroll instead of rushing to get where they're going. Beachy—like a permanent vacation.

We park the car near the big marina, where lots of massive ships are docked; Melina explains that some are ferries like the one Yiota and I took to get here, and some are day boats that take tourists to various islands. I can't believe I've been in Greece for over three months and still haven't seen one of the famously gorgeous beaches.

I ask Melina which is her favorite, and she lists a few she's been to. "But they're all beautiful, you know? Different sand, maybe, but the clear water and the sun . . . it's a beach! The beaches here are nice, too, right near our house!"

I make a note to ask how to get there—if I can't visit Santorini or Mykonos, I can definitely go somewhere local, right? Pretty sure a big part of celebrating Easter is having a nice, even tan. I definitely read that somewhere.

We keep walking. There are about a million cobbled streets that fork off the main road, and down each one is a café or bar with people sitting and reading or smoking or having coffee and playing cards, just chatting and enjoying their time together. Melina tells me they sit there all day long, and maybe never even order anything. I tell her that we do that in Athens, too, but it would *never* fly in Manhattan.

She laughs. "In New York you take things too seriously. In Crete we just live."

Nail Salon Filled With Fish Tanks Alarms Passersby

In Heraklion today, visitor Zona Lowell was confronted by an unfamiliar and vaguely disturbing sight.

"The place looked just like a nail salon, but there were fish tanks all over it, including on the floor. Big tanks with bright blue water. And thousands of tiny fish inside!"

Her cousin Melina tried to explain: "This is, em . . . this is like a place where they do your feet nicely, yes? But first you put them in the tank and the fish eat the dead skin off. To make smooth, you know? I've never tried it, though. Too, em . . . creepy. Creepy, right?"

Ms. Lowell seemed to have trouble digesting this news [Ed. Note: pun deliberate]. "You're not serious," she was reported as saying. "You're telling me there's a place where you can get a fish pedicure and you've never been inside?! Oh my God—we have to go right now. Bring your dad. This is too weird to skip."

At press time, Melina was still adamantly refusing to let fish chew on her feet.

Filed, 2:13 p.m., Heraklion.

Thios Theseus stops to talk to every single person we pass and point out every crack in the sidewalk, just like on the drive here. On the main street—the high road—there are mostly typical stores, just like in Athens (when we pass the Starbucks, Theseus lets out a grunt and Melina whispers to me, "He *hates* the Starbucks. Don't even *ask* to go in."), and also little gift boutiques and clothing stores. Everything inside is perfectly nice, but looks slightly out of date. It's like the styles here are five or six years back from NYC, or even Athens.

There are also quite a few empty storefronts, or shops with metal gates pulled down over them, covered with graffiti.

"Is it because of the economy?" I ask.

"On Crete we aren't affected so much as in Athens, really," Melina says. "We make so many things, you know, and don't rely so much on this kind of, em . . . commerce? But—you know, some businesses just close, I guess."

"Well, that's good. For the people on Crete, I mean. Not so good for the people in Athens."

At this point, *Thios* Theseus has stopped to talk to yet another person he is apparently best friends with.

194

I'm starting to wonder if he's the unofficial mayor of this place.

"It isn't so bad anymore, at least here," Melina continues. "People are learning how to live this way. Greeks are very strong people. Don't worry." She smiles. A few yards away, Theseus is jogging back up the street to rejoin us. "I dare you should ask my father to go into Ben & Jerry's."

"Ha! Yeah, right," I say.

"Girls! What are you whispering about? I can't trust you for a minute." Theseus smiles, joining us and kissing Melina on the top of her head. Seeing them together makes me wish my dad could be here, too. He'd love exploring this new place with me.

"I'm telling Zona about the Greek economy," Melina says. "Maybe her father will want to interview me for his book, yes? Me and not you?" Melina teases him. Theseus doesn't respond, but at the mention of Dad, a darkness passes over his usually sunny expression. It bothers me.

"Yes, you'll have to meet him. He's amazing," I say. "He's won two Pulitzers." Ugh, now I'm bragging about his awards—Dad would hate that. But I can't help it. Why don't they want to get to know him, to just try?

There's a chilly silence as we go around a corner.

"Ah, Zona, *this* is an important place. It is the 25th of August Street Promenade, which is a long story, and here is Lion Square, which has a very famous fountain. But no one can ever tell how many lions there are—six? Four? What is the answer, do you know?" Theseus is back to his usual self, but Melina reaches for my hand and squeezes it lightly. I let the uncomfortable moment slip away.

"Uh, how many?" I ask, squeezing back.

"Five! There are five!" Theseus crows delightedly. "But for some reason, Zona, no one can ever remember this. Ask anyone you see on the street and you'll see—it's a mystery. And tomorrow night, we will come back near here for a Happening. You will love it. Everyone comes—old, young, babies, even cynical teenagers like you two, yes?"

I decide not to risk asking what a Happening is—what if it's even more confusing than the bus system? Better to wait and see.

29

The next morning Yiota's mother, *Thia* Angela, invites me to go with her to the market, and I gratefully accept. In the beautiful white light of the morning, a quiet trip for two seems like a perfect idea.

Last night all the cousins crowded into the main house again for another giant feast of Lent-approved foods, and while I'm getting more used to being surrounded by relatives, it's still overwhelming. Plus, I'm always very much aware of the coldness from *Thios* Labis and some of the other older relatives. It's nothing they do or say; it's just that they don't really interact with me much at all. Even *Thios* Theseus changes the subject every time my parents come up.

It was a really fun night, though—don't get me wrong. Theseus played and sang some of his favorite Elvis songs, and each of the little cousins recited a poem or sang or performed something. It was really sweet. Before I knew it, it was three A.M. I don't know how they do this every night. I, for one, am exhausted.

As we drive down to the market, I tentatively ask Angela about the bus system, in case I actually want to try using it.

She laughs. "Oh, no—was Theseus explaining to you? You'll go one time and be fine. He just likes to make everything complicated. It's one bus, or take a bike. You know there are beautiful beaches right here, yes? Come, I'll show you on the way, then you'll know how to get there. And of course Yiota or Melina will go with you." She turns the car at a small fork in the road.

"So, you just go straight here, then around this bend— it's all flat, really, once you get down this far, if you are biking—and then turn in here where it says 'Public Beach,' you see?" There is a second sign made of old driftwood that says *bikini plaz*. That makes me think of SpongeBob SquarePants, which makes me laugh.

"It's funny, the sign? Well, it's old, you know. Like Greece!" Angela smiles at me.

"No, I was just . . . Never mind. Do you guys come down here a lot?"

"Oh, yes!" She stops the car in a small lot and we get out. She leads me down a little path that goes through a sort of tunnel and then opens up again at the beach.

It's my first real glimpse of the beach in Greece, and oh my God, is it incredible. The sand looks like beigey-pink powder (unlike coarse yellow Coney Island sand, which scratches your feet to pieces). The water is an opal: blue and green and white and constantly changing. I catch my breath.

"I know, can you believe how beautiful? I look at it my whole life and I still cannot believe." Angela sighs. We are leaning up against a wooden beam on the deck overlooking the sand. The only people in the water are a gorgeously tan woman and a naked toddler who is squealing with excitement as her mother dips her over and over.

I wonder if my mother would have taken me here.

"I love this beach," Angela muses. "It's nice and quiet, and the water is warm and, you know, so clear and blue. Sometimes I come at seven and spend the whole day. For only two euros, you can have a chair and stay all day if you want. I take my nap here, read . . . I used to bring my children when they were little. Now Yiota likes the busier beach, or she goes to Santorini with her friends, but I like this one."

"Where are your other kids?" I ask.

Angela looks wistful. "Well, my oldest, my daughter Christiana, she lives in France with her husband and their children. They visit sometimes, but they are too far away to me. And my sons, Vasilis and Kostas, they are living in Athens. Vasilis, he will come with his wife for Easter—their children, they are here, you met them—but Kostas is very busy, so you maybe will not meet. They are all much older than Yiota, you know? Yiota was our . . . I don't know in

English how to say. She was . . . a surprise." Angela laughs, but then cuts herself off. "Zona, I know your *thios* Labis has been a bit . . . cold to you."

He hasn't spoken a word to me since I got here, actually, I think.

Of course I say, "No, *Thia* Angela, I—"

"*Éla,* Zona, I am not blind. But I also know more of this story than you do. You understand, I was already married to your *thios* then, I knew Hélenè since she was a little girl. She was like Yiota, a surprise for your grandparents. Yes?"

"Okay," I say cautiously. This seems like big secret sharing time, and I'm not sure I'm ready for it. But she goes on.

"Labis, he is the oldest, fourteen years older than your mother. And your *pappous,* your grandfather, he was . . . not a very *warm* person, you understand? Not a bad man, but very strict, and Hélenè was the only daughter, and she was very, em . . . very spirited and curious. Always teasing her brothers, always making new friends and wanting to explore everywhere."

I try to picture my mother as a little girl, running around this place, in the fields and on the beach. It's too hard.

"When she gets older he is more strict with her, but she wants to go out, have fun. Your *thios* Labis was her trusted friend, almost another father to her, yes? She confided in him. He thought his father was *too* strict. We used to help her sneak out sometimes, or stay with us in our little place so she could meet her friends. Yiota was a baby then—

Hélenè would help us with her, though I don't think Yiota remembers. So we said . . . Well, we wanted her to be happy, she was so beautiful and so much . . . energy, so much love of life—"

"So," I interject, "when she ran away with the horrible American, *Thios* Labis blamed himself, right? He thought if he had listened to his father, none of it would've happened. So now he can't forgive himself or my father or me?" I've seen this movie. *Come on, life. You can do better than that.*

"Well, sort of this way," Angela says. "But more like he cannot forgive *her.* Because he thought what she loved so much was Greece and her life here. It never crossed his mind that she would leave, not ever. And when she met your father, who was much older—older even than Labis!—and so obviously in love with her. You know, she had many admirers, many boyfriends; she teased them all and it was a game—not a mean game, but the way a teenager is. Labis thought . . . and when she left, when he realized she was serious, he was so hurt. Like he had failed her, as a brother, as a father. As a friend, as a Cretan. I am not explaining well, I'm sorry."

"No, you are. It's just . . . I'm not used to talking about my mom very much, and I've done nothing *but* talk about her recently. It's just . . . a lot."

"Can you try to give your *thios* a chance? He is a wonderful man, and he loved Hélenè so much. I think it's that you are so like her . . . He doesn't want to risk loving you since

201

you are going away. I know, it sounds simple, but it isn't. He was very strict with our girls after that—oh, did they struggle with Labis's rules, especially Christiana, the oldest. I think sometimes, maybe this is why she moves away." Angela pauses, thinking. "Anyway, Labis has lived with this pain for many years, and then one day finds out about you. It is hard for us, too, this news. I think he always hoped that maybe Hélenè was still alive, in America, that one day she would write another letter, come back."

I'm quiet for a while. I don't really know what to say. I hadn't stopped to think about the fact that finding out about me also meant finding out, for sure, that Hélenè was gone and the possibility of seeing her again was gone, too.

But it still isn't enough. "I just don't understand *why*. Why they didn't write back, why they didn't try. Not ever. How could they . . . do that to her? If they loved her so much?"

I can feel hot tears springing up in back of my eyes, and it makes me furious. Because I know it's not really about my mother, this woman I never knew; it's about the principle of the whole thing. The hatred directed at my terrific dad for no reason by people who don't even know him. The frustration of never knowing why my mother's family gave up on her. The dichotomy of my sweet *Yia-Yia* and the woman who deserted her youngest child.

Angela sighs. "I don't know that I have good answers, Zona," she says. "Like I am saying, your *pappous* was a very . . . a traditional man. He didn't speak any English, he did not have interest in America or Americans, he was Greek through and through, and that was it. He did not approve and he told Hélenè so with his silence. *Yia-Yia* didn't question her husband's choices; she was traditional also." Angela sees me about to interject and puts her hand on my arm firmly. "I'm not saying they were right, Zona, just that . . . this was the choice they made. Not because they didn't care. They thought it was the right thing. And then, years pass and nothing . . . but at that time also, there was no Google, no e-mails, no Facebooks. You couldn't just find someone so easily—especially in a different country, in a different language."

"Come on, *Thia* Angela. People have been finding other people without the Internet for hundreds of years—my dad does it all the time! And besides," I continue quickly, "Theseus lived in America, didn't he? He speaks English, why didn't he—"

"Theseus is different story," Angela confesses, looking away. "Him, I think maybe . . . I think he was afraid to look. Or maybe even he did and didn't admit it to us. Because he didn't want to believe his sister . . . that she had passed. That they could never fix their father's mistake. Everyone's mistake."

We sit together in silence, watching the waves and listening to the birds wheel over the sand. I can't think of any more questions. At least, not right now.

"Angela," I say finally, "you never lived in America, did you?"

"Me? Oh, no! Why?"

"How is your English so good?"

She laughs. "*My* English? *Ochi,* is terrible! I try, but thank you. So, to tell—I learned some in school, and then my kids, when they learn, I learn more and we all speak together. I think it is important, to learn. In case . . ."

"In case . . . what?"

She puts her hand over mine on the wooden beam and presses it firmly. "Just in case." We watch the water for a few minutes in silence, and then we walk back to the car, her hand still wrapped around mine.

30

This Just In: Cretans Unfazed By Crowds

During today's trip to the open-air market in Heraklion, a place to which she is expected to return on a regular basis during her vacation, Zona Lowell discovered that the Cretan people are not big believers in the so-called "personal space" much beloved by Americans. In fact, Cretans will trample over one's sorry ass if one doesn't move. (This practice is in direct contradiction to the habit of stopping a car in the middle of a supposedly two-lane street to have a chat with random passersby.)

Equally upsetting was the discovery that sometimes a slow-moving American teen (taking a look around at the endless stalls and food and people and yelling that is a lot like the Union Square Greenmarket in NYC but just *more*) will get hit in the leg with a walking stick by a mean, wizened old woman dessed head to toe in black. Said teen didn't even see said woman because she was so tiny and scrunched over . . . and yet quite handy with a stick, as it turns out.

Other things for sale in the market besides every kind of fresh fruit and vegetable imaginable include spices, fish (they clean it for you!), homemade cheeses, honey, beans, rice, and newly made raisins still on their stems. In a related story, freshly caught calamari have actual eyes. They are terrifying. Ms. Lowell bought some to scare her cousins.

Filed, 8:30 a.m., Heraklion.

Before he met my mom, Dad lived on what he calls "bachelor cuisine," and after they got married, she did all the cooking and he gained twenty pounds. After she died, he went right back to his old ways (which became my ways), so this is really the first time I've ever made (or helped to make, anyway) a big meal from scratch. No microwave. No box with instructions on the back.

We chop. We peel. We boil and mix and bake and then, after a very long time, we've made a giant meal that could feed an army, but will only actually be family dinner. And man, does it look good. I personally made three perfectly shaped *loukoumades* (fried balls of dough soaked in honey, with sesame seeds on top) all by myself after only messing up five. I Instagram a picture of them immediately and am excited when Lilena, Ashley, and Alex "like" it almost right away.

I show Melina a picture of Alex from the online class directory, and she tells me about a boy in her class she thought was going to be her boyfriend but then started acting like an idiot.

"So after he was flirting with my friend, I decided to just give him the shoe," she explains.

"I'm sorry, the what? The shoe?"

"The shoe, yes, I gave him the shoe—this is an expression. You never heard this, to give someone the shoe?" She looks at me like I'm the crazy one.

Finally it clicks. "Oh—you gave him the *boot*!" I exclaim. Then we're both laughing, and the aunts kick us out of the kitchen for being too silly and annoying.

Since I already sent e-mails to Matt and Hilary when I got back from the market, I decide to text my GIS friends to say hi. Lilena and I have exchanged a few messages since my first night here (as she predicted, her mother had to go to a last-minute conference somewhere, so Lilena's stuck by herself in Kallithea), and she's fascinated by the stories about my new family.

I really like that Lilena is so interested in what I'm up to, but as usual I wish she'd open up about herself. Whenever I try to find out how she's doing—how she's *really* doing, which I have to imagine is lonely and bored and pretty pissed off—she changes the subject. I don't push her, though. She obviously doesn't want to talk about it, and I don't want her to feel even worse than she already does.

Hi from Crete, I write to Alex next. My relatives don't subscribe to the NY Times! May not survive . . .

He sends back a series of emoticons: a newspaper, a sad face, a knife, and—inexplicably—a snowman. The message makes me laugh, and Melina insists on reading over my shoulder.

"Don't write back right away," she insists. "Make him think you're so busy. This will drive him crazy."

Am I really going to take guy advice from my fourteen-year-old cousin? I muse as I watch her dash back into the house for

207

her phone. *Well, I guess it can't hurt to try it and see what happens.*

I wander into the garden to call my dad, but his phone's off. I leave him a short message saying I miss him and that I'm fine. I don't want him to worry about me and get distracted from his work. Plus, I'm not sure how to describe what I'm thinking and feeling about all these new people yet—I don't want to hurt his feelings if I say I like them, or sound defensive if I say I don't.

I'm almost glad he didn't pick up.

I get a text from Yiota: How you doing, okay? I'm at the beach with my friends—want to meet us?

The beach! Excellent idea. And I even know how to get there, after this morning's trip. I ask her which beach, and *Thia* Angela confirms that it's on the same road as the one we visited.

Now I just have to figure out how I'm going to get there.

Cretan Cycling Fad Not Quite On Par With Brooklyn's: A Report

To residents of most major cities, cycling has come to represent far more than a leisure activity; this alternative to fuel-based transportation has seen a rise in popularity and practicality over the last decade, inspiring bike lanes and helmet laws across the globe.

A recent study in a small Cretan town, however, shows this is not the new normal for everyone. Zona Lowell, visitor and novice cyclist, was offered the use of a "terrific bike, excellent condition, don't worry about it," according to the bike's owner. Ms. Lowell, however, seemed hesitant about the proffered two-wheeler, pointing out its distinct lack of safety lights, a functioning gear shifter, or accompanying helmet.

Said Theseus Marousopoulou, the bike's proud owner, "This bike, unsafe?! It is a classic—this is from 1991, an excellent year, trust me. I'm an engineer, okay? And if the brakes don't work, you just put your foot like this, see, on the tire [at this point in the interview, Mr. Marousopoulou offered a demonstration] and poof, bike is stopped." As for the lack of helmet, he said simply, "A helmet is what a good driver doesn't need. That's how you learn."

Ms. Lowell was overheard muttering, "I'm going to die in the street on a white Huffy that was made before I was born. Awesome," before heading off down a very steep hill.

Filed, 2:14 p.m., Heraklion.

I do not die on the bicycle. In fact, riding it—while definitely very dangerous—is *incredibly* fun. It feels like flying, with the sweet-salty wind whipping my hair back and the fruit-covered trees zipping by. We don't have a lot of giant scenic cliffs to cruise along in New York City.

The beach is bigger than the quiet one Angela took me to in the morning. It's packed with people and chairs and umbrellas, but I find Yiota and her friends pretty easily. I still can't get over the color of the water—it's so clear and every shade of green and blue rolled together. I snap pictures of everything, and Yiota and her friends get cold beers, which I decline (I have to ride back, after all), so they bring me the freshest, most delicious orange juice I've ever tasted.

I miss sunscreening a huge area on one of my legs, and within an hour it turns bright red and looks ridiculous. Then I see a totally naked old man walking toward us and start freaking out. Yiota's friend Danae explains to me about nude beaches here and how it's gross but no big deal. Then we realize the guy isn't actually nude but wearing a Speedo that is the exact same color as his skin, which is somehow even worse.

It's just the kind of glorious day you would imagine having in Greece. (Well, except for the creepy nude Speedo thing. Clearly.)

Glorious, that is, *until* you have to get your stupid one-gear bike back up the hill. Especially if you aren't exactly a thighs-of-steel-type bicyclist, or even a bicyclist at all. Let me tell you, you haven't lived til you've walked a bike up a giant cliff in the approaching darkness while being barked at by possibly rabid dogs who are clearly harboring a taste for young American girls.

I've never been so glad to see a house in my life as when I get back to the complex. I collapse in a sweaty heap on my bed and don't wake up until Melina comes to get me for dinner.

My *loukoumades* taste amazing, by the way. Even the wonky ones.

31

After dinner, we somehow manage to get the family—I still can't believe that everyone isn't even *here* yet—into various cars, and the entire group drives down to the town center. This takes a lot less time than yesterday's guided tour, and I realize the family complex isn't quite as far from downtown Heraklion as I'd thought.

Yiota is staying with one of her friends for the night, but earlier they talked about maybe coming to the mysterious Happening, too. I think about friends with older siblings back home, and I can't think of a single event other than, say, Thanksgiving dinner that they'd all willingly attend together with their parents. Which isn't to say that Americans—or New Yorkers, anyway—don't love their families, or that Greek kids don't ever want to get the hell away from theirs. Of course they do. But there's something here that's . . . different. Like, spending time with your parents is more important than the embarrassment of being seen with them.

It makes me understand a tiny bit more how hurt my mom's family must have been when she ran off with a stranger to a country so far away. It doesn't excuse their reaction, of course. But I never thought I'd even be willing to think about their side of the story.

We park the cars by the marina and walk as a group through the town center, past the fountain with the lions, past the Starbucks, and into the main square. There are about fifty people milling around, looking annoyed or confused or both. We stand in a small huddle, the adults trying to keep the little ones from running off, while *Thios* Theseus talks to a few people he knows.

"Well, guess what, baaaaaay-beh?" he says to Melina when he comes back, slinging his arm around her shoulder. Then to Ioanna and the group at large, he says something in rapid Greek. My *thios* Dimitris, the youngest brother, looks furious and starts shouting in Greek. His wife starts shouting back.

Melina leans over to me and explains, "Apparently they moved it! There were maybe three hundred people here before, but everyone is wandering like fools now."

"I don't understand," I say. "I thought it was, like, a community gathering. Wasn't it in the paper, or—"

"Oh, yeah, sure," Melina explains as we head back toward the parking lot, the little kids racing one another up and down the brightly lit streets. Except for Dimitris and his wife, no one seems remotely put out. "There were fliers all

212

over town. But, you know, sometimes they change their minds about where to have, or when; it happens. Baba, he is going to call the mayor to complain."

I laugh, thinking about what would happen if three hundred or so New Yorkers turned up for a show that was moved with no notice. Not a bunch of shrugs and people going to get ice cream, that's for sure. We stop at a gelato shop, and I notice Theseus on the phone.

"Who's he talking to?" I ask Melina.

"I told you—the mayor. Baba, he likes to make a point, you know? He's so embarrassing sometimes."

We walk on, licking our cones. *Thios* Dimitris, who has barely spoken to me since I arrived and seems to like me about as much as Labis does, is still arguing with his wife, both of them gesticulating wildly. Soon we've left them behind us.

"Are they . . . ?" I ask Melina.

She laughs. "Oh, they are always this way. Fighting and making up. We ignore them mostly."

"*Éla!* It's on the north side, past the marina!" Theseus crows, finally ending his call. He looks as excited as a kid who knows a secret before any of his friends. "Come on, let's hurry or we'll miss it!" He dances up the cobbled street past us until he comes even with Ioanna and the other wives.

"Excuse me, laaaaaaaaaaaaaaaadies," he croons in his Elvis voice. "But I need to hold hands with my wife, if you don't mind!" He takes Ioanna's hand, then turns back and winks at me and Melina.

I try to imagine my dad holding hands with my mother on this same street, but I can't quite get there. Actually, I can't picture him holding hands with anyone—except me, when I was little. I feel sad, suddenly, watching Theseus and Ioanna, so obviously in love after years together. I wonder if Dad ever wanted to date again and didn't because of me. Or if he's spent the last sixteen years missing my mom every day, not letting me know because I couldn't miss her that way, too.

It makes me even more furious that my Greek family won't welcome him—after all, it wouldn't bring Hélenè back, but maybe it would give him some peace. Let him feel close to her again. Something.

"Zona, you are okay?" Melina asks, poking me gently in the arm. I nod quickly.

I'm not used to having so many feelings all at once.

I send Hil a quick text: Wish we could talk.

After a minute or so, I get back: In class! Got yr email yesterday, but no chance to w/b. You ok?????

It's nice to feel connected to her a little. At least Hilary I can be sure of, even if I can't be sure of myself.

I write back: Yeah, I'm on my way to a Happening. NBD.

. . .

214

"Happening" Revealed To Be Mandolin Concert; Weird But Cool?

It seems that the annual attempt to gather a world record number of people playing mandolins in one place is a very big deal in Heraklion (at last count, it was 415). As in, seriously, approximately fifteen hundred people of all ages gathered for the yearly event tonight—including two television crews, a Guinness official, and a bunch of kids who had clearly been forced to wear traditional Greek costumes and hand out flowers.

"I guess I don't know what I was expecting, but it wasn't this," commented Zona Lowell, visitor. "Don't get me wrong, it's interesting, and it's especially intriguing how into it everyone here is. I mean, where I'm from I don't think you'd see high school kids very excited to go to a mandolin concert with their parents."

"What kind of stupid kids would miss this?" her uncle Theseus Marousopoulou was overheard remarking to his wife. "Have you ever seen this many mandolins? New Yorkers don't know about this stuff, that's why."

Ms. Lowell was unavailable for further comment, as she was busy watching a bunch of local boys break dancing on the front steps of what turned out to be the town hall.

Filed, 9:36 p.m., Heraklion.

While the adults are congratulating the mayor on a magnificent Happening or herding up the littlest cousins (some of whom are asleep on their feet), Melina and I sit at a café table with a few of her schoolmates.

"So, what do you think of Heraklion?" Phoebe, one

215

of Melina's friends, asks me. "Not like New York too much?"

"Oh, I like it a lot here. But it's definitely . . . different," I reply thoughtfully.

Melina and her friends laugh. "We aren't dying to go to mandolin shows, Zona," Melina says. "It's more like, our parents want us to be with them, so we do it. In American TV or books every teenager mostly hates their parents. Not so much in Greece."

"*Éla*, my parents, they are so annoying," a boy with a pierced nose says. "They watching me all the time and making me crazy."

"Everyone makes you crazy, Kon. *Greekgreekgreekgreek-greek*," one of the other girls scolds him.

"I guess I just don't understand why my mother left all this behind if family is such a big deal," I say. "I mean, I know she tried to get in touch with your family. *Our* family," I correct myself when Melina gives me a poke. "And I know she couldn't have predicted what happened. But the way she just left, knowing how angry they'd be . . . She wasn't a child. She must've known they'd react the way they did, considering how overprotective our grandparents were. So why didn't she do something to make sure they'd stay connected?"

Melina looks thoughtful. Her friends are riveted. I guess new gossip in a small town is pretty exciting— even at a thrilling Happening. "I guess she was in love, and being . . . wild, maybe. She was not so old. I can see how it seems like you can do anything and fix it later. I'd love to meet a man who swept me away to somewhere else, so romantic." Melina's girlfriends giggle. The boys groan. "But, Zona," she continues, "Hélenè did connect you to us. Because of your name. Didn't you know this?"

"My name? Ugh, I hate my name. It's so weird and it doesn't even mean anything good."

"What do you think it means?" she asks.

"Girdle or belt, right?" There's a flurry of Greek as Phoebe tries to explain what a girdle is to Kon. "What, is it supposed to be that I'm, like, belted to the family?"

Melina gives me an exasperated look. "Come on, Zona—do you think your own mother was this . . . how to say it . . . lame? *No.* In Greece, it is traditional to name grand-children after grandparents. So, this way if you meet someone named Stefan, you can be sure his grandfather had that same name, yes? So, my grandmother's name is also Melina—from my mother's side."

"Really? I didn't know that."

"My grandfather is Konstantinos, like me as well," Kon offers.

"Wow. Well, that's cool . . . but . . ."

"*But*, didn't you ask what is *Yia-Yia's* given name?" Melina asks impatiently.

Oh. I never did, come to think of it.

"It's *Zona*, of course!" she says triumphantly. "So you were always part of us, even when you didn't know it. You see?"

Oh. I am starting to see more clearly, I think.

"If you are not going to be smarter about these things, I will have to give *you* the shoe." Melina grins.

And I grin back.

32

When we get home, it's past midnight. I know my friends in NYC will be eating dinner, but I send a text saying I miss them anyway. I take a picture of myself blowing a kiss and consider sending it to Alex. Not exactly sexting, but it seems bold anyway. Though he did send *me* a picture of an ice cream cone, so . . .

I'm still mulling it over when I get a reply from Matt (who is apparently *not* at dinner) asking me to get on Skype. Since Yiota is with her friend tonight, I have the room to myself.

I log on, and Matty's image flashes onto my screen. He's dressed in a black shirt with mesh sleeves, his hair is spiked, and he's wearing a ton of makeup—liquid liner and glitter on his eyes and some kind of face paint on his cheekbones, like blush, but yellow.

"Whoa," I say. "Is this your new day look?"

He laughs. "I'm going with Scott and his friends to a dance club later," he explains, keeping his voice low. "Just trying out a few things. So, how's your family stuff going? Your e-mail was kind of . . . I dunno, vague. Your uncle Theseus sounds pretty crazy, though."

I laugh. "Yeah, he is, I guess—but in a good way."

"So? Are you okay or what? Seriously asking here."

"Um," I reply, hesitantly. "It's . . . interesting."

"Just *interesting*?" Matt puts his eye right up to the camera lens, so it fills the whole screen. "ZOOOONAAAAAAAA. This is me, remember? Use your words, please!" He backs away again and waits for me to answer.

I take a breath, and then the words come out in a tumble. "Well, it's . . . My cousins are wonderful. And I wrote you about my *thia* Angela, what she said at the beach, so that was an amazing surprise. Then my grandmother is, like, this tiny storybook granny who everyone adores—including me—and I can't reconcile her at all with the evil witch I've imagined her to be for the last decade. But two of my other uncles haven't been very friendly to me at all, which is uncomfortable, and the other uncle isn't here for me to meet; I guess he's sick or something, I don't know. And no one really talks about my mom at all except to say I look like her, and whenever I mention my dad, they ignore me or talk about something else, which makes me absolutely irate, you know?"

"Totally. So, do you want to leave?" Matty asks.

"Well, no. But I used to have such an unwavering stance about my Greek relatives, and now it's kind of . . . blurry."

Saying what I've been thinking out loud isn't making it any clearer, so I opt to change the subject instead. "Enough about that—tell me about this club!"

"Oh my God, Zona, it's *insaaaaane*. The last time we were there, there were these go-go dancers—guys, obviously—wearing only manties, and this one guy—"

"Sorry, what? Did you just say *manties*?"

"You know, like man panties? Panties for—"

"Okay, I get it, thanks. How do you get into a place like that?" I ask, deciding to never discuss manties again if at all possible.

"Fake ID. Scott got me one."

"Ah, okay."

"Besides, these are gay clubs. They don't care as long as you're cute or with people they know."

"Well, I told you my one and only clubbing story, so . . . yeah. But I'll take your word for it."

Matt laughs again. "Oh, right. Well, I never drink anything unless I see it made right in front of me—I don't care who's buying. So anyway, we're at this kiki . . ."

I'm glad Matt is having fun and making new friends—of course I am. I know how hard it's been for him not to have other gay guys to talk to. But he never cared about any of this stuff before. Now he seems to be *Mister* Nightlife. He's honestly the smartest guy I know; I can't imagine he'd do anything stupid, like flunk out of school or start doing drugs, but I wonder what other things Scott and his friends might be doing, or getting Matty to try. Maybe Hilary isn't so far off the mark. I think it's time for Matt to come back down to earth, at least a little bit.

By the time we hang up, I've learned a lot about the NYC club scene and been instructed to erase the kissing selfie. I do—Matty's right; it might be a bit much to send to a guy who's . . . well, a guy who I don't know *what* he is.

I wish I could reach my dad and talk over the family stuff with him—trying to explain my feelings to Matty made me realize it would be easier to sort through them with Dad's help.

I'll try again tomorrow, I think as I climb under the covers and drift off to sleep.

33

"*We* aren't going anywhere. You are," Melina says with a sly grin. Yiota laughs, then turns the laugh into an unconvincing cough.

We're sitting outside in the sun eating breakfast a few days later, and I've just been informed that I'm taking a trip to the country. By myself.

"*Nay, nay,* you going!" the little cousins squeal, delighted.

"Yeah, I'm gonna need more info, thanks."

"*Pro-Yia-Yia* wants to meet you. She lives in a teeny town near Spilli—you'll go stay with her for a few days and let her get to know you. You can see what a traditional Cretan village is like, where your family comes from," Melina explains.

"Uh . . . *Pro-Yia-Yia*? What is that?"

"Not what—*who*. Our great-grandmother. *Yia-Yia*'s mother. She's, em . . . the mother-in-law, *Pappous*'s mother-in-law. She runs the whole family, basically."

"Why doesn't she live here, then?"

"No, no—her, em . . . She has her own many people there, her own children, their children—like *Yia-Yia* and all of us. But *Pro-Yia-Yia* is the oldest of the whole family, so she is in charge. She tells everybody what to do."

"I see. From her fortress in a minuscule hamlet in the middle of nowhere. Sounds like a dream."

Melina looks at me quizzically. She still doesn't always get sarcasm. Or maybe she doesn't know what a hamlet is? Ah, well.

"Yiota, you did *not* tell me about this," I say, turning to her. She widens her eyes, the picture of innocence.

"No? I'm sure I must have mentioned it," she swears. She's bluffing. She and Melina sneak a look at each other and I can tell they're trying not to laugh again. Clearly there is more to this than meets the eye, and everyone is in on the joke but me. Time to put the old rusty journalism skills to good use.

"How old is *Pro-Yia-Yia*?"

"Oh, I have no idea. Maybe . . . ninety-five years? More?" Melina says.

"And she lives all alone?!"

"Her children and the neighbors visit her and make sure she has what she needs, and she is in excellent, em . . . healthy?" Melina nods to herself. "Health. She walks in town and cooks and gardens. She's . . . you would say, she's a 'character.'"

"Uh-huh. And does she speak English?"

Yiota laughs. "No, of course not!"

"And how am I supposed to communicate with her? Can't you come, too?! This is nuts."

Yiota looks stern. "We have to stay here and help with the olive oil and Easter preparations. Besides, I already have gone for my turn."

"Me, too," Melina adds. "Two years ago."

"I'm sorry, your *turn*? What—"

"*Pro-Yia-Yia* likes to spend time alone with each member in the family, *nay*? See that they are, em . . . how to say . . . carrying a legacy? So these ones"—she makes a face at the little kids—"are still too small. But you *have* to go. *Pro-Yia-Yia* wants to meet you—she said on the phone yesterday to Baba, and what she wants . . ." She raises her eyebrows.

Okay, I get it. This old lady has the family wrapped around her little finger.

"Zona, do not look this worried! You'll figure it out." Yiota grins at me, a gleam in her eye. I don't like the sound of this at all.

This Just In: Teen Expected To Travel To Remote Town Alone

It was with great trepidation that Zona Lowell, formerly of New York City, allowed herself to be talked into taking a series of four (predictably confusing) buses to a tiny rural village. The trip was at the behest of a mys-terious great-grandmother—a woman Ms. Lowell had never even heard of until that morning.

"My uncle told me to ask the last driver to drop me off at a nameless bakery—like the guy would just happen to know where it was!—and he totally didn't. And then some people got off in what seemed to be an empty field. I'm lucky I didn't end up in Santorini. Or Turkey."

Ms. Lowell did make it to her final destination despite myriad obstacles and managed to find the aforementioned bakery all by herself. Which was not easy to do, despite the fact that the entire "town" turned out to be one street with four stores on it.

Filed, 1:37 p.m., the middle of nowhere, Crete.

As I lug my overnight bag down the barely paved road—it has a row of stones at the edge but no sidewalk—I gaze dejectedly at the four identical square buildings in front of me. Each one has a faded, barely legible sign written in Greek letters. There are no people on the road, I don't smell any bread, and I realize there's basically no way to figure out which is the bakery without going into each building and trying not to look like a complete moron in the process.

The last thing Yiota said to me before I left early this morning was, "Have fun! By the way, you have been working on your Greek, yes?"

This. Is. A. Disaster.

In the first store—which is definitely *not* a bakery—I find a toothless old man who stares at me in total silence until I finally just back out apologetically. The second store is locked.

I head into the third little store, which is less like a bakery than a small grocery store. There are, however, racks of bread, which is a hopeful sign. It is totally empty.

"Uh, *kalimera*?" I call out. A door swings open from what

could be a kitchen and a cheerful-looking woman in a red shirt appears, wiping her floury hands on a towel.

"*Kalimera,*" she says. Then she starts off in a string of Greek that I can't understand.

"Sorry, sorry—I don't speak Greek," I say for the millionth time since January. She just stares at me now. Oh, no. "Um, I'm trying to visit my, um . . . Athénè Pelonis? My *thios* Theseus said someone at the bakery could call . . ." I mime a telephone.

Nothing.

I hold out my little notepad with the phone number written on it.

The woman takes a look, then grins broadly. "Ah, *Pro-Yia-Yia!*" she exclaims. "*Greekgreekgreek* Athénè *greekgreekgreek!*"

I smile at her, hoping this will end soon and I'll have the slightest clue where to go. She finally realizes I don't have any idea what she's saying and goes back behind the swinging door, calling out to someone.

A guy in his twenties comes out, also very floury and with one giant furry eyebrow across his forehead. He smiles at me hesitantly. "You are Zona?" he says in a soft, heavily accented voice.

"Yes!" Does this guy speak English? And know who I am?!

"Em . . . I your cousin Markos. I . . . all your cousin. *Pro-Yia-Yia.*" He points to the woman in red and to the door.

Well, that's *some* English, anyway. I'll take it. "Cousins!"

I exclaim. "Great. And . . . *where* is *Pro-Yia-Yia*? Her . . . house?"

Markos and the woman exchange some words, and then she says something to me that I don't understand. Markos says, "I take you . . . van, house. Yes?"

Sounds good to me.

We go through the kitchen—*definitely* a bakery!—and exit through a back door. After Markos manages to start what may be the first bread delivery van ever invented, we drive around a short bend behind the main street and up a hill that is lined by crumbling stone walls. It occurs to me that this might not be my cousin at all, but just a random man who likes to hide the bodies of American teens in construction sites. But since I don't have any other options besides staying put and jumping out, I hope for the best.

He stops outside a very crumbly wall and we get out. He takes my bag with a smile, and I follow him down some equally crumbly stone steps. At the bottom is a big stone platform surrounded by walls and filled with trees and plants (in terra-cotta pots of all sizes) and flowers. It's rustic and beautiful.

Bent over one of these plants is a teensy, stooped, unbelievably ancient woman dressed in all black. She has a kerchief tied over her thin white hair and the sharpest, shiniest black eyes I've ever seen. She's got to be at least a hundred. Maybe two hundred.

Pro-Yia-Yia.

Without even looking up from her plant, she barks, "Markos *greekgreekgreekgreekgreekgreek*," and he scurries down the steps with my bag.

I follow, taking in the lush greenery and the cool white stones. There's an old stove built into the wall, and I can see a river from where I'm standing. Right there, just flowing past the enormous garden.

I don't actually see a house, however.

I'm unsure what to do. *Pro-Yia-Yia*'s body looks so fragile, like she'd break if I tried to hug her—she can't be taller than four foot eight and weighs maybe eighty-five pounds. I'll let her make the first move.

"*Kalimera*," I say.

"*Kalimera*," she replies. From the low wall she picks up a wooden stick—just like the mean lady in the market!—and uses it to march right up to me. She looks me over in silence, frowning, tugging my hair, reaching up to move my head to the side to inspect my profile, squeezing my cheeks and chin. Finally she looks me square in the face and nods sharply, with a grunt.

I smile stupidly at her. She seems to be waiting for something. Does she have a magic ring I need to kiss? I feel like I'm in a video game and I don't know the password to get to the next level.

Luckily, Markos reappears at that moment—without my bag. "You, em . . . This way, to house?" he says, gesturing. *Pro-Yia-Yia* has gone back to tending her plant, so I follow him.

200-Year-Old Cottage In Crumbling Stone Village Might Be . . . Awesome?

Zona Lowell was less than overwhelmed by her first impression of her great-grandmother's Cretan home, sources say. As her cousin Markos showed her the amenities, she tried very hard not to run for the nearest bus.

"One of the walls is entirely made from a big wooden door—which is just a big slab of wood with a hole in it instead of a knob—and behind the door is a small stone room. There's a mini-fridge and a small stove with a sink built into the wall underneath a window—well, it's technically a window, I guess," Ms. Lowell told us. "Actually, the 'window' has no glass; it's just a cavity, really. And there's a plain wooden table with a bowl of tomatoes on it. Hanging from the roof beams are woven rugs, and there's a single lightbulb dangling by a cord from the ceiling, a thatched wooden chair, and . . . that's it."

Markos elaborated on the living setup, explaining, "Em . . . this your place. *Pro-Yia-Yia* live . . . other side. This, em . . . for guest, em, tourist, yes?"

"Well, at least there's electricity, right?" Ms. Lowell remarked, trying for optimism. "I mean, it's a bit *Lord-of-the-Rings*-y, but hey, I've never had a place all to myself before. In the middle of nowhere. With no lock on the door. Um . . ."

Just when the situation seemed to be unsalvageable, the tour took a surprising turn: Markos pointed to an ancient wooden ladder, at the top of which was a tiny lofted room, filled entirely with a bed. But what a bed!

"It's covered with green satin sheets and has a huge floaty green net covering it," Ms. Lowell gushed excitedly. "I guess it's a mosquito net, but the whole thing looks made for an Arabian princess. I can't wait to sleep in it! Seriously, the bed makes me feel like I'm in a Disney movie. Not that I watch those. Whatever—Hilary will die of jealousy when I show her pictures!"

Filed, 2:02 p.m., the middle of nowhere, Crete.

Maybe this will be a fun adventure, I think. After all, I'd never get my own house with a princess bed back in NYC. I start thinking about how I'm going to fill the little fridge with stuff from the market: fresh veggies, some cheese . . .

Markos is still talking, so I go down the ladder and follow him back outside. He goes through a second wooden door that's sort of mid-garden and leads onto an enclosed stone terrace. There's a detachable showerhead attached to the wall at about knee-level, and a knob. It's completely out in the open.

"For . . . wash," Markos says.

Um, for what *now?*

Next he points to an ugly brown rug hanging from the top of a little arch next to the "shower." He pulls it aside, revealing a small stone "room"—at least it's enclosed—with another little window (square hole). There's a sink and a toilet.

Outside.

I mentioned that the door to the bathroom is a weird brown rug, right? And the shower is basically a sink?! *OUTSIDE?!*

I am going to kill Melina and Yiota.

34

It's the middle of the night and I'm trying not to panic. I lie in my bed, the one I thought was straight out of a fairy tale only a few hours ago. I must've forgotten that most fairy tales have monsters.

There is something inside the wall or on the roof—which is, after all, right above my head—and it wants to get out. Badly. Or possibly, it wants to get *in*, into my room . . . and eat me for a midnight snack. There is a repetitive scratching and scuffling noise that sounds like Tony at the door when he wants to go for a walk. I wish Tony were here to protect me.

I mentally compile a list of all the things that could be making the noise:

1) A rat
2) A squirrel
3) A raccoon
4) A ghost

5) A demon

6) A psychopathic killer

I haven't seen any squirrels or raccoons in Greece. And a killer would have to be pretty idiotic to waste time trying to break in through the wall when the door doesn't lock. Oh, and when the *window is a hole*. Which leaves options one, four, and five.

I squeeze my eyes shut and pray for sleep.

More scratching and pawing sounds. Was that a squeak? Or a *voice*? Oh, God. Now I'm imagining things and I have to go to the bathroom.

I fumble for the light and tiptoe down the wooden ladder. Remember how cool I thought it was to have a place to myself just a few hours ago? What I wouldn't give now to be sleeping on the floor next to *Pro-Yia-Yia*'s bed . . . At least if a demon came out of the wall, she could hit it with her mean-old-lady stick and protect us.

I go through the little kitchen and open the back door. It's pitch-dark out. I mean, totally and completely—no moonlight or anything—and I can't find the switch for the outside lights. I take a little camping lantern off a nail by the door; a reassuring blue light flashes . . . and then goes out.

Seriously?!

Maybe I don't have to go that badly. I contemplate waiting til morning.

Nope. I'll just have to be brave.

Outdoor Bathrooms A Terrible Idea, May Cause Nightmares For Life

It was late at night when Zona Lowell, 16, stumbled through the dark to the tiny outdoor bathroom, thinking that, at worst, she'd sustain a stubbed toe. (Or possibly be eaten by a demon.) This was not the case, however.

"You know that scene in *Silence of the Lambs*? The one where they find Buffalo Bill's house and it's filled with all the moths? It was like that, only the moths were bigger and out for blood. Oh, and I couldn't see them so I couldn't tell they were moths at first, just horrible giant flapping things. Plus I was on a toilet and unable to defend myself," the stricken victim explained.

Alerted by her great-granddaughter's shrieks of terror, Athénè Pelonis (who apparently has night vision and had no trouble navigating in the dark) moseyed outside, flipped up a hidden light switch, and sniffed disparagingly at Ms. Lowell, who was at this point cowering half under the sink with her arms wrapped around her head. When asked for comment, Mrs. Pelonis would only mutter "*Amerikanitha*" repeatedly as she shuffled back to her bed.

"Look, this is the twenty-first century, okay?" Ms. Lowell exclaimed on the way back to her (most likely haunted) cottage. "I don't think it's too much to ask for bathrooms to be enclosed."

When told of the incident, Lowell's elder cousin Yiota Marousopoulou laughed until she cried. "Glass in the windows? Up until three years ago, there wasn't even a real toilet. It was just a hole! That was only put in so tourists would rent the cottage!"

Zona Lowell offered no additional comments, except to state that she will not be consuming liquids until she is safely back in civilization.

Filed, total darkness, the middle of nowhere, Crete.

You know what's less scary but just as upsetting as wall monsters and toilet moths?

ROOSTERS.

I finally fall asleep after the horrifying bathroom incident, and about two seconds later the local roosters start having some kind of sing-off, their individual cries getting progressively fancier and louder.

It goes on so long, I start wondering why roosters crow— wouldn't it make more sense for them to rooster? Do crows rooster?! I'm slowly becoming delirious, so I put a pillow over my head and try to lull myself back to sleep by calculating exactly how many hours I have left before I can return to Heraklion.

I am yanked out of a dream about windows with glass in them by a pounding on the door. I bolt upright and call out, "Yes? *Kali*—hello?"

I hear a string of grouchy Greek and more pounding, which tells me that *Pro-Yia-Yia* (and her stick) is up and ready to hang out. I crawl out of my green mosquito net, slip on my jean shorts, and head outside.

Pro-Yia-Yia is in the garden, and on the big stone table is a *spread*: boiled eggs, honey, feta, tomatoes, fresh bread, olive oil, olives, cucumbers . . . plus some things I can't identify but feel fairly certain are Greek delicacies.

"Wow, *Pro-Yia-Yia*! This looks amazing! *Efcharisto!*" I exclaim, smiling hugely and waving my hands around in a way that I hope conveys my gratitude.

She glares at me and nods her head. *Doesn't she ever smile?*

I find it hard to believe she actually wanted me to come here, because she seems like she'd rather be alone with her plants, frankly.

She gestures to a plastic lawn chair with her trusty stick and I sit. Then she piles more food than I could eat in a week onto my plate—but I've gotten used to that by now. I wait while she slowly eases herself into a similar plastic chair (she refuses my offer of help with an angry sucking noise), and then we dig in.

It's delicious. I try some of everything.

Except the olives, of course. Because I hate olives. Always have, always will.

Pro-Yia-Yia is working on her third boiled egg, nibbling her way around with limited teeth and fierce determination. I take a break from stuffing my face to look around at the river and trees. It really is beautiful out here. Boring, with no Internet access, no cell service, and no one to talk to, but glorious to look at. A very nice place to have breakfast.

I'm jerked out of my reverie by *Pro-Yia-Yia*, who is tapping a fork against my plate next to the pile of uneaten olives.

I wave my hand and shake my head, saying, "Oh, thank you, *Pro-Yia-Yia*, but I don't like olives. Do you want mine?" I hold the plate out to her and receive another tap of the fork and a string of angry Greek words.

She mimes picking up an olive and putting it in her

mouth, then points at me. She says more things I don't understand.

Why, oh, why wasn't cousin Markos invited to breakfast so he could explain? I will seriously throw up if I have to put one of those in my mouth. But then I think that she probably grew these olives herself. I don't want to hurt her feelings. Or get hit with her stick.

I look gloomily down at my plate and then back at *Pro-Yia-Yia*, who is watching me with her evilest eye. I have a feeling I will either have to eat a revolting olive or be sacrificed at the top of a hill.

The olive is about the same size as a chocolate-covered almond. Maybe I can pretend that's what it is and get it over with.

I pick it up, mentally hold my nose, and bite. It's . . . salty. It feels fleshier than I expected, and a bit juicy, and only medium terrible. I think I may actually survive this. I sneak a peek at *Pro-Yia-Yia*, who is watching me. I put the whole thing in my mouth, chew around the pit, and swallow.

I did it.

And I don't even feel like puking. *Pro-Yia-Yia* slaps her hand on the table and says a bunch of stuff, then nods so sharply, I'm worried her head will fall off.

I'm actually considering eating a second olive, just to see what she'll do. Can I win her over with my bravery? Earn a tiny smile, perhaps?

Three olives later, the answer is still no.

35

Later in the afternoon I'm reading outside on my iPad mini and trying to figure out how to mime "Where is there an Internet connection?" to *Pro-Yia-Yia* when she appears beside me. She's holding a basket of figs and prickly pears and a loaf of homemade bread.

"You want me to slice that up for you, *Pro-Yia-Yia*?" I ask politely. Since our breakfast this morning, I've been asking if she needs help with anything and she keeps shooing me away, puttering around in the house or the garden.

"Markos," she says, holding out the basket. I take it from her, and she points up the stone steps and toward town. "Markos," she says again.

"You want . . . me to bring it to Markos?" I say. I take a few exaggerated steps away from her. She nods and claps her little hands, and I feel proud of myself. (I try not to think about the fact that I *used* to feel proud of myself for things like writing a thought-provoking piece on the state of women's reproductive rights in America; now

I'm thrilled to get a nursery-school game of charades right. Ah, well.)

"Sure!"

She turns on her heel and heads back to her cottage. Finally, something to do! And town must have an Internet café and cell reception, right? I can send some e-mails, see if anyone has texted me . . . plus ask Markos some valuable questions, such as, *Did I do something to piss off* Pro-Yia-Yia, *or is she always like this?* And, *Do you think there is a ghost living in the guest cottage?*

I stuff my things into my backpack, slap on my sunglasses and flip-flops, and head up the chalky path. There is a row of stone houses similar to *Pro-Yia-Yia*'s (but falling apart) lining the hillside; they're clearly unlived-in and uninhabitable. It's so weird how all these houses look like actual Greek ruins, what I thought I'd see in Athens. I guess they *are*, technically, Greek ruins—but not famous ones where Hercules and Plato used to throw orgies and invent government or anything. They're really beautiful—so quiet, and sad. My favorites are the ones where leaves are starting to grow up from the stones, like nature is taking over again. I wonder why these places are all crumbled and empty. Is it the economy, or did people just leave? I wish I had someone to ask.

It's so incredibly frustrating to not be able to communicate, and I feel moronic for not having picked up more Greek in the last four months.

At the fork in the road I turn right and there I am—town, or what passes for it. Why is it so deserted? It's tiny, sure, but picturesque . . . and yet the streets are empty.

I go to the bakery and the woman in red is there again (in a blue shirt this time). She's probably my cousin, too, and I don't even know her name. I feel bad. *"Kalimera,"* I say, even though it's actually afternoon and not morning.

"Yassas," she says, smiling. (I know that one—it means "hello!") She looks at me expectantly.

"Um, is Markos here?" I hold up the basket from *Pro-Yia-Yia*

"Oh, *greekgreekgreekgreekgreek,"* she says. I shake my head, frowning. She puts a finger on her chin, thinking. "Other town," she says slowly. "Markos . . . other town."

"Markos is in another town?"

She looks at her hands, then calls to someone in the back room. A guy comes out—another cousin? They exchange a few sentences in Greek, and then he says, "Markos next town. Is . . . this way," and points down the road.

"Oh," I say. "Uh . . . should I . . . go there? And do you guys have Wi-Fi?"

"You go . . . Markos," the man says again. He says a word that I'm guessing is the name of the town.

"It's just down the road," says a woman's voice behind me in accented English. Australian maybe? I turn around and see a woman with gray hair but a young face, wearing a long colorful skirt. "I can give you a lift, if you like?" She speaks in fluent Greek to the man at the counter, then turns back to me. "There's a café there with Wi-Fi, too. It's a much bigger town than this one."

"That would be terrific, if you don't mind," I say. "Thank you so much!"

I do realize I've only been without Internet access for about two days, by the way. But I can't help getting excited by the word *Wi-Fi*—I'm losing my mind without it. I'd never make it on a deserted island. I guess I really am a city girl at heart.

I take a second to consider whether it would be a terrible idea to get in a car with a stranger, but she seems nice enough—plus my cousins (all the people at the bakery are related to me, I'm almost sure of it) know where I'm going, and with whom. It'll be fine. Right? She must sense my thoughts because she says, "Don't worry—everyone gets rides from people here. It's completely safe. The buses are very sporadic, though it's pretty close if you want to walk instead."

"No, no, a ride would be great, thanks. Sorry—I'm from New York, so not really used to hitching rides."

"You're from the city?" she asks as she loads her bag into the car. I open the passenger door.

"Yep," I say, climbing in beside her with *Pro-Yia-Yia*'s basket. "Where are you from?"

"South Africa, but I've lived here for over twenty years." She pulls away from the curb and continues down the main road. "I came here on my honeymoon and never left."

"Wow, that's so romantic."

"Well, not so romantic—my ex didn't like it as much as I did!" We both laugh, her boldly and me hesitantly. "It was too small for him. But I love it—the simple life, everyone neighbors, easy days . . ."

"It is . . . small," I say carefully, not wanting to insult this nice lady. "The streets are all so empty. Are the people inside napping, or . . . ?"

"They're napping, or working in other towns nearby, or just having a coffee in their kitchens. There's no rush here. People take their time; they enjoy everything. It's a very magical place," she says, pulling to the side of the road outside of a small general store that looks an awful lot like the bakery. In fact, for a "much larger town," this place looks almost exactly the same as the one we just left. "Your cousin is in there. Have fun!"

"Thanks!" I call as she pulls away.

I go into the store, locate Markos, and ascertain that the only Wi-Fi connection here isn't working. He gets me a soda and we sit together for a few minutes.

Teen Learns $$ Truth About Family Matriarch

At an impromptu sit-down meeting today, Zona Lowell learned about the differences between Greek and American financial security, inside sources report.

"Apparently *Pro-Yia-Yia* is in-sanely rich," Zona said, clearly surprised. "The wealthiest person in the whole family, and she controls all the money—but she lives like it's the eighteenth century! Apparently these cottages are over two hundred years old and, except for the plumbing, haven't been updated at all."

Zona's cousin, Markos Pelonis, tried to explain: "Here it is land that means wealth. She owns [the young man spreads his hands wide to indicate a large amount] very very much land, and many olives, grapes . . . for make oil, rakí, wine . . . Also many houses of people on her land. New houses, yes?"

Zona was even more shocked to learn that Athéné Pelonis's direct descendants— with the exception of Zona's own grandmother, who as the only daughter went to live with her husband's family—all live in a modern complex a few miles away that actually belongs to the family matriarch. "Why doesn't she live there, too? She's a million years old, for God's sake!"

Once again, it was Markos who illuminated her: "She doesn't want to. She likes how she lives, how she grew up as a child. It's what she wants. My father, he had to insist on the electric lights outside!"

Zona seemed stumped, but impressed. She wondered briefly about the contents of the old woman's will, but felt pretty certain that Athéné Pelonis was destined to outlive them all.

Filed, 1:46 p.m., the middle of nowhere, Crete.

After Markos goes back to work, it becomes clear there's nothing to do in this town but watch him stack boxes or walk back and forth wondering where all the people are. At least back at my little cottage I could take a lovely, very Greek, midafternoon nap.

But first I have to get there. And my South African friend is nowhere to be seen.

I start walking, waving my cell phone around until I actually get a faint signal. I call Dad, hoping to finally get through.

"Hello?" he says. "Ace, is that you?"

"Dad! I've been trying to call you for days—where have you been?" I'm so relieved to hear his voice. I have a thousand things to tell him.

"Something's been going on with the cell service over here—everything's a mess," he explains, sounding annoyed and very far away. "Believe me, I've been trying to reach you, too! So how's it going? I got your voice mail. Are you . . . okay?"

I think for a second before I respond. "Yes," I finally say. "It's exciting and interesting. But also weird and overwhelming. Mostly everyone is great, but—"

"Hello? Zona, can you hear me?" Dad is shouting into the phone. I look at the screen—one measly bar.

"Dad? Dad, I'm here!"

"Zona, if you can hear me, try to call me again later, okay, kiddo? I miss you. Tony misses you, too. We love you! Have fun!"

"I love you, too!" I shout, not caring if anyone hears (not that there's anyone around *to* hear). "Give Tony a kiss from . . ." But the connection is gone. I sigh. "Wish you were here, Dad," I say quietly, shoving the phone back in my pocket.

I plug my headphones into my trusty iPad mini and keep walking. I enjoy the distracting music and think that walking isn't actually *so* bad, even in flip-flops—a beautiful, cloudless, sunny sky, flowers everywhere, only the occasional maniacal driver blazing around a curve and forcing me to jump into a hedge . . . and anyway, it's something to do. I figure I've got a solid two hours or so before it starts to get dark, and if I can't walk three miles by then, I need one of those old lady walking sticks myself.

Twenty minutes later, I'm bored. You know what the worst possible shoes are for walking three miles along a questionably poured highway? Flip-flops. I've scraped two of my toes on a rock, and I have about fifty mosquito bites. I'm sweaty. This *sucks*. Man, was I this pathetic back in New York? I don't think so—I mean, I walked everywhere and never thought twice about it. But here it's like all this nature is destroying me, slowly but surely.

Also, I have to admit my feelings are a little hurt. I mean, that lady said people in Crete offer rides all the time, that it's a regular thing to do, just to be friendly. How come all these cars have gone by and not one has stopped? I'm cute and nice! I consider putting my thumb out, but that seems too desperate—I don't think I can take the added layer of hitching rejection.

Then a Jeep-like car slows down at the crossroads. There's no light there, so the driver either wants to offer me a lift or ask for directions. I hope it's the former, as I haven't seen a sign that indicates I'm even close to my destination.

I approach the car and the guy rolls down the window. He's swarthy and has a big mustache and tiny squinty eyes in a big face. Hmm. I had hoped it would be a nice woman driver.

"I hope you don't want directions, because I'm the wrong person to ask," I quip, wondering if he even speaks English.

"Where you go?" he says.

I tell him the name of the town and he looks confused, which isn't exactly reassuring. He reaches over and opens the door for me to get in.

Which maybe isn't such a great idea. But I remember the South African woman has lived here for twenty years. Surely she wouldn't give bad advice to a new girl in town, right?

This is how women end up hog-tied in shallow graves, Zona, says the wise field reporter in my head. *Hello?! What is the point of being up on your true crime reading if you aren't going to utilize the information? Do you want to be a serious journalist or cover local bake sales?*

He starts driving. "Where you live?"

"With my *pro-yia-yia.* Athénè Pelonis?" I use the name like a shield, thinking maybe he knows her or lives on her land, even. As in, *Don't screw around with me, pal. I'm connected.*

He just grunts. "No, no . . . where you from? France?"

Well, that's sort of flattering, actually. Odd, but definitely a compliment. "No, New York. United States," I clarify. Another grunt. "This is really nice of you, sir. I really, um . . . appreciate—oh! That's the place, just stop—"

But he doesn't stop.

"Sir, wait, I need to go there, my cousin . . . *Stop!*"

The man looks at me, grinning—evilly?!—but still doesn't stop. "New York, I have not been," he says.

I'm feeling a little panicky. He's not going very fast, but he's still driving and clearly ignoring me. *Oh, Zona, Zona, you dummy—you need to listen to your instincts!*

"Sir!" I say more loudly. I wonder if I could jump out like in the movies. I can't reach for the handle preemptively, though, or he'll guess my intentions and maybe lock the door. Then I'll be screwed. "Sir, please stop—I have to be back there. STOP."

"You want stop here?" He is still going. Then, finally, he slows down and stops. "Why, you sure? Right here?"

The relief flows over me like water. I throw the door open before anything else can happen. "Yes, yes, thank you, *efcharisto*, thanks!" I jump out of the car quickly.

Did I imagine that whole thing? Did he change his mind when I got insistent? Anyway, I'm okay, I'm not kidnapped.

I'm never hitching a ride again—I don't care *what* the local custom is. I'll wear sneakers and I'll walk the whole way. Or better, I'll stay put in my Arabian-nights bed.

36

By the time I get back to the cottage I'm dusty, hungry, and grouchy. I just want a shower and a huge plate of something delicious.

Then I remember the shower. Oy.

Well, I need to stop being such a baby. It's not like I have to go bathe in a river covered with ice, for crying out loud. I want to travel the world and write about it someday, and I'm not even prepared to take a cold shower? *Pull yourself together, Zona.*

I strip off my dirty clothes, wrap a towel around myself, and head back outside, careful to switch on the garden lights in case dusk falls quickly like it did yesterday.

On my way to the shower closet I notice there's a big white bird with a long neck and a round yellow beak standing on the stone table. I think it's a goose. I've never really seen a goose up close before. Maybe at a petting zoo as a kid, but I don't remember. Its feet are also bright yellow and look rubbery.

"Hi, goose," I say. *Great, Zo. Two days away from civilization and you're chatting up birds.*

The shower is cold. The shower is as cold as a river covered with ice. But I am brave! I use the handheld nozzle-thing and get my hair wet right away—the chill takes my breath away, but I shampoo! I condition! I wash the dust from between my toes! And I survive. So there.

I wrap myself back in the towel, slide on my flip-flops, and open the wooden door to the shower. The goose is standing right there outside it.

"Oh, hey, goose. Did you miss me? You want to shower, too?" I start to walk out and it hisses. It HISSES, like an angry cat. I immediately step back, and it stops.

First of all, since when do geese *hiss*? I definitely remember the goose going *honk honk* in the "Old MacDonald" song. Secondly, what does the hiss mean? It sounds terrifying, but maybe it's more like a friendly greeting. How do I know?

I peek out from behind the door again. Now there are *three* geese: two white, one black and white and bigger. Fantastic.

I step, they hiss. I take another tiny step and the big goose—the male?—*snaps* at my foot. Do geese have teeth? No, right? *Right?!*

I don't wait to find out. I dash back inside the shower.

This is ridiculous. I'm trapped inside an outdoor bathroom because of a gang of crazy geese? Not acceptable. I think about calling for *Pro-Yia-Yia*, but that seems too pathetic. I don't need a geriatric woman half my size to scare away the mean birdies.

Well, I might, actually.

I think about what people say about bears when camping, how you just have to make a lot of noise and frighten them away. I try to stomp my feet, but flip-flops on cement do not sound intimidating. Maybe if I wave my towel at them like an angry flag? I open the wooden door again, planning to whip the towel out at them—if that doesn't work, maybe the sight of a naked teenager will do it?—but the big goose is *right at the door*. I scream—he does not get scared but barges *into the shower*, hissing and snapping and trying to eat me. He has a terrifying gray tongue that looks like a corpse's finger, only with pointy, jagged edges. Kind of like teeth!

I back toward the sink/toilet area, clutching my towel around me, praying for a quick death. The big, mean goose—clearly the gang leader—continues to snap at me until I throw the towel over him and make a break for it, hoping his friends will be distracted enough to let me by.

He's faster than I thought he would be. In a flash he's out from under the towel and, before I can snatch it back to cover myself, the whole flock has formed a blockade, preventing my escape.

When *Pro-Yia-Yia* finds me a short time later, I'm under the sink again, hiding behind the gross brown rug that used to serve as a door. (It's thicker than a towel, so harder for a crazed goose to gnaw through.) She bangs her stick on the floor and the geese immediately scatter. No hissing, no argument.

As I collect myself and follow her out, she grumbles a bunch of stuff in Greek that I assume means, *There is something seriously wrong with this girl. I think she may be mentally deficient. Afraid of geese, honestly? No way she's related to me*, or similar.

I spend the next two days inside napping, in the garden reading, studying, or playing games on my iPad, and taking "artsy" pictures of the rocks and trees surrounding the cottages to show off to Alex when I get back to Athens. At meals with *Pro-Yia-Yia* we are both silent—me, embarrassed and always watching for vengeful birds; her, probably wondering how many more times she'll have to rescue me from the bathroom before I get the hell off her property.

When Markos finally comes to get me for the bus, I am long past desperate to relieve poor, disappointed *Pro-Yia-Yia* of the burden of a citified, gadget-addicted American great-granddaughter. Markos smiles broadly after setting down a big basket of supplies for *Pro-Yia-Yia*.

"Sad to go, yes? Is paradise here, yes?"

I smile halfheartedly. "Yes, it's beautiful," I say. I really do feel bad that I wasted so much time doing nothing in such a pretty place, but I guess it's my own fault. If Hilary were here, she'd have painted every tree and rock and ruin. If Matty were here, he'd have talked to everyone in town—English-speaking or not. Not me. Too shy, and too frustrated with my own limitations. If I'd been able to communicate I could've at least written about the history of the village, learned about the construction of the stone cottages, done an exposé on the tourist industry in tiny towns . . . a million things. Instead I got chased by a pack of geese and then gave up to play Angry Birds.

(Is that ironic? I'm never sure.)

Pro-Yia-Yia shuffles out of her cottage, her black kerchief tied snugly under her chin as always, her eyes bright. "Markos!" she hollers. "Markos, *greekgreekgreekgreekgreekgreek* HISSSSSSS *greekgreekgreek*!"

Markos looks at me incredulously. "You . . . Geese chase you naked in the garden?"

When I don't immediately respond, he turns to *Pro-Yia-Yia* and says something to her, a question.

She starts making hissing sounds and lunging forward with her stick, then miming hiding behind her hands, all the while chattering away excitedly. She stops talking and starts to laugh—a loud, cackling, pealing laugh that would be terrifying if it weren't so flat-out shocking to see it coming out of this diminutive, stern old lady.

Markos is trying *not* to laugh, I can tell.

Finally, she runs out of steam and hobbles over to me.

She puts her gnarled hand up to my face and pinches my cheek. "Zona," she says. *"Greekgreekgreekgreek."*

I look at Markos. He is smiling again. "She says . . . thank you for make an old woman to laugh."

As I gently hug her good-bye, I think, *Maybe I wasn't a disappointment after all.*

37

By the time I navigate the seventeen (fine, *four*) buses I need to catch to get back to the family homestead, I've forgiven Yiota and Melina for tricking me into leaving civilization.

Thia Angela picks me up that afternoon at the bus stop, and I collapse into the front seat. "You had fun?" she asks coyly.

"Oh, yes, very fun," I reply, pretending to scowl. "Markos and *Pro-Yia-Yia* send you their *warmest* regards. So do the geese." Angela giggles like a little girl and leans over to kiss me on both cheeks. I'm so happy to see her warm smiling face, and it surprises me how easy it is to feel welcomed home. By someone other than Dad, I mean. I finally reached him on the bus ride back and got to tell him more about what I've been doing and who I've met. But despite insisting he wasn't, he sounded completely distracted by work, so I let him go. It's weird to feel lonely talking to him and then *not* lonely with my *thia*, who

I barely know. But I'm trying to not judge my feelings, to just let them happen.

"We have been hard at work at the house. I hope you are ready for Greek Easter, because it will not be egg hunts and fancy hats."

We pull up to the family complex, and Yiota and Melina are outside waiting. They rush to the car, practically pulling me out and kissing my cheeks and hugging me. I missed them, too.

"Girls, why aren't you inside? We have lots of work to do still," Angela scolds them, but she's smiling.

"*Thia*, it's too hot in the kitchen," Melina groans. "The *tsoureki* is baking, everything is waiting for you."

I follow them into the house and Angela heads to the kitchen, which, as promised, feels like the inside of a volcano. *Thia* Ioanna and a few other women I don't know are in there stirring and mixing and chopping. Angela starts rattling off names—I guess even more family has shown up since I went on my jaunt to the countryside. I smile, but my attention is distracted by a huge bowl of bright red eggs.

"You *do* have colored eggs!" I exclaim, reaching for one. "Are they hard-boiled?"

I discover that they are *not*, in fact, hard-boiled when the one I grab cracks open in my hand and dribbles through my fingers. Everyone laughs, except for Ioanna, who shakes a wooden spoon at me before going back to stirring.

"They are in the fridge, the hard-boiled ones, for the

tsoureki," Melina explains. "This is a sweet bread, is baking now, and you put the egg on it. Then on Sunday we play a game where you crack these eggs together." She indicates the bowl. "Whoever's egg doesn't crack until last will have the best luck for the year."

"I hope you do better with your next egg, Zona!" Yiota adds. *Thios* Labis comes into the kitchen carrying a large carton. "Baba, look at Zona with her first red egg," she calls to him. Labis nods at me politely, then turns away. I make myself smile at him as I wipe up the mess with a rag.

"Angela, *greekgreekgreekgreekgreekgreek*," he tells his wife, and she clucks in agreement to whatever he's said, simultaneously checking on the loaves in the oven.

To me she says, "We have church tomorrow night, Zona, you will see how beautiful it is for Holy Friday. More flowers than you can imagine, you will see."

And she's right—the church is absolutely *bedecked* in flowers when we get there late the next evening after a quiet day spent not doing much (Greeks don't work or cook on Holy Friday). There are garlands and banks of flowers, and urns filled with them, just piles and piles of flowers and petals in every color. It's a solemn service that I don't understand, but it's soothing, with beautiful music, and is really like nothing I've ever been to. I sit with Melina and her parents; the little ones are in the pew in front of us, all dressed up and tidy for a change. Even the older boys have been dragged away from their electronic games and they manage to escort their aunts and grandmothers to their seats without looking too put out. Afterward, we all walk back to the house, through streets that really have been splashed with rosewater.

Saturday morning I come down later than usual, and I'm absolutely ravenous. In the kitchen all the women are crammed around the various counters, hard at work.

Yiota looks up from kneading a bowl of something covered in flour. "I hope you aren't looking for breakfast," she says in a warning tone. "I'm starving, too. It sucks."

"Pffft! Don't say this word, Yiota!"

"What word, 'starving'?" Yiota sticks her tongue out playfully at *Thia* Angela, who waves a hand at her and then turns to me. "We fast on the day before Easter, for Holy Saturday," she explains. "Like for a Jewish holiday, too, I think, yes?"

"Oh, my dad and I don't really do any of that stuff . . ." I say, trailing off. Um, does this mean there will be no lunch, either? My stomach rumbles grouchily. This is going to be a long day, especially if I have to spend it in a kitchen full of delicious food. There is a row of amazing-smelling loaves of bread on a table by the wall—the *tsoureki*, I guess, since each loaf is studded with at least one bright red egg. Actually, it sort of looks like the loaves are wearing clown noses.

Then I notice what *else* is on the table, and it immediately quashes my appetite, at least for the time being. Perhaps forever.

It's a . . . Well, I don't know what it is, actually. It's definitely an animal, and it's big, and skinned. In a huge wooden bowl next to it are its insides. I shriek, backing away. Yiota laughs.

"It's not a little cousin, don't worry. Just the lamb for tomorrow."

"But . . . but why is it . . ." I stumble over my words, trying not to gag. "Naked?" That's the best I can come up with.

"What do you think fresh meat looks like—cut in squares?" Angela chuckles. *Um, yes, I much prefer to think that, thanks.* Even at the market the meat is . . . Well, come to think of it, I haven't seen any meat since I've been here. Because of Lent. Ah, I get it now. I feel a wave of vegetarianism washing over me.

"Come on, girls—I need help making the soup," Angela continues. "Zona, you go find your *thios* Theseus. You can help him get the effigy ready for later."

"I'm sorry—the what?"

"An effigy is—" Melina says.

"I know what an effigy *is*, but why would we need one for Easter?"

Melina sticks her hands into the bowl of horrifying, slimy innards and starts doing something I don't want to think about. Yiota is cutting up lemons. "To burn Judas, of course.

You'll see. *Thios* Theseus is in the backyard, I think. He's in a bad mood."

"He's *always* in a bad mood when he's hungry," Angela says.

I head for the door, shaking my head. Melina lifts a hand out of the scary lamb-insides bowl, waving a piece of I-don't-know-what at me. I shiver. "Wait til you taste the soup! It's delicious."

I practically run out the door.

In the yard, *Thios* Theseus is wrestling with a larger-than-life-size mummy of sorts, which I guess is meant to be Judas. It looks more like the Scarecrow from *The Wizard of Oz*, but I decide to keep that information to myself. He's trying to get it to stay on a complicated wooden frame shaped like a gallows with a cross attached to it. It keeps leaning to one side. This is probably another reason why he's in a bad mood. As I approach, *Thios* Dimitris slinks away into the garage.

"Dimitris, *greekgreekgreekgreekgreek*!" Theseus calls after him, stepping back from the leaning effigy-on-a-stick. "Your *thios* Dimitris is such a quitter, eh?" he says to me, wiping his face with a rag from his back pocket. "So, Zona, you like our Judas? Tonight, up he goes! And he will *not* be sideways, you can trust me on that one, baaaaaaaaay-beh."

I giggle. His Elvis voice always cracks me up.

"Obviously I have no idea what this is supposed to look like," I reply carefully, "but wouldn't it be easier to just put him on a regular . . . cross? That's supposed to be a cross, right? Did Judas . . . go on a cross?"

Theseus shakes his head at me. "No, this is my own concept—a cross, yes, but hanging as well, you see? Ah, Zona, my treasured *anipsiá*, I am an engineer. I have three advanced degrees, you understand? I cannot build a simple cross when my neighbors expect more. Of course, I'm used to working with sophisticated materials, yes? *Éla*, if I had some pistons and a steel frame, I could really *make something*, but for the burning, it has to be wood. And this wood, it is . . . substandard! Well, you can see. You understand your poor *thios* now, yes?"

I do *not* understand, and I'm honestly trying not to laugh. He looks so upset, but he's fussing with a giant stuffed doll on a wonky coatrack. I try to cheer him up. "Melina is making a scary soup out of lamb insides right now," I offer. "I think she intends for us to actually eat it."

Theseus brightens immediately. "Ah, my favorite thing—lemon intestines soup! Don't worry, she's just preparing the ingredients. *I* will make it tonight to break the fast; it's my specialty, and so delicious. Of course, by midnight you will be so hungry, you would eat poor Judas if you had to, yes?" He laughs uproariously, then looks back at the effigy and starts scowling again. He kicks the structure.

"Wait. We can't eat until *midnight*?" I gasp. I'm pretty sure that most other religions have a sundown break-the-fast system, and I was definitely counting on that being the plan for Greek Easter. My stomach rumbles again.

"I know, it is impossible. And yet, we have to focus on God and our blessings, yes? Besides, there is so much to do. Did you see the fireworks yet? Come with me."

Greece Continues To Have Questionable Ideas About Public Safety

As part of the Easter celebration on the quaint island of Crete, adult citizens think a terrific plan is to set up thousands of fireworks on a big wooden structure and then set them off. The best part? They are aimed at a church across town! The other best part? That church is doing the same thing in the opposite direction!

It seems that fireworks battles between rival churches have long been a tradition here and take place all over Crete on this holiest of days. Angela Marousopoulou, local resident, commented, "Oh yes, this is all in fun. Everyone loves it—especially the children!"

Zona Lowell, American visitor, seemed skeptical at first. "Am I the only person who thinks this is a really bad idea? I mean, exciting, yes . . . but seriously?"

Her uncle, Theseus Marousopoulou, scoffed at his niece's reservations. "This is a tradition! Americans are so worried about being cozy and safe—this is Greece. Here we live, we are exciting! Besides, the men lighting the rockets tie cloth over their faces for the smoke. That is plenty of protection, *nay*?"

Ms. Lowell's suggestion to watch the classic film *Easter Parade* and eat Cadbury Creme Eggs instead was unanimously rejected.

Filed, 4:12 p.m., Heraklion.

I have never been so hungry and so terrified about an impending meal in my life. By the time we are dressed and at church again, I don't think I'll last another minute, but I do. (An Easter miracle?) After the service, around eleven P.M., the priest lights a candle, and then each person in the congregation lights a candle from it. Then we all have to carry our candles back to the house without the flames going out, which is not as easy as it sounds. Especially if you happen to live at the crest of a giant hill.

When we finally get there, I think I'm going to pass out from hunger. I'm wondering, *How bad can intestine soup be, really?* when Melina and Yiota pull me into the street in front of the house. Apparently we aren't up to the newly-slaughtered-animals-eating part of the program yet, because Theseus's Judas effigy is planted in the middle of the road and surrounded by massive piles of sticks and other branches. Church bells ring for the millionth time that day as our whole family and the neighbors and their families gather around. *Thios* Labis, who I suppose is Head of the Street, comes forward, swinging a lit torch. The little kids are freaking out with excitement as he lights the brush and the whole thing goes up in flames. Flames that rise higher than the house. The heat is blinding.

It's insane and surprisingly beautiful.

(Did I mention *insane*? I mean, my uncle just started a giant bonfire in the middle of the neighborhood! Next to his own house! And the crowd *loves it*.)

"They do this in every village, you know, at the same

time," Yiota tells me over the cheering. "Next is the fireworks; we can see best from the edge of the hill."

Why *wouldn't* we go stand directly in the path of thousands of fireworks? It seems like a perfectly logical thing to do. Just as I'm mentally outlining a Greek safety awareness profile, the show starts.

Imagine the climactic finale of a Fourth of July fireworks display. Times a hundred. The sky is so bright with color and light, it almost looks like it's daytime. The noise is deafening. The smell is overwhelming. The crowd is losing its mind, especially when the fireworks from the other side of the battle start firing in *our* direction. Cries of *"Christos anesti!"* (Christ is risen!) come from every direction. Even gloomy *Thios* Dimitris and his wife seem to be on good terms.

For that ten minutes, I can see why it might be okay to forget about things like health hazards and fire codes. It may be the most incredible sight I've ever seen in my life.

The organ soup, however, is exactly as revolting as I knew it would be. For the record, I'd rather starve than try another bite. Luckily there's enough other food to feed about six armies, so I don't have to.

The entire rest of the family gobbles up that intestine soup like it's manna in the desert. I just smile and have an extra slice of delicious, chewy clown-nose bread instead.

Then, after we sleep for what seems like five minutes, Easter Sunday arrives in a beautiful burst of sunshine.

There's another church service that I'm barely conscious for and then it's back to food, food, family, music, and more food. The celebrating starts at dawn and goes on until we're all bursting at the seams. I'll say this: the Marousoupolous *really* know how to do holidays.

Kalo Pascha to all!

38

The next morning, I pack my things to go back to Athens. I want to see my dad and my friends . . . but I'm not quite ready to go. I feel like this huge part of who I am is different now, but that I should have had some kind of great epiphany or realization . . . and I don't know what it is. I want a specific thought or item to carry back with me. I want a ribbon to tie around the experience. And I don't have one.

What I do have is a lot of studying that I blew off. And a very heavy heart when I think about leaving Melina, *Thia* Angela, and *Yia-Yia* behind. Being with them and *Thios* Theseus (and Yiota, of course, but she's coming back with me) was really the best part of this trip. I still don't feel like I know my mother, exactly, but I do have a better idea of where she came from. And where *I* come from.

While Yiota is saying good-bye to her friends, I finish packing, then decide to go find Melina. One of the older cousins I met yesterday is in the kitchen eating (how can anyone ever eat again after last night?) and tells me she's at her house.

Ioanna lets me in and I knock on the door of Melina's room. I poke my head inside. "You busy?" I ask.

"No, come in," she calls, smiling. I flop onto her bed. Melina is looking at a bunch of glossy brochures.

"What's all this stuff?" I ask, picking one up. "College brochures? Are you worried about this stuff already?" Great. Melina's a grade below me, and all I can think about are the repercussions of eating too much meat in such a short amount of time.

"Well, I have to think what classes to take because school here isn't so . . . comprehensive. We have to take extra courses on our own to qualify for all the tests to go to college outside of Greece. It's expensive, but very important if I want to study engineering like Baba."

"Oh." I leaf through the brochure. "But why wouldn't you stay here? I mean, your family is here, and all your friends."

"There's nothing for me here," Melina says sadly. "Not just me, but my friends, too. We will go to school abroad and find jobs . . . even Mama knows it is for the best. To do anything with engineering, or computers, science, most things, there's no place here for us now to work. People study all these years and have nothing to do with it after. We don't know where we will get our next money, or if we can raise a family here."

I can see her eyes filling with tears, and I know she doesn't want to admit these things out loud. I feel like I'm going to cry, too. Melina drops her head and looks at the bedspread. "Greece is sending her kids away," she whispers. Then she looks me in the eye. "So we have to go."

Visitor Finds Suitcase Filled With Sundries, No Room For Clothes

After exchanging a bitter-sweet farewell with her newfound and very special cousin Melina Marousopoulou, Zona Lowell was surprised to find herself doubled over with laughter mere moments later.

"Clearly *Yia-Yia* snuck in while I was across the street," Ms. Lowell explained through her giggles. "I went to get a hoodie out of my suitcase and discovered half my clothes had been taken out and replaced with food and other presents— bottles of olive oil, fresh bread, olive oil soap, grape leaves, little trinkets . . . I don't even know what else."

Whether the family matriarch intended her granddaugh- ter to simply wear all her clothes onto the plane is unclear at time of printing. What is clear is that Mrs. Marousopoulou has little understanding of airport luggage content/weight restrictions.

Ms. Lowell was touched by the gesture, but uncertain how to handle it. "It's not like they're going to let me take this on the plane," she lamented, sniffing a freshly baked loaf of bread. "Maybe if my cousin Yiota takes half . . . ?"

UPDATE: It was later discov- ered that Ms. Lowell's cousin had been gifted with a suitcase full of foodstuffs herself. Miss Marousopoulou had, however, anticipated this eventuality and brought an extra bag with her.

Filed, 10:36 a.m., Heraklion.

Finally, everything is eaten, packed, shoved somewhere, or hidden away.

There's nothing left to do but say good-bye.

After spending so much time together, *Yia-Yia* and I are able to communicate much better, but words aren't really needed at this particular moment. She kisses me on both cheeks for the last time and pulls me into a long hug. We stand together in the doorway to her house, me bending down so my head rests on her tiny shoulder, and I can tell—no, I can *feel*—what she's thinking: her regrets, her hopes . . . and I know she can feel mine.

All the lost time, the mixed emotions, neither of us really understanding why she let my mother slip away so many years ago. But I can also feel her love for me, and I'm sending mine back to her.

We can't rewrite history, so a fresh start may have to be enough.

Finally, *Thia* Angela pulls me gently away. Then there are many, many more hugs from a thousand people. Yiota and I get into her parents' car and drive to the airport with Theseus, Ioanna, and Melina behind us in the beloved Fiat.

We park and get out of our respective cars. Labis and Angela surround Yiota and talk a mile a minute in Greek while Ioanna kisses me good-bye and slips a bar of Greek chocolate into my carry-on bag.

Theseus gives me a big hug, then grins at me slyly and hands me a silver disc in a plastic case. "A big surprise for you, baaaaaay-beh," he says. "You watch this when you get home on your computer, then you tell me what is what!" Suddenly distracted by someone standing too close to his precious car, he dashes off, and I look at Melina in confusion.

"It's a DVD of him performing. As Elvis. I can't talk about it," she says, rolling her eyes. We laugh and hug good-bye. Then I feel a soft hand on my arm, and of course it's *Thia* Angela. She folds me into her embrace, smelling of lemon and spices as always.

"We are so lucky to have you," she says quietly. "Remember that we are always here for you. For anything at all, *nay*? Too many years going by, we will not let this happen again, *aqapi mou*."

I hear Labis clear his throat behind me. "Not much time to talk now," he says gruffly. I'm sure Yiota makes a face at him from behind me, because he reaches out a hand stiffly and pats me on the arm. He opens his mouth, then shuts it. Then he says, "Be safe."

And . . . that's it. He hugs Yiota again, and they drive away.

Labis's continued coldness confuses and disappoints me. He's not the only one who acted that way, but he's the only one whose behavior really makes me feel bad; it's like he's showing everyone else this other nice Labis he won't let me see. *Thios* Dimitris seems to be a bit of a weirdo, so I didn't really care that he mostly ignored me. The other adults who weren't especially friendly kept to themselves and didn't speak much English, and the boy cousins ignored pretty much everyone. But after everything Angela and Yiota told me about *Thios* Labis, I thought I'd see a different side of him eventually. The side that loved my mother so much.

But at the end of the day, I guess he couldn't get past blaming my dad for taking her away. And, indirectly, me.

It was easier when I didn't know any of them, honestly. Now I have hurt feelings, and it feels really unfair. On the other hand, I wouldn't want to have missed out on meeting *Yia-Yia* or Angela, Yiota or Melina or Theseus . . . so it's hard to know what to feel. Like I said: no pretty bow to wrap up the experience with. Just more questions.

Yiota and I fly back to Athens, which only takes about forty minutes. I use my old train ticket to get on the Metro like the sneaky abuser of public transportation I am. When I arrive at Kallithea, I practically sprint to the apartment, not even stopping to respond to texts from Hilary and Lilena. I dash inside, expecting to be greeted by an ecstatic Tony and a festive meal prepared by my father, who has missed me beyond measure.

What I get is an eyebrow lift and a giant yawn from Tony, who is lounging in his dog bed, and a visual of an apartment that looks like it's been hit with a paper tornado.

No sign of Dad. Not even a Post-it with a headline.

You know, sometimes it's nice to be treated like an adult by your parent, and sometimes it's upsetting. On the other hand, after being surrounded by people for two weeks, it's not such a bad thing to have some time to myself. I unpack and coax Tony into leaving the apartment for a walk in the beautiful spring air.

I can't believe it's over. This event that I've dreaded for so long has come and gone. I have a family now—a big, boisterous, funny, kind, complicated family. And I can't pretend that it's just me, Dad, and Tony any longer.

When something you've been anticipating is over, it's hard not to feel depressed or empty, and I do feel that way. Filling up the space with my GIS friends and studying— even the prospect of seeing what happens with Alex now that I'm back in town—just doesn't feel like enough somehow.

39

When Dad finally turns up a few hours later, he looks like he hasn't shaved in at least a week. He's got ink stains on every one of his fingers. But he also has bags from the grocery store and the bakery—filled with my favorite spanakopita and yummy flaky pastries—and I forgive him immediately for not being home when I got here.

I hug him so hard, you'd think I'd been away for two years instead of two weeks. But it's scary to reevaluate my idea of "family," and Dad has always been the center of that idea for me. I want to make sure he knows that he still is.

We put the spanakopita in the oven, then sit down to catch up. I try to insist that Dad tell me about his work—how far along he is and who he spoke to while I was gone—but he waves the idea away.

"Are you crazy?" he asks incredulously. "Ace, you just had the biggest adventure of your life! No way am I going to bore you with interviews about economic policy. At least not until after dessert, anyway."

I pause, unsure how to begin. I'm still worried that

he'll feel betrayed if I admit I had a good time, even though it was his idea that I go. But then it's like I can't get the words out fast enough. I want to tell him everything, without forgetting a single detail, but there are too many names and feelings and geese-related stories. I start getting mixed up, and soon he's totally confused and we're both laughing.

The timer on the oven chimes. "You know," Dad says, pretending to be stern as he grabs two plates, "this is *not* the way I taught you to report a story, young lady. Where's my clear but intriguing opening, followed by meticulously arranged details? I can't tell if you have forty cousins or four with multiple personality disorders. And who is this Pra-La-La? Is she even a real person? I'm worried you've devolved into—I can't believe I'm saying this—*fiction.*"

I gasp theatrically. "I can't believe you'd say something like that to your only child!" I start cutting up the spanako-pita. "I don't know if you deserve any dinner. In fact, I think I'll give your share to Tony."

Tony's ears perk up at the sound of his name, and he pads into the kitchen hoping for a handout. "I've always known you'd choose that mutt over me," Dad says, shooing a very insulted Tony back out the door. "I can see the head-lines now: Cub Reporter Deserts Dear Old Dad, Sets Off on World Tour With Dog."

I look carefully at him as he takes a big bite and wonder if maybe he's saying something without saying it. The very thing I was worried about, in fact.

I put my fork down. "Dad, I'd never desert you—not for anyone. On the Gray Lady's legacy, I solemnly swear it."

He glances up at me again with his familiar lopsided grin. "Oh, sure—until you meet some handsome hunk in your history class or something . . . then it'll be 'Dad *who*?' No more treats for the pooch then, either—you hear that, boy?" he calls toward the living room. But I know he heard me, and that's enough. So I let the conversation slide back into our usual teasing repartee.

Dad loads up another forkful and points it at me. "Now— tell me more about this Theseus fellow. He sounds like a character!"

School Exactly The Same As Before, Students Lament

Turns out it's pretty easy to get back into the swing of things," revealed Zona Lowell, GIS sophomore, upon returning from an emotionally taxing spring break trip this week. "And having exams, friends competing over who has the best vacation stories, and the glorious reveal that is full spring in Athens certainly helps distract a person from major life episodes."

Ms. Lowell's concerns that she'd be unable to quickly readjust to school life were indeed unfounded. Despite meeting no less than thirty new relations and having myriad perception-changing experiences, she found herself able to get right back down to the business of education and socialization as though nothing much had happened at all.

"She's totally been texting with Alex Loushas, and I think they're going to the movies or something this weekend," said an inside source close to Ms. Lowell. "Zona's cousin only has two classes this semester, too, so she can hang out with us. She's cool."

Whether or not Ms. Lowell will pass her hurriedly-studied-for exams remains to be seen. One hopes that she managed to squeak by despite an unprecedented lack of preparation.

Filed, 2:08 p.m., Athens.

I'm actually having fun being back at school (despite the exams, obviously). It's easy to slip back into my place at the lunch table, the text-message chain, the worrying about whether the guy I like is going to make a move or not.

And speaking of guys, it looks like Melina was right about playing hard to get; Alex was waiting by my locker after first period on Monday, wanting to hear all about my trip and tell me about visiting his family in Egypt.

"Well, if it isn't Miss *New York Times*," he said, gray eyes sparkling behind his glasses. I felt myself blushing—I don't think having a cute guy pay attention to me in public could *ever* get old. "We were worried you'd decide to stay on Crete and leave all this behind."

"Who's 'we'?" I asked, pretending to be very busily organizing my locker. Alex leaned in, working hard to get my attention.

"You know, inquiring minds. The masses." I give him a questioning look over the top of my stack of books. "Okay, me," he continued, smiling. "Hey, you free for coffee later?"

Of course I wanted to shout *Yes!*, but I actually really had to study, and besides, I didn't want to seem too eager. I silently prayed that Melina knew what she was talking about, took the risk, and told him I wasn't available.

"Wow, busy girl," he said, looking disappointed. "How about Saturday night? Exams will be over by then, and I know your little gang doesn't make plans that far in advance."

I just got asked out on my first real date! I shrieked inside my head. I couldn't wait to tell Hilary and Matt and—well, everyone on the planet! I forced myself to remain outwardly calm, however.

"I think that works," I said coolly. "Can I text you later and let you know?" The bell rang above our heads. "Oh, gotta run," I said, then boldly leaned in and kissed him on the lips for half a second. No one even saw, but I felt empowered and very brave as I walked away, reminding myself not to look back.

I started grinning like a maniac the second I was out of his sight. So I suppose being back at school hasn't been too bad.

Less happily, Lilena looks even worse than she did before I went to Crete, and I decide I can't keep quiet any longer. I have to do *something*.

The night I got back from Crete, she and I met at our usual blue-tiled table. I was really excited to see her. I wanted to tell her details of my trip and see how she was doing—I felt so sad that she'd been by herself for the whole break, just waiting around for school to start again.

She was standing by the counter when I got to the café. I didn't even recognize her at first—from behind, she looked like a child. Maybe seeing her constantly had made her thinness less noticeable; not seeing her for a while made it all the more jarring. Her face was gaunt and ashy-looking, her eyes had dark smudges under them, and around her mouth were tiny lines that made her look much older than sixteen. Even her hair looked dull and thin. It broke my heart. I wondered if, without being under the scrutiny of Ashley and her snarky comments—which, while not very helpful, did sometimes goad Lilena into eating a bite or two—she had ingested anything at all besides coffee since I last saw her.

Every time she moved I was sure I'd hear her bones snapping inside her skin. I spent the whole time thinking that the second I got back to the apartment I'd figure out a way to help her.

But it's hard to know what to do or who to talk to about the situation. Hilary and Matt don't know Lilena, though they are sympathetic and agree that I have to follow my instincts. Yiota is worried that Lilena might react badly and thinks I should think carefully before I do or say anything. My dad is up to his ears in his latest draft and transcribing translated interviews obsessively—I don't want to distract him with details of a friend he doesn't know and a problem he can't do anything about. I can't ask Alex about it, because that would be . . . too weird. So I settle on Betony.

If I can get her on her own, without Ashley around, she might actually hear what I have to say.

I ask her to meet me to hang out a few days later. I figure I'll warm her up with some idle chitchat, throw in a few details about Alex to get her interested, and then tell her what I've decided is the best course of action. My plan is to ask her to be a united front with me; I hope maybe she'll get Ashley on board, as well.

But my plan doesn't work out as I'd hoped.

"Zona. You can't just . . . you can't just call someone's mother! Especially if you don't even know her!" Betony says, looking shocked.

We're sitting with mugs of tea at a corner table in Starbucks after school on Wednesday. I picked one in her neighborhood, Glyfada, knowing we'd be unlikely to run into anyone we knew there. I should be home cramming for tomorrow's exam (especially considering how terribly I probably did on the previous ones), but I know I won't be able to focus.

"Why not?"

"Because . . . because for one thing, it's intrusive." Betony is getting exasperated, which, with her high-pitched voice, would be funny if we were talking about something else. "I mean, what would you even *say*?"

"I don't know, maybe something like, 'Your daughter needs help, please do something'?" I suggest.

"You can't do that! She'll be so offended!" Betony looks

like I suggested lighting a cross on fire on Lilena's parents' lawn.

"Why would she be *offended*?" I ask, incredulous.

"Because you're saying there's something wrong with her daughter!"

"Her daughter is sick!" I practically yell. Heads turn, and I duck my head, embarrassed. I just can't believe she's being so obstinate about this. I guess hoping Betony would be on Team Help Lilena was wishful thinking. And forget about Ashley. *Am I really going to have to do this by myself?*

"I think this is a really bad idea." Betony sniffs. "It's like tattling. Like we're six years old."

"Would it be like tattling if I called to say she'd been hit by a car?"

"All I'm saying is, I think this is a really bad idea," she repeats. "But you do what you want. You Americans always do."

"What the hell is *that* supposed to mean?!" Now I'm pissed.

"Look, I just think Lilena's going to be furious if she ever finds out. Do you want to lose a friend? Because I don't." She crosses her arms over her chest.

"I'd rather her not be my friend than have her starve to death! Maybe that's just very *American* of me?"

"Oh, come on, Zona. You're being so overdramatic and twisting everything I say around. Lilena just wants attention, and you're giving it to her. No one actually starves to death on purpose. I don't think she looks that different than she did before, anyway."

I just stare at her. Either she's being deliberately stubborn for reasons I don't understand, or . . . I don't know what.

And what if she's right?

Maybe this *is* a terrible idea. Maybe Lilena's mother will hang up on me—she doesn't know me, after all—and tell Lilena I called and she'll . . . hate me forever? Get everyone in school to hate me for the rest of my Grecian tenure? Have me taken to jail by her family's fancy embassy connections?

I don't know what to do.

But the thing is, I *do* know what to do. I just wish I didn't have to do it all alone.

I tell Betony not to worry about it, that I have to go home and study, and give her a quick hug good-bye.

Slightly Out-Of-Practice Investigator Jumps Back In Feet First

Despite taking time off from the writing biz to have her entire world turned upside down, intrepid reporter Zona Lowell was able to reach back into her journalist's tool bag today like no time had gone by at all.

"Good reporting means being willing to take on the hard tasks nobody else wants," Lowell said. "And being meticulous about covering your tracks."

On Friday, Lowell asked her friend, Lilena Vobras, if she could borrow her cell phone to use its calculator, alleging that her own had a dead battery. After scrolling through Ms.

280

Vobras's contacts, Lowell was able to text herself the cell phone number of Vobras's mother. Mrs. Vobras, a high-ranking government official, would have been impossible to reach without this inside path to her contact information.

"I was very careful—I erased the text from her phone as soon as I sent it and scrolled everything back so she wouldn't know what I was looking at. I triple-checked," Lowell explained confidently.

At press time, it is unclear whether Lowell was able to reach her target.

Filed, 1:02 p.m., Athens.

40

When I get home after school, I have second thoughts again. But I summon Lilena's face back to my mind, her sharply defined eye sockets, her sunken cheeks. It hurts my heart.

I take a deep breath and switch roles for the first time: I'm no longer a reporter, but a source.

I will myself not to hang up as the phone rings. Then a woman's voice answers, sounding rushed and a bit annoyed—probably because she doesn't recognize the number.

"Yes? Hello, who is this?"

"Hi, Mrs. Vobras, um . . ." I pause, trying to remember my prepared speech. "I'm a friend of Lilena's. From GIS. I'm calling because—oh, my name is Zona, Zona Lowell, um . . ." All those years of honing my vocabulary, and when I could actually stand to sound smart and authoritative, I'm reduced to the word *um*?! This is awful.

"How did you get this number? If you need Lilena, she—"

"No, no, Mrs. Vobras, I'm sorry. I'm a little nervous. I . . . I called to talk to you. About Lilena. I'm worried about her. She doesn't eat, Mrs. Vobras, and I think . . . I think she may have an eating disorder. She's so thin now, and I don't mean to be ratting her out, I just . . . I'm really concerned. I . . . I didn't know what else to do."

The total quiet on the other end of the line seems to stretch on forever. She's going to hang up on me. I can feel it. Then:

"I thought I was the only one," she whispers. "No one else has . . . I've been so busy, so I thought, if no one else noticed, maybe . . . because . . ." She takes a ragged breath, and I wonder if she's going to cry, but she doesn't. "Because no one said anything, you understand?"

"Yes," I say in a small voice. "But I'm saying something. Because I think she's really sick, Mrs. Vobras. I think she needs help."

Mrs. Vobras clears her throat, and her voice snaps back to all business. "Okay. Well, thank you, Zona. I'll make sure she gets help, now that—yes. Thank you for calling. I'm sure it wasn't an easy thing for you to do."

"Please, um, please don't tell her it was me, okay?"

"No, I certainly won't. Okay, thank you. Good-bye." She hangs up.

I press "End" on my phone and stare at it for a while. When you're writing a story, it's pretty easy to tell when you're finished and when you've got it just right. When you're a source, it isn't easy to tell at all. There's nothing to turn in or edit. You just have to wait to see what happens.

I don't see or hear from Lilena at all over the weekend. I'm scared to reach out, and also scared that her not reaching out to *me* means she knows. I run the conversation through my mind on an endless loop, telling myself I did the right thing, but unable to stop the doubt from creeping in.

I meet Ashley and Betony at one of the gigantic state-of-the-art malls that keep popping up in Athens; this one was built on the site of the 2004 Olympic stadium, which led to a huge real estate and finance scandal. (My dad has devoted a whole section of his research to the mall.) We window-shop for a few hours (I can't afford anything in these places, but they are sparkly and shiny and fun to explore), and the girls don't mention Lilena, so I don't, either. But of course I'm wondering where she is and if they've talked to her.

But I don't want to give myself away.

Even on my date with Alex, I'm distracted. I try not to let my thoughts wander—which should be easy, considering there's a cute guy who seems to be perfectly content to listen to anything I have to say (when he's not trying to kiss me, that is)—but it's hard. I just wish I knew what was going to happen, and that I could be sure my friendship with Lilena was going to be okay.

• • •

At school on Monday, my heart is beating so fast and loud that I'm sure everyone around me can hear it. Lilena isn't in first period. By lunch, the rumors have started spreading. Rumors that most likely aren't rumors—everyone is saying she's been sent to a treatment facility. Instead of being happy that she's getting help, all I can think about is whether everyone knows what I did. I keep reminding myself that I did a good thing, out of concern and care for my friend . . . so why do I feel so guilty?

By the end of the day, I can't take it anymore. I don't even hang around to see if Alex will come say hi at my locker; I rush outside to find a quiet spot where I can text Lilena.

Are you okay? Missed you at school today.

I pretend like I don't know a thing. Like no one was talking about her. Like maybe she's got a bad cold and I'm checking in, that's all.

After two minutes, I get a reply.

GO TO HELL, TRAITOR.

I've never heard Lilena talk like that, *ever*. I can't believe her mother threw me under the bus. My stomach turns inside out.

Sometimes, doing the right thing means losing everything. Journalists learn this every day—it's nothing new. But it's new to me.

And it hurts so much.

At home I fling myself into my room, feeling certain no

one has ever felt as bad about anything as I do about Lilena hating me. I want to call Hilary, but she's in school. I'm considering telling my dad everything, even if he has no idea what I'm talking about, when my phone rings.

It's Matty, who should also be in school. When I answer, he's crying. I've never heard him cry before, and it stops me cold. Maybe there *is* someone who feels worse than I do right now.

"Scott rejected me. Outright," Matty sputters through tears. "I tried to kiss him last night, I thought after all this time, I just . . . and he pushed me away, Zona. He *pushed me away*."

"When did you—"

"He said he was flattered, but I'm way too young for him," he continues. "He didn't even let me . . . I just wanted to kiss him. I'm totally in love with him, and all he can think about is age—he's not even that much older! I didn't think he thought of me like some stupid kid. I thought we were friends. I thought . . . I thought he just didn't want to rush things, I don't know . . ."

"Matty, I'm so sorry. But was he at least nice about it? He could've been a jerk," I say. "Or worse, he could've hooked up with you and then ditched you and you'd feel twice as bad. Right?"

I am trying very hard not to say *He* is *too old for you!* right now. Because that wouldn't be helpful. And my heart aches for Matt—I know how it feels to like someone you can't have. And I know how much he wanted Scott.

"I guess." Matty's calmer now, sniffling. "It just felt so patronizing, you know? He was like, 'You should be with someone your own age, who's having the same kind of experiences you are.' Then he said a bunch of crap about how cool it is that I'm out and confident with who I am, and how when he was my age he was really confused and closeted and he wishes he'd been more like me. Basically, he just isn't into me." He takes a deep, shuddering breath. "Whatever. How was the rest of Crete?"

Matty loves to suddenly slam the door on a topic, but I'm not ready to let this one go—even though he could just hang up and end it if he feels like it. "Matty, don't change the subject. Look, I don't think Scott was being patronizing. I think he was probably being serious and trying to give you advice. He obviously cares about you and admires you. Couldn't he be like . . . a mentor?"

"Do *you* need a mentor?" Matt sounds bitter now. "Why do I have to have a mentor? Because I'm gay? That's pretty damn—"

"I would freaking *love* a mentor. Are you kidding me? Go find me one, seriously," I jump in. "Find me two."

"I just . . . I just wanted to finally actually date someone. Is that so much to ask?" Matt says quietly.

"And you will, I promise. There are a zillion cute guys out there. Who are the right age and want the same things as you."

"I can't wait to be in college, Zo, seriously. I'm so sick of being the one who's different. I mean, there are, like, five guys off the top of my head at school that just *need* to come out of the closet. And it's like they're scared to just admit it. It's so lame."

"Matty, not everyone is as self-assured as you are. It's not fair to try to force everyone to do things at your pace, right? Look, life can suck sometimes. You can either deal with it or let it be who you are. So . . . don't let it be who you are. Please?"

Matt sighs. "I'll try. Thanks for listening."

"Of course. That's what I'm here for."

"I'm totally going in late today. I don't even care if I get in trouble," he says.

I swallow hard, grateful that he's on the other end of the line just when I need someone—someone who really knows me.

"Matty, I need to talk to you about something, too. Something that happened . . . I need you to tell me if I did the right thing. Honestly, okay?"

Sometimes you can see yourself a lot more clearly when you look at someone else. That's another thing I learned in Greece.

41

I'm in math class the next week, mostly ignoring the teacher and coloring in all the vowels on the pages of my book, when Mr. Pelidis, a guidance counselor I have spoken to maybe one time, opens the door and comes straight to my desk. He doesn't look happy as he tells me to collect my things and follow him. Ms. Blasi's voice trails off, and I shrug at Betony and Nikos as I follow Mr. Pelidis out the door.

Field Report: Getting Called Out Of Class Seriously Uncool

Previously perfectly behaved sophomore Zona Lowell was summoned from class today in front of her peers and had no idea why, according to witnesses.

"I've literally never been in trouble at school in my entire life. There must be some kind of mistake," Ms. Lowell insisted on her way out the door. Her classmates weren't as sure.

"Everyone knows she's the one who ratted out Lilena Vobras to her parents," said a student who did not wish to be identified. "Probably it's about that. I mean, yeah, I guess it's good that girl is getting help, and I guess no one is, like, mad at Zona, but come on. Lame."

Ms. Lowell was adamant in her belief that she had done the right thing, however, and that this summons had nothing to do with Ms. Vobras. In brighter news, Ms. Lowell stayed mostly cool and collected on her way out the door.

Filed, 1:16 p.m., Athens.

Mr. Pelidis closes the door to the guidance office and asks me to sit. My palms start to sweat.

"Mr. Pelidis, I don't know what you think I—"

He cuts me off. "You haven't done anything wrong, Zona. I just wanted to talk to you in private. Please, don't panic until I've finished explaining what's going on, okay?"

You know what a great way to keep someone from panicking is? Not saying "don't panic" to them. Because that will *make them panic.* My hands start shaking.

"Wait—what's wrong?" I ask, instantly terrified.

"There was a major demonstration today, at the Parliament. You knew about it maybe, yes?"

"Of course," I blurt impatiently. "My dad is covering it for his story; he has an interview with . . ." I put the pieces together. "Oh, no."

"Someone brought tear gas. Your father . . . Well, the details don't matter. There was a riot, things got violent, and he was caught in the middle when things got very bad."

I feel my chest caving in on itself, and I can't get any air into my lungs. Tears roll down my face and my throat is on fire. I grip my legs, trying not to fall out of the chair.

"Zona, please don't panic—he's alive! Please, I need you to listen. Can you do that?" Mr. Pelidis waves his hand; I realize he's signaled his secretary to bring me a cup of water, which I take but can't drink.

"He is at the hospital. He was trampled and they know his leg is broken and they think his spleen has ruptured. He is in surgery and will be there for several hours. He—"

Now that I know he's alive—that I'm not being told I'm an orphan by a man whose first name I don't even know—I manage to breathe. And I'm sobbing.

I'm sobbing all the tears I never cried for my mom, I'm dropping the cup of water and only sort of feeling the wetness as it splashes against my legs, I'm falling into my own lap and heaving giant gulps of noisy air into my body.

I can't stop sobbing, even though I can tell that Mr. Pelidis is trying to tell me more things that are probably important in a calm voice he probably learned at guidance counselor college.

And then, suddenly, I *can* stop. I take a big, difficult breath, I wipe my eyes on my sleeve, and I focus.

He's alive, I remind myself. *You are not all alone. He's alive, and this man is trying to help you. So listen to him.*

"Zona. Zona, okay. Okay, good. So, your father, he is at the hospital across town. Miss Papadakis has offered to drive you there." His secretary puts her hand on my shoulder; I'm too upset and simultaneously weirdly calm to even be embarrassed about the fact that she was probably standing there during my meltdown. "So you can go right now, okay?" Mr. Pelidis stands awkwardly.

I wipe my face again and stand up, too, but my legs are shaky and it takes me a second before I can follow them out of the office.

I don't even stop at my locker. I follow Miss Papadakis down the hall and out the door. I see Betony outside our math classroom holding the bathroom pass, obviously waiting to see what happened. She starts to come over when she sees my red, blotchy face. I shake my head at her, and then Miss Papadakis and I are outside.

In the car, I send a short group text to my GIS friends so they don't think I've been hauled off to jail. Then I ask Miss Papadakis, "How did the hospital know where I was? Was he . . . conscious? Was he in *pain*?" I feel the tears starting again and I swallow hard to try to keep it together.

"He told them your name and your school before surgery. I'm sure he's in very good hands, Zona, okay?" she says. "Now, who can we call to meet you at the hospital?"

I have no idea how to answer this question. Dad's my legal guardian. What if they won't let me see him? What about paying for the surgery and everything else—I don't know anything about our health insurance or . . . do they even take health insurance in Greece? Is it free here? Is it only free for Greek citizens?

I take a deep breath, trying not to panic. "I can call my cousin," I say, bringing up Yiota's number. At the very least she might know how to help.

Miss Papadakis pulls into the parking lot while the phone is ringing. I get Yiota's voice mail. I send a text saying it's an emergency, hoping she's just in class or something and will step out to take the call. I try again as we cross the parking lot, getting closer to the doors and to my dad.

Yiota picks up, sounding out of breath. "Zona, are you okay? Sorry, I was—you guys, *greekgreekgreekgreek*!—Sorry, Zona, I'm just with some friends and . . . Where are you?"

"I'm at the hospital," I gasp with relief. My voice breaks and the tears start again, but I fight to get my words out. "My dad was at the riot, he's in surgery, and I . . . I don't know what to do. Can you come?"

I hear Yiota yelling in Greek to her friends, who are laughing and playing music in the background. She comes back to the phone. "Of course, Zona—please, do not worry, yes? At which hospital are you?" I give her the information and hang up.

Miss Papadakis looks nervous. This is not what she signed up for, and she can't really do anything to help but sit with me until my cousin arrives.

We walk through the sliding doors, her hand on my back and my heart in my mouth.

42

Thirty minutes later, Yiota rushes down the hospital hallway and collapses into the hard plastic chair next to me. She throws her arms around me in a bear hug. I didn't realize until that moment how clenched my entire body was, and it takes me a second to relax even a little. I'm so drained from crying and trying not to panic that I can barely find the strength to hug her back.

Miss Papadakis stands up awkwardly, twisting her hands together, which is what she's been doing since the hospital people told me (through Miss P) that Dad is still in surgery and might not be out for a while, and that, by the way, I couldn't see him anyway because I'm a minor and this is the critical care unit, and would my mother be getting here soon?

"It's okay, you can go, *efcharisto, greekgreekgreekgreek,*" Yiota tells her, and with a last awkward pat on my arm, Miss Papadakis is gone. I'm relieved—watching her feel uncomfortable has not been helping, though I'm grateful she came with me, of course.

"They won't let me see him," I whisper to Yiota. "When he comes out of surgery, I mean . . . and they won't tell me anything! I—"

"Shhh, it's okay," Yiota murmurs. "We'll take care of it, of course. Don't worry about that, you just send prayers to your father. Okay?"

My phone buzzes with another text; my GIS friends and my NYC friends (I texted Hil and Matty to let them know what was happening) have sent me a hundred messages, and I haven't known how to respond. What could they do, anyway? Hold down the doctors until they let me see my dad? Take up a collection to pay the bill? Find a way to turn back time so I never came here in the first place?

Because right now, the last plan is the one I'd like to implement most. We came here because of me, no matter what Dad says—and now he's hurt and there's nothing I can do.

We sit there, listening to the clocks tick. Every ten minutes or so, Yiota gets up and tries to talk to the hospital staff, mostly getting ignored because she looks so young and isn't a close relation—technically, she isn't related to him at all. As far as we know, he's still in surgery, and that's all they'll tell her.

Yiota keeps checking her phone, clicking it in and out of its case, and it's annoying the hell out of me. It's not her fault, I'm just on edge and upset, but I swear I'm about to throw it across the waiting room. I wish Tony were here so I could—Tony!

I suddenly remember that he's been cooped up in the house, all alone, without being walked or anything. I turn to Yiota in a panic. I feel hot tears of exhaustion and frustration starting to leak out of my eyes. "I can't leave, and I know he's just a dog, but I can't—he's old, he can't be all—"

"Honey, this is no problem, okay?" Yiota says, squeezing my hands. "I'll go. You stay here, just tell me what to do, okay? I can be there in no time—I borrowed Nik's scooter to come here. Your place is very close."

I drag the back of my hand across my eyes for what seems like the millionth time in the last two hours and explain where the leash is and the plastic bags and the food. Yiota gives me another hug. "I'll be back really quick, okay, so don't worry. But if he gets here before me, just . . . let him help, okay? He loves you."

And she's gone before I can ask what she's talking about.

What a weird thing to say, I think. Maybe it's a Greek saying that doesn't translate.

I take a deep breath and start returning texts to my friends. Not like I have anything else to do. Thanks for checking in. Can't really talk, but scared. Don't know anything yet. XO

About an hour later, I'm reading a long text from Hilary when I hear a deep, accented voice calling my name. I look up, startled.

It's *Thios* Labis. He's carrying a small suitcase and looks harried and purposeful at the same time.

I'm so surprised, I don't do anything for a long minute. "Um . . . *Thios* Labis? What are you—"

He comes over, puts down his suitcase on a plastic chair, then puts his hands on my shoulders.

"Yiota calls me, I take the next flight to here," he explains gruffly. "These doctors, you have to be firm to them, understand? Not for two young girls to handle alone. So you leave this to me now. We will take care of it, so do not worry."

This Just In: Teen Stunned By Surprise Appearance Of Uncle

For Zona Lowell, today was a day rife with twists and turns. The last person she anticipated seeing on this, the most frightening day thus far in her young life, was her cold and unaffectionate uncle, Labis Marousopoulou.

"I didn't know what to say," Ms. Lowell shared with us, her voice faltering slightly. "My uncle had never said that many words to me, maybe even cumulatively. And the prideful part of me, the part that still felt responsible for defending my wonderful dad, wanted to tell him to go back to Crete and not bother worrying about us Lowells, because we could take care of ourselves. You know?"

But the bigger part of Ms. Lowell knew that she *did* need help. It was up to her whether or not to accept that help, of course, on behalf of herself and her badly injured father.

"The truth is that I have never been so grateful to see a relative since I got to Greece," she admitted finally. "And he's certainly not the one I expected to be grateful for. But life keeps surprising me, I guess."

Filed, 4:07 p.m., Athens.

297

I start to cry again, but these aren't desperate tears—they're relieved ones. Labis pulls me into his arms; he smells like tobacco and salt and olive oil soap, and it makes me think of Crete. He pats my hair gently, and the man *Thia* Angela tried so hard to describe peeks out a little from behind his high walls of emotional defense. I know Yiota loves him, and know that my mother must have loved him, too. I guess he isn't good at getting over being hurt by people, either. Maybe we have more in common than I realized.

He steers me back into my seat and tells me to stay put. The next thing I know, he's over at the main desk, going off on a nurse in rapid-fire Greek and clearly refusing to take no for an answer. She makes a phone call and a doctor comes scurrying out within two minutes. I can't believe it. I haven't laid eyes on an actual doctor—one who wasn't rushing somewhere and ignoring me, anyway—since we got here.

Thios Labis says some things, and the doctor says some things, and then my uncle reaches into his coat and takes out what appears to be a thick envelope. He hands it to the doctor, who smoothly pockets it, nods sharply, and walks off.

Labis comes back over to sit down. He looks annoyed. "What did you give him?" I ask tentatively.

"Ah, this country, you know, you have to give someone a little gift if you want them to do their job right. Is ridiculous, but this is the way we do it." He pulls a Greek newspaper out of the front pocket of his suitcase and unfolds it.

"You mean you gave him money? *Thios* Labis, I can't accept—I mean, I really appreciate your . . . I just don't have, I mean, to pay you back . . ." I start calculating in my head. A last-minute plane ticket, plus whatever was in that envelope, not to mention whatever my dad's bills are going to be . . . I don't know if Labis can afford to spend that kind of money, but my dad and I definitely can't. We just don't have it. My chest starts to constrict.

"Zona," he says quietly, looking up from the paper, "this is just money, these things. Money is like water, you understand? It flows . . . one person who needs it to another. There is always more money, from somewhere. There is *not* always more family. I am . . . *Éla*, my English is not good for talking so much, very sorry." He pauses, searching for a word, then giving up. "I am realize now, I was wrong, I . . . not know how to say. Please, *agapi mou*, do not worry. I will take care of this all. Okay?"

"Okay," I say. "Thank you, *Thios*." Because what else can I say? He nods and goes back to his paper. And I go back to listening to the clock tick.

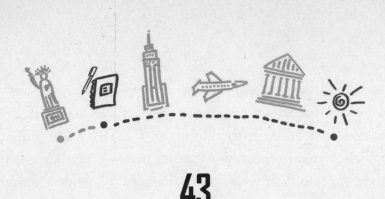

43

I slowly become aware that someone is shaking my shoulder and calling my name. I open my eyes, taking a second to remember where I am. My neck and shoulders hurt from sitting in this chair so long.

Then I snap my head up and I'm wide awake; Yiota is there holding out a cup of coffee. And smiling, which I take as a good sign.

"Tony is fine," she tells me. "And your dad is out of surgery. He is awake, and my dad is going to make them let you see him." She indicates Labis, who is gesticulating broadly at another doctor and talking to him very sternly.

I almost feel bad for the doctor.

Almost.

A nurse finally comes over, and I follow her down a corridor into a barely lit room. I look out the tiny window and see it's already dark outside. The whole day has passed since I got here.

I don't know if it's all the machines surrounding him, or the white sheets, but for the first time in my life, my dad looks frail. Frail . . . and old. It scares me. His leg is in a massive cast and supported by a sling hanging from the ceiling. His face is swollen on one side. That's really all I can see without moving the covers.

I can't tell if he's awake, and I'm not sure if I should say anything, but then he whispers, "Ace. That you?"

I let out a little laugh, wiping away yet more tears. "Yeah, Dad. It's me."

"This is gonna be one hell of a story, am I right?" He coughs, and I leap to grab a cup of water from the bedside table. I hold the straw out for him to sip, then he closes his eyes. "These drugs are terrific. Find out what they are, willya?"

"Dad!" I scold him, but I'm thinking, *If he can make jokes, that means he's going to be okay. Right?* "This is serious. Renowned Journalist Presses Luck, Goes One Step Too Far. You are a mess."

"I know." He opens his eyes again, and they look worried. "I don't know how long I have to . . . You may have to call my editor about a loan. He'll do that, I think . . . I got traveler's insurance, but this is—"

I reach out and touch his shoulder carefully, not sure where he might be in pain. I hear the door opening behind me; it's *Thios* Labis. I gesture for him to come in.

"It's okay, Dad. This is, um, Yiota's father, Labis. He . . . he flew in from Crete. Just now, I mean. And he talked to all the doctors and . . ."

Dad is squirming a bit, like he's trying to sit up. I can tell it's hurting him to move, and his eyes are unfocused from the medication. He would never have wanted to face my mother's relatives—especially this one—in such a weak position. My heart aches and I let my words fade away, because I don't know what to say or do.

Labis surprises me again. He puts a strong hand under Dad's back and helps him lean against the pillows. "David, you remember me, *nay*?" he says quietly in his gruff voice. "I am sorry you are in hospital and I . . . I say already to Zona, I will take care everything. Bills, is all taken care of this. So you are not to worry."

Dad looks as shocked as I feel, but also like he's trying to stand his ground. "Labis, I don't think that would be . . . I can't accept . . ." he murmurs softly. He clears his throat.

"I hope you will accept from me also an apology," Labis interjects.

Dad is quiet. I think maybe he's drifted off, but then he says, "You were very important to Hélenè, always. She never—"

The door opens and a nurse comes in. "Your father needs to rest, cannot have infection," she says in heavily accented English. "Sleeping very important now, yes?"

Dad's eyes are closing, and whatever he'd been about to say is gone. Labis puts his hand on my shoulder. "We let him rest now, *nay*?" So I kiss Dad on the cheek and we creep out of the room.

Back in the world of blue plastic chairs, Yiota is waiting.

"He's resting," I tell her. "His leg is in a cast and he's all banged up . . . and they didn't tell me how long it'll take to recover yet. I don't know how he'll be able to . . . do anything." I slump into a seat next to her and put my head in my hands.

Of all the disasters I anticipated coming to Greece, this isn't close to anything I imagined. Will I have to find a nurse to take care of him? I can't leave him and Tony alone all day while I'm at school, obviously. Back home, we have people who would help—friends, neighbors—but here . . . the only adults I know live on Crete. I don't think the powers that be will let me quit school and nurse him myself. Which, considering the implications of a ruptured spleen and a broken leg, I don't think I'm capable of doing, anyway.

I feel hopeless and lost and helpless and *young*.

Yiota interrupts my train of thought. "Zona. My mother is going to come. She and Baba will stay here and help you. So you don't have to be scared or worried, okay?"

I look up at her. "But—"

Thios Labis reaches across his daughter and puts his hand on mine. "I am already tell you, we are family. That's all to say."

So I don't say anything. I just let out the breath I didn't know I was holding.

44

When I get back to the apartment, I'm so exhausted—physically, emotionally—I can barely make it up the stairs. Yiota steers me to the bathroom so I can wash the dried tears off my face; *Thios* Labis is still at the hospital making arrangements. Yiota makes tea and tries to get me to drink it, but I'm too tired. I'm vaguely aware of her pulling my shoes off and draping a blanket over me, and then I'm asleep for hours.

When I wake up, I feel better, but I panic when I see the apartment is empty. I find a note on the fridge from Yiota, saying she's meeting her mother at the airport. I call her immediately, and she tells me that the hospital is keeping my dad for observation but I can go visit him whenever I want to.

I breathe. I drink about a gallon of water and eat a breakfast bar and text my friends. They're all being so sweet and offering to stop by or get my homework for me, but all I can think about is my dad. Who cares about stupid homework? Even the concerned text from Alex doesn't chip away at the shell of dread that's all around me. Because what if, what if, what if . . . ?

At the hospital, Dad's in much better spirits, even though he still can't sit up or eat regular food. "These drugs are fantastic, Zona. Did I tell you that already? It's like being in the seventies again." He giggles like a little girl. "Or the eighties. Or the nineties!"

"Okay, Dad. Glad you're feeling better. Father Shares Too Much While Under the Influence, Scandalizes Only Child." A nurse pokes her head into the room and tells me it's time for Dad's sponge bath. Definitely don't need to be here for that. "Dad, I'll go wait outside, okay?"

Dad is singing quietly to himself, which I interpret as a yes. Even though seeing him all trussed up in that room is still awful, he seems so much better already that I feel calmer and safer. And able to think more rationally about what comes next.

I spend the next few days setting up the apartment for an extra person to stay (Labis and Angela will take turns staying with Yiota at her apartment) and trying to make my dad comfortable after he comes home.

My friends keep touching base with me, but it's really my aunt, uncle, and cousin who are there, taking care of everything. It's amazing how, when you hear "Family means taking care of each other" enough times, you start to accept it as true—even though you believed the exact opposite for your whole life.

Getting Out Of School Not As Great As Previously Imagined

Certainly, Zona Lowell has always shared the typical student's dream of getting to skip school indefinitely and not having to do homework. Following the deadly incident in Athens earlier this week, Ms. Lowell received her assignments along with a note "wishing her well" and imploring her "not to worry about due dates" from her school's administrative office. We caught up with Ms. Lowell to find out if playing hooky without repercussions was as terrific as she thought it could be.

"My dad was in a life-threatening accident. Of course I'd rather go to class than have him be hurt! Are you completely insane?!" she is reported to have screeched angrily before slamming the door.

Ms. Lowell has refused to make herself available for additional interviews. Sources say she will be leaving her father in the care of relations when she resumes her studies at the Greek International School next week. We strongly recommend that reporters not attempt to contact her at this time.

Filed, 4:36 p.m., Athens.

The change in *Thios* Labis over the next month is shocking: here, suddenly, is the cuddly man Yiota and Angela swore was hidden inside the stolid, gruff one I'd known before. I come home from school and he's made me a snack. He jokes with me. He even teases my father, especially when he has to carry him from the couch to the bathroom. (Dad insisted on ditching the bedpan after the first few days.) I can finally see how he might be Theseus's brother after all.

I can't help but feel guilty about accepting so much generosity—financial, physical, and emotional—from my aunt and uncle, though. I mean, I have a vague idea of how much this must be costing, and it's not like they're wealthy people. But every time I try to bring it up, or even buy groceries, they rebuff me. I don't want to insult them, but I feel like I have to do something to show them how grateful I am. To acknowledge that I could never, ever have gotten through this without them.

Finally, after weeks have gone by, I think of just the right thing: the blue box.

After dinner, while Dad is sleeping and before *Thios* Labis goes to Yiota's apartment to spend the night, I bring the box out from my closet. I remove the stack of my mother's letters and put them on the table, then leave the room so they won't feel like I'm watching them.

After about an hour, Angela knocks lightly on my door. "Can we talk with you?" she asks.

"Of course." I roll off my bed, where I've been pretending to read but have really just been waiting impatiently for their reactions.

I go into the living room and sit down. "Before you say anything, I have something else to show you." I reach into my pocket and pull out my mother's wedding ring, which I hand to Angela. "It was a gift when I turned sixteen, from my dad," I explain, pointing out the engraving on the inside of the band. "They really, truly loved each other."

Angela hands the ring back to me, and her eyes are wet. "We know," she says quietly, smiling. "Her letters . . . *éla,* they are full of joy—in your father, New York, being so young and having a wonderful . . . a wonderful adventure. Thank you for sharing them with us."

Labis clears his throat. "I miss your mother," he says hoarsely, staring at the floor. Then he looks up at his wife, and then at me. "I miss my sister, you understand?" He puts the stack of letters, all neatly folded back into their envelopes, back in the box. He places the lid on it and strokes the top of the box softly. "And again, I must tell that I am sorry, Zona. For missing *you* all these years."

"It's been . . . hard, trying to sort out my feelings, *Thios* Labis. But you don't need to keep apologizing—I forgive you. And I know my mom would, too."

Angela puts her hand over her husband's, and I decide to leave them alone with their memories. I go out onto the terrace with my laptop, wondering if I have any e-mails from Hil and Matty. The sky is such a beautiful shade of blue that it looks fake. The sunlight bounces off the white buildings on our street, and I have to put my sunglasses on to see clearly.

There's one new e-mail in my inbox.

It's from Lilena.

She hasn't responded to my attempts to reach out to her since . . . well, since April. And now it's mid-June. It's not that I haven't thought about her, but there has been so much going on lately. And now here she is, appearing out of the blue.

I can hear Angela in the other room now, fussing over Dad, who is almost certainly trying to get to his notes when she wants him to keep resting.

I'm afraid to open the e-mail.

But I'm not a coward. At least, I don't want to be. And facing things that are scary is an essential part of getting to the core of a promising story.

Zona,

I'm not really sure what I want to say. They haven't let me use a computer or my phone since I've been here, so I didn't get any of your messages until today. I wasn't sure at first that I wanted to even respond, because I'm still really mad at you. The only reason I'm even here is because of you. I can't believe what you did, I really can't.

But I guess the truth is that the real reason I'm here is because of me. Well, that's what they tell me, a million times a day, here. And maybe they're right. The doctors keep saying that if I hadn't gotten treatment when I did, I could've had a heart attack, which I don't know if I believe. But if that's true then I guess I should thank you.

But I don't think I'm ready to do that, either.

I know you called my mom because you were
worried about me. I'm trying really hard to
appreciate that you were concerned and not be
furious that you couldn't just mind your own
business. I really am trying to do that. But I
hate it here, and I hate being treated like some
kind of invalid or something, and I hate not
being in control of my own body anymore. It
still feels like your fault. And that makes me
hate you, too.

But anyway, I wanted to tell you I'm working on
forgiving you. I heard about what happened to
your dad and I'm really sorry. I hope he's okay.

Lilena

I close the laptop. I don't really know what to think.
I guess it wasn't realistic to hope she'd realize she had a
problem right away. Or that she'd forgive me. But her
words hurt. I don't want to take them personally—I know,
deep down, no matter what anyone says, that I did the right
thing.

But it sucks to be hated by anyone, and especially a
friend who you took a risk for. It hurts just as much now as
it did when I got that awful text from her.

I'll be going back to New York soon. Dad's much better,
and our sublease ends in a few weeks anyway, so we'd have
to find a new place if we were going to stay. Besides, Dad is

itching to get back to work and not be fawned over by well-meaning caregivers, as much as I can tell he is touched by the attention. Not to mention the 360-degree shift in attitude from my mother's family.

Of all the people I've met—besides my cousins, of course—Lilena is the one person I imagined staying in touch with after leaving Greece. I see Alex at school, and we still text each other every so often; while I obviously like him, I'm not sure we'll talk after I go back to New York. Maybe we'll exchange the occasional Instagram message or something. I feel bad saying it, but worrying about whether or not he likes me and when I might see him again just stopped seeming important after dad's accident. When I think about how crazy I acted after that first kiss, I feel kind of silly. And while the other GIS kids are nice and we've had fun, I don't feel that connected to them, really.

Now I guess it's a wait-and-see situation with Lilena.

Saying good-bye to my Greek family is going to be even harder after everything we've gone through together with my dad. And then, going back to my old life, I wonder if the Zona-sized space I left behind is still there, or if it's changed. If focusing on myself the last six months—*experiencing* life instead of reporting on it—has changed me. If I'm different now and if anyone will notice. If maybe I *want* to be noticed. If maybe there's more to me than two best friends and a lifelong dream of being a journalist. Or if maybe there isn't, and if that's still okay.

45

"Dad. Stop admiring yourself and let's go," I call. He is mesmerized by the sight of himself with his fancy new cane (he prefers "walking stick," which I think sounds pretentious) and pauses in front of every reflective surface to pose with it. Which, in an airport, is a lot.

Tony snores, sedated, from inside his carrier, and I pat his furry head through the top panel before dragging him—along with the rest of our carry-on luggage—farther down the hallway.

It's seven A.M. on a Tuesday in early July, and we're going back to New York.

Back to sticky hot summer and Italian ice vendors on the street; back to searching for treasure at the Strand bookstore and reading the *New York Times* over cappuccinos in our tiny kitchen; back to Hilary and Matty and my journals full of article ideas. Back to reality.

But reality is different now, I think as we find seats in the waiting area. *Now it's full of cousins and aunts and uncles and Greek phrases and strange new foods and a sense of freedom.*

I had to turn my Greek cell phone in to be recycled, and it feels weird not to have it anymore, though I don't think there would be any messages. Yiota went back to Crete with her parents two weeks ago, and we had a massive Skype chat with the whole family several times so my dad could finally "meet" them all and I could say good-bye. We've promised to write letters—real letters, not e-mails—which I intend to put in the blue box with the others. Maybe my mother's letters will be less lonely in there that way. Eventually, there will be a new box.

I already said good-bye to Betony and Ashley, Nikos and a few other kids on the last day of classes, and we promised to keep in touch. Maybe that will actually happen. I don't know if they ever found out exactly what happened between Lilena and me—they never said so, and I never asked. I haven't heard from Lilena again since her surprise e-mail. I did write back telling her to take her time, and that I'd always be there if she wanted to get in touch. I hope someday she will.

I take a bite of a terrible airport breakfast sandwich and lean back in the hard plastic chair. I'm so tired—I was out late saying good-bye to Alex. I was a little surprised he asked me to meet him, since I've hardly seen him lately. Sure, we grabbed the occasional coffee after last period, and once he left a copy of the *New York Times* by my locker as a joke . . . but I was never able to get caught back up in the crush/dating hamster wheel of excitement. I wanted to—he's just as cute and funny as he always was. My friends think I'm crazy for not paying more attention to him. But none of that stuff seemed as important after my dad got hurt.

If someone had told me I'd meet an adorable guy in Greece and then decide I had better things to do than make out with him every chance I got, I wouldn't have believed it. But if I've learned anything this year, it's that life is full of surprises.

Anyway: last night. Alex asked me to meet him in a little park sort of near school, which couldn't have been more romantic.

"So, uh, going back to New York tomorrow, huh?" he said as we walked around in the warm night air. He took his glasses off and started polishing the lenses. He seemed anxious, which made me anxious, too.

"Yes, well, that's the plan . . . unless you're planning to abduct me?" I replied, trying to lighten the mood. "I have to warn you, my dad has no money for ransom. Although he does have a snappy new cane that he may use as a weapon if you get too close."

Alex laughed and put his glasses back on.

"How's your photo project coming? I meant to ask you about it before, but I—"

"You and your dad are super close, huh?" he interrupted.

He said it like a question, but I knew it wasn't. I stopped walking.

"Alex, look—I'm sorry if I . . . I mean, I didn't mean to . . ." I trailed off.

The truth is, I didn't know what to say. *I'm sorry being with my dad was more important to me than hanging out with you* didn't seem quite right. In fact, it seemed pretty lame. But that didn't make it less true.

"No, don't feel bad, Zona." Alex plucked a leaf off the tree we were standing under and started ripping it up. *Is it possible I make him as nervous as he used to make me?!* "I just wish I had gotten to spend more time getting to know you. I mean . . . it sucks you're leaving. That's all."

"Well," I said with a smile, taking the shredded leaf bits from his hand and tossing them onto the grass, "I'm not leaving yet."

I couldn't tell if he kissed me or if I kissed him, but we were suddenly just *kissing*; the familiar sparks shot up and down my spine like fireworks. We lay down on the grass and he wrapped his arms around me and I almost couldn't believe it was me, Zona Lowell, doing something so daring and sexy and exciting.

Being the story was definitely getting easier.

When we finally broke apart, it was almost midnight. I had to get back to the apartment, and I had a feeling that if I stayed things might go too far. We brushed ourselves off, kissed one last time, and then said good-bye.

I wanted him to turn back and wave as he rode away on

his bike, but he didn't. And I knew for sure my time in Greece was done.

For the moment, anyway.

I feel the silver-tipped end of my dad's ridiculous cane tapping my foot, and I'm yanked out of my reverie.

"Hey, Ace. We're boarding. World's Most Spectacular Father-Daughter Team Anticipates Ticker Tape Parade at JFK, right?"

"Why do *you* get a parade?" I ask, pretending to be annoyed. "I'm the one who's had my whole life turned upside down. Shoved to the edge of a cliff and left to figure it out all by myself. All you did was do a bunch of research and get knocked around a little." I grab Tony's carrier with one hand, sling my carry-on over my shoulder with the other, and shove my passport and ticket between my teeth.

"True," he says, balancing on his good leg as he hoists up his computer bag. "But I'm still the only one who pays the bills around here. You wanna walk home?"

"Maybe I *will*," I mumble around my mouthful of cardboard, but I'm smiling, too. We walk together toward the gate.

"Well, Ace, that would make for a hell of a good story."

"Yeah, I think I'm all set in the 'good story' department. At least for this year," I reply drily.

"Ha. I'll second that." Dad chuckles.

Then he stops and turns to me, taking my free hand in his like he used to when I was little. "Hey, Zona?" I look up at him, and he's smiling my favorite lopsided Dad smile. "I'm really proud of you," he says. "I don't know if I've actually told you that. Sometimes I assume you already know what I'm thinking."

Other passengers are swarming around us now, anxious to get to their seats. One bumps into me and gives me a dirty look.

"We should—"

"Don't worry about them; let 'em rush," he scoffs. "I want to say this before we board, okay?"

"Okay." I feel a little silly, to be sixteen years old and holding hands with my father in an airport.

"I just want you to know that *I* know how hard this experience was for you. Especially with my being mostly MIA and working all the time, and then with the accident . . . I pushed you to come to Greece with me because I knew you could handle it. And you *did*, Zo, and with such aplomb and grace and brains, and I'm just . . . I'm just in awe of you. I really am."

I can feel the blush climbing up my cheeks. "Thanks, Dad," I whisper.

He squeezes my hand, then puts his arm around my shoulder, leaning on me a little as we head to the gate with our tickets.

And after that, we're flying through the sky and all the way home.

Adío yia tóra.

46

Readers Love Neatly Tied-Up Endings, Studies Show

It has come to the attention of this publication that people like to know what happened next. In the interest of keeping newspapers from becoming obsolete, the editors wish to offer the following items for consideration:

Nikos Hadjimarkos finally admitted to having feelings for Betony, who knew perfectly well that Ashley had feelings for Nikos. Betony told Nikos she couldn't hurt Ashley and they all remained friends . . . until Betony hooked up with Nikos at a party and Ashley found out. The status of their friendship is still pending.

Giorgos Hadjimarkos is still really weird.

Pro-Yia-Yia is still telling everyone the story of Zona and the geese. The locals say they've never seen her laugh so much in recent memory.

Lilena Vobras was able to leave treatment at the end of July and will be back at school in the fall. Her parents have agreed to stay in one place for a while to make sure she gets the help she needs. Lilena and Zona have started e-mailing again, tentatively at first, but then more regularly. Zona is hoping Lilena might visit her in NYC sometime soon.

Matt Klausner went to the Pride March with his friend Scott *and* his friends Zona and Hilary . . . and that's where he met Bill Marini, 17. They are enjoying a summer romance.

Hilary Bauer did a pretty good job as features editor, but

her heart wasn't in it. She started taking a sculpture class at School of Visual Arts during the summer, telling her parents that art was her passion and she was sticking to it. The Bauers agreed that taking a college course was indeed a "serious endeavor." Ms. Bauer would also like to collaborate on a graphic novel recounting Zona's year in Greece.

David Lowell's book scored a hefty advance, and his publishers expect it will be a huge success. Tony was unimpressed by the news.

Zona Lowell is back to writing, and still plans to be a journalist. She got a job at a local paper doing fact-checking and is saving her money to visit her relatives in Crete next Easter. This time, she's bringing her dad along.

Filed, 8:41 p.m., NYC.

ACKNOWLEDGMENTS

I am so grateful for the support and encouragement of my incredible family, friends, and readers-I-have-yet-to-meet (you guys know who you are, right? Your names are all over these books, for crying out loud).

Extra-specific appreciation goes to the following superstars: My editor, Shauna Rossano, who has been a champion for Kelsey, Zona, and all their crazy misadventures since 2008; I'd be lost without her guidance and enthusiasm. My glorious agent, Victoria Marini, who makes her job look easy and always has my back. Anne Walls is the reason half of you even knew about *Freshman Year,* and is also credited with bullying me into finishing *Sophomore Year.* Thanks, you guys.

Tony Montenieri, you do this on first dates, don't you? (Maybe *j'adore.*) Sara Sellar, you are not—and have never been—a downer. *(J'nai.)* Robby Sharpe, I'd happily attempt to reach the first-class train carriage with you forever. Ellen Shanman, your enviable success is what made me think I could actually do this in the first place, and your advice is always so appreciated. Jessica Goldstein, without you, no one would know what I really look like. Aunt Rhea, your brilliant novels always made me wish I could someday write one myself, and I am so proud to be able to place this one next to yours on my bookshelf. Carly Robins, thanks for yelling at me when I didn't feel like doing my editing homework. Ben "Apricot" Howard, you have always been my best early reader, for every page of every draft. This is why you're royalty.

The people I met in Greece were unbelievably welcoming and made the challenge of researching this book a pleasure. My incredible hosts, Pamela and Emmanuel Pascalodimitrakis (plus Leo and Julia), Christiana Polyviou, and Yiota Yiotini, inspired me, took such good care of me, and taught me more about Greece and Greek people than I could ever fit in one book. The students and faculty at ACS Athens—in particular Peggy Pelonis, Melina Vassiliadis, John Papadakis, and Alexander Vassiliadis—blew me away with their generosity. I was hoping for a brief tour of the campus and I ended up with a three-day residency that was absolutely invaluable, not to mention a blast. Finally, to the very nice guy in Rethymnon who gave me a lift on his moped when I was hopelessly lost, all the while yelling at me for taking a ride from a stranger: thank you for not kidnapping me. And as for the evil geese of Mixorouma? I hope you've been broiled for someone's dinner by now.

Okay, that's enough of that. Stop reading this list and go read the book. (Unless you've already finished it, in which case go read it again. Or lend it to somebody else and then send me an e-mail or something.)

Keep reading for a look at

FRESHMAN YEAR & OTHER UNNATURAL DISASTERS

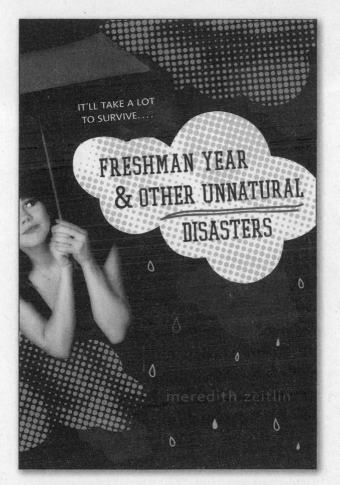

1

Here it is, practically mid-September, and it's *still* too hot to live. I'm in the den trying to find anything worth watching on TV (fat chance on a Sunday night), and I can feel myself melting all over the couch. I love how my parents spend a million dollars putting in central air and then don't want to use it because it's "technically fall." Everyone in the tristate area is wearing shorts, and my delusional parents seem to think a cold front is going to hit Brooklyn in the next five minutes. Um, global warming, anyone?

My three best friends—Em, JoJo, and Cassidy—are on their way over here right now, so all I can do is hope that they're prepared for the Sahara-like conditions. Of course, they've been to my house about a zillion times, so they're familiar with the endless cycle of injustice that is my life.

I give up on the TV and head upstairs to the kitchen to get some snacks ready—and to make sure I'm closest to the front door. That way I can guarantee that my friends aren't intercepted by any nosy family members. Tonight is the last time we're all getting together before the first day of school on Tuesday, and I can't risk letting our important strategy session get sidetracked by my dad wanting to know if Em's dad is free for a thrilling racquetball game next Saturday, or my mother telling Cassidy she just *loves* her new earrings and had some just like them when she was our age and who wants to see pictures of her back in the glory days?!

Seriously, the things I deal with.

Em and Cassidy arrive just as I'm fishing a giant bag of Twizzlers from the back of a cupboard. They toss their overnight bags on the floor in the kitchen and pull up stools at the breakfast counter. "I thought you guys were meeting JoJo at the train," I say.

"We were," Cass explains, ripping into the Twizzlers with relish. "She texted that she was—"

"Running late?" I chime in simultaneously. JoJo is *always* running late.

"Yep." Em grins. She gets a can of root beer out of the fridge and takes a long sip. "Maybe it's time to give up on her. I mean, we've only been friends for a decade. Maybe enough is enough?"

It always amazes me how Em is sarcastic and silly around us but so sweet and shy at school. I wish more people got to see this side of her—but of course, she's been my very best friend since nursery school, so I know her better than anyone.

Cass adds, "Maybe we should start telling her we're meeting half an hour before we really are so she'll show up on time." She grabs a handful of Wheat Thins from a box on the counter. "Think that would work?"

"You guys have so little faith in me!"

JoJo suddenly appears in the door frame. Her hair has new turquoise streaks in it, which means she's been hanging out with her dad today. He was a guitarist with a semi-famous band when he was young and refuses to let go of the dream. He has a Mohawk and lots of tattoos and is always encouraging JoJo to express herself. And he doesn't believe in rules, which works out great for the four of us when we go to her house.

Of course, right now we're at *my* house, and my mother absolutely cannot resist putting in an appearance. "Hi, girls! Eating us out of house and home for a change, I see?"

Ugggghhh. "Mom! Can you not?"

"Kelsey, have you been fiddling with the downstairs television set again? We put those parental controls on there for a reason, and it's a pain in the neck to keep resetting them all the time."

"I was just trying to—"

"Ooh, I like the new hair, JoJo. Very hip. And Em, I hear you had quite the romance at summer camp this year—I want to hear all about the lucky guy!"

As usual, the woman is unstoppable in her efforts to

embarrass me in front of my friends. I start scooping up our snacks, saying, "Mom, we'd love to chat, but we have a lot to do tonight, so we'll just relocate upstairs, if you don't mind. . . ." The girls and I start heading for the stairs.

"Big day on Tuesday, huh?" she calls, following us. "I know, I know, you don't want to talk to your horrible mother. Tell me, do you girls treat *your* mothers like this?"

I herd my friends into my room and close the door, but not before we hear: "No, that's fine, just ignore me—I'm used to the Typical Adolescent Behavior around here!"

She is seriously more annoying than any other person on the planet, including my dad. "Sorry, guys—you know how she is," I groan, flopping onto the floor.

"Yeah, exactly like everyone's mom. Except JoJo's," Cass points out. "And mine, obviously. But that's because I only see her, like, once a year."

Cass's mom decided one day that she felt like living in Paris and left, so now Cass lives with her dad and older brother a few blocks from me in Park Slope, Brooklyn. Some people have all the luck, I tell you.

"Twizzler, please!" JoJo sings, holding out a hand. Em passes her a fistful. "Thanks. I'd've gotten them myself, but I'm working on my Typical Adolescent Behavior."

"You didn't really tell her about James, did you?" Em asks me. James is the guy Em has been dating from camp for the last two months.

"Em, are you crazy?" I gasp. "Of course not! She sneakily read one of your letters—I left it on the kitchen table for about eight seconds, and by the time I got back it was too late. She's like the Secret Service."

"Hey, I know!" JoJo says, pausing to swallow a mouthful of licorice. "Let's spend all night talking about Kelsey's mom. Oooor . . . we could talk about Tuesday."

"Seriously. You only get one first day of high school, guys," adds Cass. "What's the plan?"

"Um, not get lost?" Em suggests. Em is brilliant, but she has the world's worst sense of direction.

"Not get expelled?" JoJo offers.

"Wow, we're really setting our sights on glory here," I say. "Way to aim high, you guys."

"Well, what did you have in mind, Kels? Like, streak through the cafeteria?"

"Yeah, Cass. That's it exactly—I thought we could streak through the caf."

I roll my eyes at her and she shrugs. "Well, just let me know what day so I can be sure to shave my legs."

I'll say this for Cass—she may be a little slow to catch up sometimes, but no matter what any of the three of us wants or needs, she's behind us one hundred percent. Of course, as our resident drama queen, she'd probably love the attention we'd get if we *did* streak the caf.

Cassidy grabs the Wheat Thins and lies down with her back on the floor and her legs straight up against the wall. It's part of a theater exercise or something—she's been doing it since she started taking acting classes in sixth grade. I'm used to it by now, but it's always fascinating to watch her eat upside down. And gross.

JoJo gives me a raised eyebrow. "What's going on, Kels? You have some big plan in mind or something?"

"No, not really. Just . . . well, we're in high school now. Obviously. And . . . it's time to defy expectations! To . . . change people's perceptions of us! I mean, I just feel like this year could be—"

"High school is still *school*, you know," JoJo scoffs. "Lame, unlikely to result in anything useful, and—"

"*Anyway*, I've decided to really . . . *do* something this year. To make a mark. Stand out. Revamp myself for a new era. You know, like Lady Gaga."

"You want to start wearing wigs and plastic bodysuits?"

"What? No. Okay—better example: Joan of Arc. You know, she wouldn't settle for the expec—"

"Wasn't she burned at the stake?!"

I sigh. "You're killing me, Cass."

"I'm just trying to understand what you mean!" She frowns.

"We might be here all night, then," JoJo says.

Cassidy sits up and swats her playfully on the arm. "Seriously, though, what are you going to do to make your big mark?"

"Well . . . I was thinking I'd start with soccer."